The
MEMORY
TREE

ALSO BY LINDA GILLARD

Emotional Geology
A Lifetime Burning
Star Gazing
House of Silence
Untying the Knot
The Glass Guardian
Cauldstane

The

MEMORY TREE

LINDA GILLARD

LAKE UNION
PUBLISHING

Previously self-published as *The Trysting Tree* in Great Britain in 2016.

Published by Lake Union Publishing, Seattle

www.apub.com

Amazon, the Amazon logo, and Lake Union Publishing are trademarks of Amazon.com, Inc., or its affiliates.

ISBN-13: 9781542009539
ISBN-10: 1542009537

Cover design by Debbie Clement

Printed in the United States of America

For my friend, Erica Munro

War is the normal occupation of man. War – and gardening.

Winston Churchill, 1918

PART ONE

THE BEECH WOOD

She has forgotten what she saw long ago, what she found. Daily she walks in the wood, a woman now, who walked beneath our boughs as a child. Alone then; alone now.

The tree still stands, one of our number, where the child swung back and forth, laughing, clutching the thick ropes the man had slung over one of its branches. Now the woman gazes up at the leafy canopy and shivers.

The swing is gone, taken down long ago, but the rope left scars. She doesn't see them, doesn't remember. But she's beginning to wonder if she has forgotten. And what she has forgotten.

There is a hole at the heart of the tree, a dark place that holds secrets. The woman looks up at the hiding place the child could never reach and she wonders.

She is scarred like the tree, with a secret hidden in her heart. Something dark. Forgotten. Unreachable.

ANN

When the old beech tree came down in the storm it was as if someone had died. Someone who'd been around forever, who'd seemed immortal, like an elder statesman or the Queen.

I actually cried. I pretended it was fear. The tree had missed the studio by inches and we could have been crushed, pinned to the ground like dead butterflies, transfixed by its branches. I allowed my mother to believe it was shock that made me weep, but it was grief. I'd lost a childhood friend. A link with my father.

When I'd calmed down, I photographed the tree, carefully recording the two centuries of graffiti incised on its smooth grey bark. Don't ask me why. It seemed important at the time. When the tree surgeons came, I couldn't bear to watch, so I hid indoors, but I still had to listen to the cruel whine of the chainsaws.

It was distressing because I knew the tree wasn't actually dead. It was weak and very old, but not dead. Even though it had succumbed to the storm, it might have continued to live, horizontally, maintaining a tenuous hold on life through its massive root system, part of which still clung to the damp earth. They were killing a living thing with many other living things growing in it and on it. It was a massacre.

The beech had flattened the shed and an outhouse. Even if we'd removed all its branches, the trunk, five metres in circumference, would have filled the garden, like a bus. It had to go, so I let them carve it up and cart it away. It took days.

On the second day, one of the men knocked on the back door and handed me what looked like a rusty biscuit tin. 'We found this in a hole in the tree. Thought you might like to see if there's anything valuable inside. Maybe the lost family jewels, eh?' he said with a smile before going back to his noisy work.

I had to take a chisel to the lid. Inside I found something wrapped in oilcloth. I hesitated before touching it, wondering what on earth the cloth might contain. There was no unpleasant smell, so I concluded the contents were inorganic or totally decayed. Cautious still, I donned rubber gloves and picked up the bundle. Despite its size, it weighed very little. I unwrapped the cloth to find it was protecting seed packets, beautiful antique seed packets, maybe a hundred years old. The delicate flower paintings were the sort of thing you'd frame nowadays and hang on a wall. But these were originals, glued by hand.

I wondered why anyone would go to so much trouble to preserve seeds. They weren't rare varieties, just humble cottage garden flowers: hollyhocks, lupins, nasturtiums, nothing special. I picked up a packet of nasturtium seeds, turned it over and read the back, wondering if the seeds would still be viable. As I held the packet between my gloved fingers, I realised it was empty. Nasturtium seeds are the size of petit pois. So are lupin seeds. I took off my gloves and felt the packets, then shook them vigorously, close to my ear. Every single packet – and there must have been twenty – appeared to be empty. Sealed, but empty.

I put the packets back in the tin and filled the kettle, averting my eyes from the dismemberment outside. As the water came to the boil, I was already preoccupied with the question that would come to haunt me in the coming weeks. Why would anyone hide empty seed packets in a hollow tree?

But the story doesn't start there. I need to go back. Back to a time when the beech tree still stood, when I didn't know the truth about my family and Connor didn't know the truth about his. Right back to a time when the twentieth century was young and the beech still kept its secrets.

When I was at art school we studied the work of a contemporary artist, Phoebe Flint, celebrated for her portraits. Her career fell into two distinct periods. During the first, which ended in the 1970s, her work was considered interesting, if derivative, and occasionally outstanding. Then, during the second period, she came into her own. Her mature work was consistently original and brilliant. Looking at a Flint portrait, you were never in any doubt as to the identity of the artist. Her work was as distinctive as Lucian Freud's and often as unsettling.

There was a third stage in Phoebe Flint's life: the period after she stopped painting. She produced her last portrait in 2009 and the art world assumed she'd died. Some critics even wrote about her in the past tense. But Phoebe Flint didn't die. It's true she nearly died, but she's still very much alive.

I know because she's my mother.

Phoebe got cancer. She fought it for some years, but in the end it wasn't cancer that stopped her painting, it was the chemotherapy – and not even the chemo itself, but its side effects. The vicious drugs that poisoned her body and saved her life also trashed her nervous system. She was left disabled by something called peripheral neuropathy.

Phoebe suffered constant pain in her feet and fingers. More importantly, she lost her fine motor control. She continued to paint – or tried to – but she couldn't stand for long. She found brushes hard to control and frequently dropped them, along with her palette. She dropped other things too: teapots, kettles, bottles of wine – a *lot* of bottles of wine – and sometimes she ended up in A&E, scalded or bleeding, fulminating against the ravaged body that had let her down.

Her agent persuaded her to hire an assistant, so Phoebe appointed a charming young man to mix her paints, prepare her canvases and meals and occasionally warm her bed. My mother and I were barely in touch and I didn't know the details of the arrangement. We'd never been close and treatment for cancer did little to mellow her irascible temperament. I visited as often as she permitted, but Phoebe made it plain I was neither wanted nor needed. Since she had a posse of friends and ex-lovers dancing attendance, I had few concerns about her welfare, other than the fear that chemo might actually kill her. (We got on so badly, there were days when I feared if the chemo didn't, I *would*.) I tried to keep in touch via phone calls, which she sometimes declined to take, and emails, which she never answered, claiming it hurt her fingers to type.

Phoebe continued to hold court at Garden Lodge, improbably red-haired, balding, pale and imperious, like a latter-day Elizabeth I, but despite the encouragement of her acolytes and her agent's nagging, she produced no more portraits.

Cancer wore Phoebe out and almost broke her spirit, but convalescence gave her an opportunity to reassess. I suspect she held a private retrospective and saw what hitherto no one else had seen, except, perhaps, me. Her prodigious output of portraits had something else in common, apart from a capacity to leap out of their frames and buttonhole the viewer. Post cancer, Phoebe might have stepped back from her easel long enough to see that every single portrait she'd painted since 1976, young or old, male or female, resembled Sylvester. Perhaps my mother finally realised that however many times she painted him and in whatever form, my father wasn't ever coming back.

Silvestre Esmeraldo Luis de Freitas. Or Sylvester, as he was commonly known.

Even after Jack and I married, I kept my own name. Nothing would persuade me to relinquish my Madeiran surname, not when it was coupled with a name like Ann. Could Phoebe have expressed her disdain for her firstborn more clearly? My parents were called Sylvester and Phoebe and I was called Ann. Just Ann, not even a middle name. I felt like somebody else's child and sometimes wondered if I was.

Sylvester called me Anna, softening my plain name. I don't remember much about him. In my memory he's tall, but I know he wasn't. Like many Madeiran men, he was short, dark and very handsome, with refined features and pale-blue eyes that looked startling even in photographs.

Sylvester was a gardener and an importer of Madeiran wines. He spent a lot of time abroad, at least before I was born. He set up a wine import business in Bristol and made a lot of money. An impulsive and cultivated man, he bought one of Phoebe's paintings, then contacted her to commission another. She declined the commission but asked if she could paint his portrait.

They fell in love and married. Sylvester bought Garden Lodge, originally the Head Gardener's cottage on a Victorian estate called Beechgrave. He turned what had been the walled kitchen garden serving a large country house into something like the kind of sub-tropical paradise he'd left behind in Madeira. Somerset's mild, wet weather combined with the heat-retaining brick walls meant the garden flourished until Sylvester left for good when I was five.

I barely remember the garden in its heyday, but I do remember running along narrow gravel paths, chasing butterflies and stalking frogs. I have one particularly vivid memory of sitting on my father's lap, on a bench in the sunshine, eating a warm peach he'd plucked from the wall. No fruit has ever tasted as good since.

But Phoebe wasn't interested in gardening. After Sylvester left, she neglected the garden and it soon became overgrown. Perhaps this was a form of revenge. Perhaps she was just preoccupied with her work. My memories of the time are hazy, but when I think back, I have a strong sense of a geographical divide. Phoebe was always indoors, shut away in her studio, painting furiously. I was usually outside, playing on my own in an abandoned garden, which quickly became a wilderness.

I have no memory of asking Phoebe where Sylvester had gone or why, and she made no attempt to explain. How do you explain marital breakdown to a five-year-old? She dealt with my father as she dealt with everyone who offended or betrayed her. She cast them off into outer darkness and pretended they were dead.

But I do remember asking repeatedly if he would be coming back. Her answer was always the same. Just the one word.

'No.'

It was Phoebe's agent, Dagmar, who summoned the cavalry. I've known Dagmar for over forty years. I grew up with few relations and she was like an aunt to me. Dagmar took an interest – as my mother did not – in my artistic aspirations. She encouraged me to pursue a career in textile design and when I became a student in London she served as a sort of mentor.

If I was in trouble, I'd ring Dagmar. Phoebe had no phone in her studio and I had no reason to believe she read my letters as I never got a reply. So when, at nineteen, I thought I was pregnant it was Dagmar I rang, Dagmar who marched me off to a chemist and bought me a pregnancy test kit. It was Dagmar I rang to say, thank God, I wasn't pregnant, the test was negative.

As was every test for the next twenty years.

'Ann? It's Dagmar. Sorry to bother you, darling, but I need to talk to you about Phoebe.'

'Is something wrong?'

'No, not *wrong* exactly, but I just wanted you to know . . . I really don't think she's coping. Not any more.'

'Did she ask you to contact me?'

'No, of course not! And while we're on the subject, this call didn't take place. I'll deny all knowledge if she asks me.'

'Dagmar, I know you're the soul of tact, but I'm sure you're aware I haven't seen Phoebe in months. We're barely in touch – and that's her choice, not mine.'

'Yes, I know things are a bit strained, but I really thought you ought to know and I wasn't sure who else to ring. I mean, I've done my best to stand by her, but I'm not family, I'm just her agent.'

'And it's a long time since she earned you any money. You'd better tell me what's going on.'

'Well, I visited her the other day and, frankly, I was appalled to see what she's been reduced to. She's living alone now and she's decamped to the studio. The house is like the *Marie Celeste*. Abandoned. She's made up a bed and she's cooking stuff in a microwave – that is, when she bothers to cook. When I was there she offered me cold pizza. She said she gets them delivered and I think she must be living on them. There was a stack of boxes piled up in a corner.'

'But don't her friends visit any more? There used to be so many. I've often worried about Phoebe, but I've never worried about her being alone.'

'Well, let's face it, darling, she's upset a lot of people over the years, not just you. And she's no longer the glamour puss she was in her youth. Though she did mention she'd invited one of the pizza delivery boys to stay and share her *quattro stagioni*.'

'Oh, God.'

'Don't worry, I gather he declined. But she's become a sad old lady and, though she'll never admit it, I think she needs someone to look after her. Or at least *organise* her. She gave me a hug when I left and I could tell she hadn't washed in a while.'

'Oh, Dagmar, I'm so sorry you've had to deal with all this.'

'Don't worry, darling. Phoebe wasn't picking up the phone and she's stopped replying to email, so I thought I'd better check up on her. And I'd heard rumours she was painting again.'

'Is she?'

'No. Her hands are just the same. She's still in pain, but I think she hides it better now. Or maybe she's just drinking more.'

'Was she drunk when you saw her?'

'No, not drunk, but she definitely needs someone to take away all the empties.'

'Oh, if only the wretched woman would keep in touch! Believe me, I have tried, Dagmar.'

'I know you have. Phoebe just won't admit she needs help.'

'She can't bear the thought of being dependent. On *anyone*. Not for money, not for love, not for anything.'

'Well, she either needs some sort of companion or she needs to sell up. I saw some nasty bruises and she wouldn't tell me how she came by them. I suspect she's had a few falls.'

'Oh, no, really?'

'And she really struggled to make us instant coffee. My heart was in my mouth watching her with the kettle, but she wouldn't let me help. Well, you know what she's like. She won't ever admit there's a problem. But I suspect that's what the pizza is all about. She's given up cooking. Given up on everything. So I think you'd better pay her a visit, Ann. But don't say I sent you.'

'Of course not. I'll go and see her. I have some news I've been meaning to tell her anyway.'

'Good news?'

'No. Well, not unless you like nice tidy endings. Jack and I are finally getting divorced. We said we wouldn't bother, but he's met someone he wants to marry. And she's pregnant.'

'Oh. I see.'

'So it's time to draw a line. And I thought I should let Phoebe know. Not that she'll care, but I like to go through the motions of filial duty. I'd hate her to hear about Jack's marriage through a third party.'

'You've done all you could, Ann. You've tried to be a good daughter, but the fact is, Phoebe just didn't *want* one.'

And that was it in a nutshell. Phoebe wasn't the least bit maternal. I was her only foray into motherhood and it was a disaster – for her, for me and apparently for Sylvester, who deserted us, leaving no forwarding address.

I assume he's dead now, but a part of me wonders if he's still alive, if he remembers anything about the little girl he abandoned to the care of a reluctant mother. I spent years missing him, then years hating him. Finally, I tried to forget him. Now I just wonder, where did he go? And why? And why would Phoebe never talk about it?

My mother ignored my letter, so I rang. I got the answering machine for several days but I kept leaving messages until one day, she finally picked up. I enquired after her health and asked if I could pay her a visit. I told her I had some news.

'Good God, you're not pregnant, are you?'

'No, of course not. I'm forty-three. I gave up on all that years ago.'

'So why do you want to see me?' she asked suspiciously.

'Well, as I said, I have some news. About Jack.'

'Is he dead?'

'*No!* Look, Mum, could I just come and visit? I'd really like to see you. I'm concerned about you living alone.'

'How do you know I'm living alone?' Phoebe snapped. 'Has Dagmar been telling tales?'

'Not at all, but she's concerned about you too.'

'I'm fine. Couldn't be better. There's a constant stream of visitors – some of them young, male and good-looking, so you don't need to worry about me. I'm in the pink! Now, if you don't mind, I'd like to get on. I'm very busy.'

I shouldn't have asked, but I did. 'Are you painting again?'

There was a brief pause, then Phoebe said 'No', and hung up.

PHOEBE

From where she lay in bed, Phoebe Flint could see her easel, with its blank canvas, her paints, brushes, oily rags, all the paraphernalia of an artist's life. When she used to be able to work, Phoebe would lock up the studio at the end of the day and stroll across to Garden Lodge, where, with paint-stained hands, she'd pour herself a large gin with very little tonic. She was happy to forget her work for a few hours, knowing she'd make the journey in reverse the following day and the next. Work was the great cure-all. It didn't mend broken hearts or bodies but, like gin, it dulled the pain.

There was a rhythm and a routine to Phoebe's days and friends and lovers knew it shouldn't be disturbed. But Sylvester hadn't understood. Sylvester had been unpredictable, emotional, romantic – in a word, *foreign*. He expected Phoebe to drop everything to meet him at the airport. He liked to go out to dinner when she'd forgotten to cook. As a Madeiran, he didn't share her enthusiasm for buttered cream crackers and a lump of stale cheddar.

Ann had proved to be another distraction. The child expected Phoebe to play games and read stories, especially after Sylvester had gone, but once Ann was settled at school, Phoebe established a routine again, one that lasted decades, until it was disrupted by the discovery of a lump that turned out to be malignant. Surgery and punishing chemotherapy confined Phoebe to bed or a wheelchair for months.

The loss of a breast and lymphoedema in her right arm made work impossible. In any case, her hands and feet hurt too much for her to work at an easel. Even sketching was difficult.

Phoebe's condition was notoriously difficult to treat. The disabling side effects of chemo were usually temporary. Her oncologist assured her many patients suffered, but most made a full recovery. Phoebe didn't. Her GP referred her to a pain clinic, but nothing from their pharmacopeia soothed her damaged nerves, apart from drugs that reduced her to a swollen, confused heap, slumped in front of the TV, too exhausted to reach for the remote. Phoebe preferred to live with her pain.

Her dogged efforts to paint were never witnessed by friends or even Dagmar. Phoebe's humiliating failures were a private affair. She stopped complaining about her disability when several well-meaning friends cited Matisse and his famous paper cut-outs, executed from his wheelchair using a pair of wallpaper shears. Phoebe vowed privately that all she'd be executing with wallpaper shears would be the next person to mention Henri bloody Matisse.

Her attempts to produce new paintings yielded work so disappointing she felt compelled to destroy it in case she dropped dead and some future art historian came upon these daubings and concluded they were a new departure in her final years, one rather less successful than Matisse's cut-outs.

To reduce the number of footsteps she was required to make, Phoebe moved into the studio. She refused to accept her painting days were over and, as a staunch atheist, she declined to pray for a miracle, but she didn't stop hoping for one. Sometimes she dreamed of waking full of energy and pain-free, able to swing her legs out of bed and stand without wincing. In dreams she strode over to her easel, picked up a brush and palette and wielded them deftly, confidently, her brain and hand so closely connected, it was as if she only had to think the brush strokes for them to appear on the canvas.

Phoebe lay still and stared at her easel for a long time before attempting to get out of bed. As soon as she moved, she knew the overnight miracle had not occurred. As the duvet grazed her damaged toes, she braced herself for the worst part of her day: the moment when she placed both feet inside her thickly padded slippers and stood, putting her whole weight on the ground.

She grunted and, stiff with inactivity, lurched across the floor like Frankenstein's monster, aiming for the kettle she'd filled the night before, when her hands still worked. She flicked a switch and hobbled over to a chair, eager to take the weight off her feet.

'It gets better,' she told herself. Mornings were always bad, but she would loosen up as the day wore on. She'd get used to the pain which had become her constant companion and things would seem brighter after the first cup of coffee. Once it had been filter, but nowadays Phoebe settled for instant. Last thing at night she would tip a generous spoonful of Carte Noir into a mug, ready for the morning. Every little helped . . .

Phoebe wondered what it was about chronic sickness and pain that brought out the clichés in people. If ever a situation required imagination and ingenuity, it was surely one like hers. Matisse knew what he was doing. You had to think laterally. There was more to art than paint.

Already Phoebe felt tired. Maybe she'd go back to bed. She obviously wasn't going to be doing any painting. Not today. As the kettle came to the boil, she looked up longingly at the mug beside it, then her eyes swivelled across the room to her tiny fridge. She estimated the number of footsteps, then remembered the powdered milk stored on the shelf above the kettle. Finally – thinking laterally – she considered drinking her coffee black.

Tired of her deliberations, Phoebe opted for the shortest route. She kicked off her slippers and clambered back into bed. She'd get up eventually, but not now.

As she fell into a doze, Phoebe wondered if there was a thermos flask in the house. If she made a flask of coffee before retiring and left it on the bedside table, she could get a caffeine fix without setting foot on the floor. Her spirits rose until she realised she would have to negotiate the uneven path and several steps on the way back to Garden Lodge. Even if she still had one, the flask was probably on the top shelf in the scullery, which would mean climbing on to a chair.

Life drove some hard bargains.

ANN

Some weeks later Dagmar contacted me to say Phoebe was in hospital. She'd fallen in the garden, putting the rubbish bin out on a rainy morning. She hadn't broken anything, but she'd twisted her ankle and had been unable to get up again. I suppose she might have died of exposure if one of the bin men hadn't heard her calling for help.

Phoebe was admitted to hospital for observation and gave Dagmar as her next of kin. Brave Dagmar took it upon herself to ring me and, with her usual efficiency, informed me of the visiting hours.

She also wished me luck.

Phoebe was sitting up in bed wearing silk pyjamas and a man's tweed cap. I saw her before she spotted me and was able to study her face before surprise rearranged it. I'd steeled myself, but the sight of her wrung my heart. I suppose one always remembers parents as younger and more vigorous, but Phoebe looked a decade older than I was expecting. She was thin and pale, like a plant deprived of sunlight. She lay collapsed against her pillows and gazed, apparently aimlessly round the ward, but I knew my mother. She was observing with her artist's eye details, lines, textures. She would be recording them in the sketchbook of her mind, maintaining the habit of a lifetime.

I was at her bedside before she registered my presence, so when she turned her head, she was startled.

'Good God! Who sent for you? Is there something they aren't telling me? Should I expect a visit from the chaplain next?'

'Hello, Mum. How are you feeling?'

'Lousy. But you didn't need to come. I really don't know why they kept me in.' She started to cough violently, demonstrating why they'd kept her in.

'Dagmar said you'd had a fall, so naturally I was concerned.'

'Dagmar should mind her own bloody business.'

'Well, fortunately for you, she doesn't. She knew they'd let you out of here sooner if you had someone to look after you at home, so I've volunteered. But of course, if there's someone else you'd rather ask . . .'

Phoebe stared stonily into space, but her eyes were misty. 'It's been a hell of a year for death . . . Dodie went, finally. And Jim just dropped down dead one day. He was only fifty-six! And Peter's in a nursing home now, poor old thing. Dementia.'

'Uncle Peter? I didn't know he was still alive.'

'Sebastian's in prison. Not sure what for. Art forgery, probably. He was very good at it. Though not good *enough*, obviously.'

'Sebastian? Wasn't he your—'

'*Assistant*. That's what I used to call them. My assistants.' She turned and glared at me. 'You didn't bring any flowers then?'

'You aren't allowed to these days. Health and Safety regulations.'

Phoebe swore and the woman in the next bed looked up and sighed audibly. I shot a conciliatory smile in her direction.

'But I did bring you some chocolates,' I said, changing the subject. 'I didn't bother with fruit because I knew you wouldn't eat it.'

'What kind of chocolates?'

'Belgian.'

'Good! Thank you,' she added as an afterthought, without looking at me. 'But your services as a babysitter will not be required.'

'Mum, I think you need someone staying with you for a while. Till you get back on your feet.'

'Ha!'

'Sorry, but you know what I mean. I don't rate your chances of getting through a winter on your own.'

'Well, there's a first time for everything.'

'I know, but I'm offering to come and look after you for a while. Until we can arrange something suitable.'

'I've shut up the house,' she announced. 'I'm living in the studio now.'

'But why?'

'Fewer footsteps. It's easier to heat. And cheaper.'

'Have you considered selling up?'

'No.'

'Why not?'

Phoebe treated me to a withering look. 'Because it would mean conceding my painting days are over. Admitting that bloody cancer has won!' The woman in the next bed tutted and turned the page of her magazine with a theatrical flourish.

'On the contrary,' I said, playing my hand carefully. 'Rejecting ancient bricks and mortar in favour of a comfortable, modern flat would demonstrate you still meant business. That you were moving forward after . . . a setback.'

My mother didn't miss a beat. 'And where would I paint?'

'Well, you're living in one room now, so you could rent or buy something open-plan. One of those exciting warehouse conversions in Bristol, perhaps? Bare brick and loads of character. Or you could opt for a conventional layout and just turn the biggest room into a studio. There are some lovely waterside flats in Portishead and Clevedon. Good for the light.'

Phoebe eyed me suspiciously. 'You've obviously given this some thought.'

'I've done more than that. I've been to some estate agents in Bristol.' I reached into my bag and brought out a large box of Belgian chocolates and a sheaf of estate agents' brochures which I placed on the bed. Phoebe ignored the leaflets and started to rip open the chocolates, saying, 'I can't afford to move.'

'Mum, you can't afford to stay. And Garden Lodge is a desirable country property – or would be, if we tarted it up a bit.'

'And what about *you*?' Phoebe asked, chewing, her words indistinct. She set about selecting a second chocolate before she'd even swallowed the first. 'Don't you have a job? A home?'

'You know perfectly well I do. But my work is all freelance now. I can work anywhere. Until we get you sorted out anyway. I've got a friend staying in my flat at the moment. She needed a place for a few months so I said she could have the spare room. She'll keep an eye on things while I'm here. But I've been thinking about moving anyway. I fancy a change. Getting away from all the old haunts.'

'From Jack?'

'I hardly ever see Jack.'

'But that's what you meant, wasn't it? Get away from Jack. The clinics. The hospitals. All the memories.'

'You are *so* tactful, Mother.'

'Should have done it years ago. No point in waiting for men to come back,' she added, shaking her head.

'I *wasn't* waiting. We parted amicably and we've both had other relationships since. Which is what I wanted to tell you about. Jack and I are getting divorced. He wants to marry his girlfriend. She's pregnant.'

Phoebe narrowed her eyes and sneered, 'So Jack finally gets to be a daddy.'

'Yes. And I'm very pleased for him.'

'After all you went through? When he wouldn't even consider adoption?'

'Jack wasn't desperate for a child, Mum. Why should he compromise? He held out for what he wanted. And eventually he got it.'

'Life stinks.'

'It doesn't, Mum. We just don't get everything we want.'

'And sometimes,' she said, rounding on me, 'we lose the things we had! Life *stinks*.'

She was probably talking about painting, but she might have been talking about her health, or even Sylvester. I thought it best not to enquire and, after a pause, said, 'Why are you wearing a hat? Are you cold in here? Shall I have a word with the nurses?'

'It's the hat I wear when I have to go outdoors. To do the bins. I was wearing it when they brought me in.'

'But why are you wearing it *now*?'

Phoebe looked a little shifty and lowered her voice. 'My roots need doing.'

'Your roots?'

'My hair. Most of it's *Copper Flame*, but the roots are white. And there are some damned fine-looking doctors in this place, so I keep my hat on. I like to look my best,' she added, adjusting the cap to a jaunty angle. 'Haven't been to a hairdresser for months and I can't do it myself. Bloody arm doesn't work.' By way of illustration, she raised an arm in the air as far as it would go, then let it fall. 'Useless.'

'I can do it for you. Or let me take you to a hairdresser. Whatever you want. You only have to ask.'

'Thank you. That's very good of you,' she added grumpily.

'Mum, it's what families *do*. Stand by one another. Try to help.' Phoebe said nothing but pressed her lips together, as if she disapproved. 'But I must say, I do like the cap. It's very stylish. I think you should continue to wear it after we've fixed your hair.'

'You do?'

'Yes, I do. It's very you, somehow. Very Phoebe Flint.'

My mother looked at me and smiled for the first time since I'd come on to the ward.

Ignoring her lamentations, I evicted my mother from her studio and installed her comfortably indoors, but not before I'd hired someone to clean up. It looked as if Phoebe had moved out to the studio when there was no longer any room in the kitchen to prepare food. Every surface was covered in empty wine bottles, mouldy milk cartons, dirty glasses and plates. I'd seen nothing like it since my student days. But perhaps I did her a disservice. Maybe she threw a gigantic party before moving out, but I suspect the domestic detritus had accumulated over weeks. Without consulting her, I ordered a small dishwasher. I forestalled any protests by telling her she needed to save her hands for work, not washing up.

I left downstairs to the cleaners and dealt with the upstairs rooms myself, then moved back into the bedroom I'd occupied until I left home. Though small, it enjoyed a view of the garden, the studio and the wooded grounds of Beechgrave, once a Victorian merchant's grandiose country home, now recycled as a rehabilitation centre for alcoholics and drug addicts.

Phoebe grumbled about the move back to the house, but showed every sign of enjoying regular meals, TV and a comfy sofa on which she frequently dozed. I was relieved she no longer had to confront her disability as she did in the studio. My mother probably missed painting more than sex, youth and pain-free walking, but at least she could now blame someone else for her failure to work. She liked to claim she'd been bullied into leading the life of an elderly invalid. If that helped her come to terms with her difficulties, I didn't mind being her scapegoat. I was used to it.

Phoebe liked to see herself as the tragic victim of unplanned motherhood and a wastrel husband who never understood her, but that was only half the story. She'd fought cancer like a fiend, refusing to make any concession to rest or even slowing down, driving herself until the brushes dropped from her ruined hands. Phoebe might rant about the visual illiteracy of British culture, but she never complained about pain. To acknowledge it openly would have been to acknowledge defeat.

Now she was up against a new enemy – old age. I sympathised. At forty-three I was no longer young myself, or no longer *felt* young. Phoebe didn't help matters by telling me my face had become 'more interesting with age'. She then surprised me by asking if I would sit for her. I say surprised because I'm the image of my father. Phoebe couldn't help but be reminded of Sylvester whenever she looked at me – a fact that might have contributed to our strained relationship. She made no reference to the likeness and never failed to point out that I owed my limited artistic ability to her genes, but as I matured, even I could see a marked resemblance to the few photographs I owned of my dark and handsome father. If Phoebe had wanted to forget Sylvester, she stood little chance while I was at home, a living reminder of what we'd both lost.

The walled kitchen garden attached to Garden Lodge used to supply all the fruit, vegetables and flowers for the big house. There were also various outbuildings for special purposes: growing vines, mushrooms and peaches; storing fruit, flowerpots and tools; housing the donkeys that pulled the lawnmower. One of the larger outbuildings was an orangery, a long building like a conservatory, but with less glass. It was this that had persuaded Sylvester and Phoebe to purchase a large overgrown plot, blessed with a piece of ancient woodland and a sheltered walled garden.

The orangery was duly converted into a spacious studio for Phoebe, with new windows and skylights installed on the north wall. Little more than a large cottage, Garden Lodge became the family home in which Sylvester hoped to raise a big family. Once restored, the walled garden was to provide that family with food, flowers and an excess to sell.

It was a natural adventure playground and once my father had gone, I had it all to myself while Phoebe worked long days in her studio. She would allow me to enter and watch, but if she had a paintbrush or a stick of charcoal in her hand, conversation was forbidden. Consequently, I loved school for the social life. There was always someone to talk to, but in fact, mostly I listened. Listening seemed to make you more popular, especially with boys, and I was desperate to be popular. My father had done a bunk and my mother ignored me. Grandparents, aunts and uncles were dead or distant – mostly in Madeira – so I used to long for Monday mornings when I could get on the school bus and hear what everyone had been up to at the weekend. Their lives always seemed so much more exciting than mine. Other children's parents provided a taxi service to and from shopping centres, cinemas and parties, but Phoebe refused to ferry me about, insisting that, as the breadwinner, she didn't have time. I was dependent on an irregular country bus service.

Phoebe occasionally gave me money for a taxi and my pocket money was generous, but we did little together apart from go into Bristol to buy art materials. Much to the envy of my friends, she even allowed me to buy my own clothes and shoes. She didn't mind what I looked like. I doubt she even noticed.

I enjoyed our excursions to the art shop. Phoebe would chat and explain what things were for and how they were used. Whenever I showed an interest in something, she'd pick it up and put it down on the counter, adding it to her purchases. I wasn't allowed to paint in the studio, but I didn't mind. I liked to work at an old table in my bedroom with its view of gloomy Beechgrave up on the hill, looking, to my fanciful teenage eyes, like Jane Eyre's Thornfield Hall.

Long after Sylvester had abandoned his family and garden, there were still flowers and seed heads to be gathered. I developed an interest in botanical illustration and pattern which led to a career in textile design. My work now appears on kitchenware and stationery, as well as textiles. It earns me a comfortable living, but Phoebe was disappointed that I pursued a commercial branch of art. She took a dim view of my draughtsmanship and knew my artistic options were limited, but she deplored my lack of ambition. I just wanted to earn a living doing something I enjoyed, something that would fit in around raising the family I assumed I would have. So I acquired a suitable job, a suitable husband and a suitable home. I even knew which room would become the nursery.

In the end, in an act of despair and defiance that I hoped would ensure conception, I resigned from a perfectly good job and went freelance, creating a studio for myself in the large, light room I'd set aside for my babies. My career flourished, but my marriage didn't. By the time I was forty, I was on my own, working hard, making lots of money, rarely leaving the house. Just like my mother.

When Jack rang to say he wanted a divorce, I decided it was time to face up to my future. I was ready to abandon the nursery-studio and return to my roots in Somerset. I'd never had the big family I'd longed for, both as a child and as an adult, but I decided I would do my best with the family I had, which was Phoebe. It seemed the right thing to do. She had nobody else and, really, neither did I.

Phoebe wouldn't countenance anything in the studio being moved, so I had to work with her set-up, which wasn't difficult. It was distracting, but also inspiring to be surrounded by my mother's work, to sense the creative energy those walls had witnessed and absorbed.

When I moved in there were two easels, both supporting work in progress, though the paint was long dry. At one end of the long room stood an oriental screen dividing the space into bedsit and studio. Behind the screen was an old wooden dresser with kettle, teapot, a jar of coffee and a few empty wine bottles. There was a single Z-bed standing on the bare boards with a rug beside it. There was no wardrobe, but Phoebe had hammered a few nails into the wall and hung clothes from them – the paint-stained jeans and overalls she wore for work. Thick jumpers spilled out of a chest of drawers, topped with a hairbrush and comb, but no mirror.

The studio half of the room was more organised, with paints, brushes, jars and other equipment neatly arranged on shelves. Sketches and postcards were pinned up on a cork board, alongside various takeaway food menus. There was a faded and threadbare chaise longue and a full-length mirror hanging on the wall. I assumed this was to reflect more light until I realised one of the unfinished canvases was a self-portrait of Phoebe at work in her studio, an almost geometric study of squares and oblongs, lozenges of light and shadow. It made me think of Vermeer and I admired it very much.

When I sat for Phoebe in the studio, I took the risk of telling her so.

'You know, that unfinished self-portrait is very good.'

'Sit still.'

'Sorry . . . Why don't you finish it?'

'I got bored with it. Bored with me as a subject. And irritated. I kept *moving*.'

I suppressed a smile. 'I suppose that's the trouble with self-portraits.'

'You said that without moving your lips. No, don't smile. This is a study for a series I'm planning and there'll be nothing pretty about it. I want it to be *forensic*,' she added with relish.

'Oh dear, that doesn't sound at all flattering.'

'I had the idea of doing a series of portraits. *The Seven Ages of Woman*. I thought it might make a good comeback show. The journey from untouched adolescent girl into raddled old age. That one of me would be the last in the series. The one of you hanging in the sitting room would be the first.'

'The one with the flowers?'

'Yes. You were twelve. It would be a good place to start. Dagmar's had her eye on that one for years, but I said I'd never part with it. It's some of my best work,' she hastened to explain.

I wasn't hurt because I knew Phoebe hadn't meant to hurt, probably didn't even understand that I *could* be hurt. She was just an artist at work. Observant. Impersonal. I was no more to her than an inanimate object in a still-life arrangement.

Altering my position minutely to relieve tension, I said, 'It's a great idea for a series.'

'Stop fidgeting! You were much better at this when you were a child. You'd sit for hours. A model model, in fact.'

'Tell me more about your portrait series.'

Phoebe didn't reply. I thought she'd decided to drop the subject when she suddenly said, 'I wanted to show how women have lived, what they've experienced, just by showing their faces. *I* see it and I think I can make other people see it. Well, I could have done once. Not sure now. Not sure about anything any more. Bloody cancer,' she muttered. Her charcoal stick snapped and she tossed the remainder aside, saying, 'That's enough for today. I'm tired . . . Is it gin o'clock yet?'

I knew better than to ask Phoebe if I could see the sketch, but I could tell she was happy with it. Later, when she was taking a nap, I went back over to the studio and examined her work.

My first reaction was to look away, shocked, as one might turn away from the sight of an open wound. I steeled myself to look again and the second time wasn't so bad. I was prepared for the thin face with its sharp chin. The lines on my face weren't deep yet, but they were there. Life had already sketched them in and so had Phoebe. My eyes looked good – large, challenging – but she couldn't catch their pale blue in monochrome.

It was a good likeness and it wasn't just a likeness. Phoebe's sketch showed me a quality I never see when I'm putting on my make-up or when I'm in front of the mirror at the hairdresser's, but which I know is there.

Emptiness.

An emptiness that longs to be filled.

Phoebe and I rubbed along. She was both grateful for and resentful of my presence, but there were few sulks and no rows. We both knew we were avoiding a discussion of the big issue: putting Garden Lodge up for sale. I waited for her to raise the topic and she waited for me. It was emotional stalemate. Every day I promised myself I would tackle the subject of Phoebe's future, but the longer I was there, the harder it became.

Matters were finally brought to a head when she fell again, slipping on frosty paving stones. It could have happened to anyone, including me, but I took it as a sign and decided to broach the painful subject of selling the home she'd loved, lived and worked in for more than forty years.

'No.'

'Mum, *please*. Can you at least give it some thought?'

'I've already given it a great deal of thought,' she said loftily. 'This is my home and my workplace. I cannot leave.'

'I'm not asking you to give up work, you know that. I'm just asking you to think about moving to somewhere more manageable. You can continue to live independently with a bit of assistance. Someone to clean, a freezer full of nutritious food, a flat close to a doctor's surgery – all of this would make your life so much easier. And just think of the cash you'd raise.'

'Cash?' Suddenly alert, Phoebe fixed me with a look. I realised she had no idea what Garden Lodge was worth.

'You're sitting on a small fortune here and what use is that to you? You could sell this, buy a comfy flat and have enough left over for a luxury cruise.'

She snorted. 'And who would I go with?'

'You'd have enough money to treat someone to a holiday.'

'I would?'

'My preliminary research suggests an asking price of half a million would not be out of the question.'

'*What?*'

'It depends what the land's worth as a building plot. But the house itself has a certain historical appeal. The two combined could fetch a good price. Then there's the woodland. People get emotional about things like that. Someone could view this place and fall in love with it, just like you and Dad.'

In the silence that followed it occurred to me how rarely I mentioned my father to Phoebe. I felt awkward, guilty almost, as if I'd sworn in church.

'I didn't fall in love with it, actually. But I was in love with Sylvester and he was mad to have the place, so I went along with his hare-brained scheme. I humoured him and he humoured me. It worked up to a point.'

Talking about Sylvester seemed to lower her mood still further, so I decided to drop the subject, contenting myself with the suggestion that it might be useful to have the house valued. Phoebe said nothing for a moment, then looked at me warily, as if she suspected a trap. 'Half a million, you say?'

'It's possible. There's no knowing what someone would pay for a quirky one-off property like this.'

'It would have to be someone with more money than sense!'

'Well, fortunately there's no shortage of those.'

Phoebe fell silent again, but I knew she hadn't finished, so I waited.

'I suppose I'm not getting any younger.'

'Nor do you have one foot in the grave. You're semi-disabled, not dying. You just need to adapt. Like you did after Dad left. It was very hard, I'm sure, but you did it. You started over. You could do that again. Especially with me to help you.'

'What do you mean?'

'I think if I moved closer . . . I mean, if you had someone dependable living locally, I'm sure you'd manage better.'

Phoebe raised a hand in protest. 'I wouldn't want you cramping my style, Ann. I have to have my own place, with my own front door.'

'Of course. I wasn't suggesting we'd share a home, but I think the time has come for me to live closer. Closer to my roots. It's what I'd like to do. I could help set you up in a new home and be around for . . . well, for any emergency. And then I could stop worrying about you.'

Phoebe looked surprised. 'You worry about me?'

'Of course I do.'

'Why? There's absolutely no need.'

'I know I don't *need* to worry, I just do. You're my mother. It's natural to worry about people you love.' Phoebe looked blank and I began to flounder. 'That's what love is, isn't it? Worrying something bad will happen.'

'Well, I never worried about Sylvester.' She looked away and added, 'I suppose I should have, but you never see these things coming.' She looked back at me and lifted her chin. 'I *observe*, Ann, I don't empathise. That's why I was a lousy wife and a lousy mother.' She shrugged. 'Sorry, but that's just the way I'm made.'

'You weren't a lousy mother,' I lied. 'And I'm sorry if I've depressed you with all this talk of selling up. Just give it some thought and let me know what you decide. When you're ready. No pressure.'

As the year wore on and the trees surrounding Garden Lodge shed their leaves, the house and garden became lighter. As a child, I would take myself off to the wood in autumn and lie under the beeches, gazing up at their golden leaves. Sometimes I'd pretend I'd been abandoned – not a huge leap for my imagination. I'd lie there, feigning death, waiting to be buried under a blanket of leaves by robins, like the Babes in the Wood – a vain hope, since beeches retain their leaves until the spring. In the end cold and hunger would effect my resurrection and I'd run back to the house in search of warmth and food, wobbling inside my oversized wellingtons, glad to be alive.

When I was older, I liked to watch from my bedroom window as autumn stripped the other trees and their dark outlines emerged, stark against a pale, wintry sky. As the leaf canopy fell, trees became easier to draw, I could spot birds and the occasional foraging squirrel, so I rather liked the West Country winter, despite what seemed at times to be perpetual rain. My father fled to Madeira whenever he could and found excuses to linger. He wasn't like Phoebe or me. We observed the weather with our artists' eyes or we ignored it, carrying on in our phlegmatic British way. But Sylvester must have suffered.

Autumn was made bearable for him by his dahlias. Bold flowers with no scent, they collapse at the first frost, but they're the last big colourful blooms before the onset of winter, gaudy and short-lived, like a firework display. Sylvester gathered bunches of them and brought them into the house where, to Phoebe's horror, they would shed earwigs. Whenever I see them now – dahlias or earwigs – I think of my father.

There's a photo of me, standing gap-toothed next to a cactus dahlia, its flowers as big as my head. For many years I wondered if, whenever he saw one, Sylvester thought of the shy, smiling child who'd posed beside one of his giant blooms. I liked to think that he did.

Phoebe caved eventually and agreed – 'just out of curiosity' – to have Garden Lodge valued. Two agents told us it was difficult to price, but suggested we test the market at around £495,000. They also warned us there would be little interest until the spring. Nevertheless, Phoebe agreed to put the house on the market, reassuring herself, 'I don't have to accept an offer. I'd just be interested to know, that's all. Half a million for this place seems bloody ridiculous to me. I'm sure it's just greedy estate agents, trying to boost their commission.'

It was a start. My mother was at least thinking about her future.

Weeks passed and we heard nothing. Phoebe said, 'I told you so.' We discussed reducing the price, but the agent advised us to hang on until the spring when things would apparently get moving again, but I sensed Phoebe was disappointed. She was also irritated by my continuing attempts to keep the house tidy for potential buyers, so in the end I gave up and turned my attention to the neglected garden.

Phoebe had let the walled garden become completely overgrown. Renovating it was beyond my modest capabilities, but I'd cleared the paths and swept up fallen leaves so people could at least walk round and see the size of the plot.

The cottage garden, as we called it, was situated at the back of Garden Lodge, enclosed by old outbuildings and glasshouses, a shed, the studio and a gate that led to a rutted lane and the outside world. It had once been riotous with colour and crammed with plants. I could vaguely remember its decline in the years after Sylvester's departure. The roses had persisted, as did the shrubs. Marigolds, cornflowers and nasturtiums had self-seeded, but gradually the weeds took over. Plants died and weren't replaced. Phoebe wasn't interested. She simply passed through the garden on her way to the studio. It was just a thoroughfare to her and probably a source of unhappy memories.

I chose a fine, still November day to make a start. We had no near neighbours, so I decided to have a bonfire. I collected fallen twigs and small branches from the wood and carried them back to the piece of waste ground that once hosted Sylvester's dahlias. Nothing but weeds had grown there for almost forty years. I forked it over and felt cheered as a blank canvas of damp, dark soil emerged. Soon a robin joined me and, keeping a cautious distance, picked over the crumbling soil for worms. I was glad of the company.

When some ground was cleared, I arranged my kindling to form a sort of wigwam and added some of the driest vegetation. When I struck a match, the dead leaves sizzled and soon a plume of smoke rose straight up into the air. The smell was almost intoxicating and I experienced a sudden craving for sausages. I remembered a Bonfire Night, my father lighting Roman candles and launching rockets from empty beer bottles, while Phoebe handed round charred sausages in rolls. After he'd gone, I was allowed sparklers and a few small fireworks, but there were no more bonfires or al fresco bangers.

As I tended my bonfire and contemplated my early childhood, I wondered why I spent so much time thinking about something I could hardly remember. Was I trying to fill in the blanks? Or did I ponder my own childhood because I'd never had a child? No childhood had ever superseded mine in importance, so perhaps I remained shackled to mine, even though it seemed distant, strange, almost forgotten.

I stared, hypnotised, into the crackling flames, looking for answers, but found none.

By the time the agent finally rang to make an appointment for someone to view Garden Lodge, I'd almost forgotten it was on the market. The phone call threw me and I must have sounded off-hand, even a little confused.

'Someone wants to *view*?'

'Yes. A Mr Grenville would like to view the property.'

'Is he a serious buyer?'

'I've no idea, but we haven't exactly been inundated with enquiries, have we? He does have a property to sell. In Bristol. I don't have any more details, I'm afraid.'

'I see. When does he want to come?'

'As soon as it suits you.'

'Well, tomorrow would be okay. I need to have a bit of a tidy up. Indoors and out. It's the worst time of the year for viewing the garden unfortunately. There's nothing to see in January.'

'I doubt he'll be interested in the garden. It will be the cottage and the building plot. It's a great business opportunity.'

But the agent was wrong. Mr Grenville wasn't looking for a business opportunity.

He was punctual. As a damage limitation exercise, I'd settled Phoebe down with a cup of tea and a DVD of *Murder, She Wrote*. At three o' clock I opened the door to a tall, shabby-looking young man with muddy shoes and over-long hair. Not my idea of an entrepreneur, though I suppose the hair was a bit Richard Branson. I decided he looked the self-sufficient type and must be in search of a family home with a plot of land. Alternatively, he might be casing the joint to see if we were worth burgling.

He held up the agency brochure and, as he extended a large hand, his wide smile was reassuring. 'Mrs Flint? Connor Grenville. I hope I'm not too early?'

'Not at all. Do come in. I'm Ann de Freitas and I'll be showing you round.'

'Thank you,' he said, stepping on to the doormat where he scraped his shoes thoroughly. As I shut the door behind him, I realised he wasn't that young – early thirties maybe, fair, with a high forehead that made him look academic, as did the worn cord trousers and shapeless woollen jumper. Looking at him, I doubted he had the financial resources to buy Garden Lodge. Then I told myself there was no uniform for millionaires. Perhaps they made their money by economising on clothes and haircuts.

I felt nervous. This was the kind of thing Jack used to do. Jack was good with people and could talk to anyone. He'd been the one who'd bought and sold houses. I'd decorated, gardened and cooked. I'd been the home-maker, but it had always been a home of Jack's choosing.

Mr Grenville was still standing on the doormat, waiting for me to show him round, so I pulled myself together. 'This is the hall,' I announced superfluously. 'There's plenty of storage,' I added, opening a glory hole cupboard and shutting it again quickly before the contents could tumble out. 'And through here we have the kitchen.'

'Have you lived here long?' he asked, examining me and not the kitchen.

'I don't actually live here. I'm staying with my mother until she's sold the house.'

'Has she lived here long?'

'Yes. Since the early seventies. My father renovated the house and garden.'

'Ah, yes, the garden. It's very old, isn't it?'

'It was the kitchen garden attached to the big house.'

'Beechgrave.'

'That's right. Would you like to see inside the kitchen cupboards?'

'No, thanks, that won't be necessary.'

'The dishwasher's brand new,' I said, pointing.

'Is it?' He gave the machine a cursory nod, said, 'That's useful to know,' and looked eager to move on.

He showed no interest in the scullery or the downstairs cloakroom, but stood in front of windows, looking out in various directions. The burglary option seemed increasingly likely, though unless he knew about paintings, he would see nothing worth stealing. Phoebe owned a decent art collection which she'd assembled over the years, often buying when an artist was unknown and still affordable, but Mr Grenville ignored the paintings. When we got to the sitting room and I introduced Phoebe by name, there was no flicker of recognition, so I concluded he either knew nothing about art or was a very good actor.

He viewed each room politely and briefly, showing no inclination to linger until we came to my room with its view of the wood and distant Beechgrave up on the hill. He stood at the window and looked out in silence until I asked if he had any questions. That jolted him out of his reverie and he said, no, he didn't want to take up much more of my time.

I was starting to feel slightly annoyed, or perhaps it was disappointed. 'Would you like to view outside? The orangery was converted into a studio for my mother, but it would make a lovely big summer house. Or an office.'

'Yes, please. I'd really like to have a look round the garden.'

'There's not a lot to see at this time of year, but the building plot is sizeable.'

'Building plot?' He looked surprised.

'Well, yes. We assume that's what most people will be interested in. The walled garden is a nice level plot and the old brick walls are very attractive. Or they would be if you removed all the ivy. But you don't have to take the land. We're selling in two lots. The house and woodland are one lot, the walled garden and outbuildings are the other.'

He looked crestfallen. 'I didn't realise you were breaking it up.'

'All the details are in the brochure,' I said, sounding rather curt.

'I see. Sorry, I hadn't really registered . . .'

I glanced out of the window and said, 'It's started to rain again, I'm afraid.'

'I won't keep you long. In fact, you don't even need to show me round. I can explore on my own. I know my way round a Victorian garden,' he added cryptically.

'I'll have to unlock the studio for you. It's a bit of a tip, I'm afraid. It's where I work.'

'I thought you said your mother—'

'She used to work there until she became ill. She hasn't been able to paint for some time now, so I've taken over the studio while I'm staying with her.'

'You paint too?' he asked, following me down the stairs.

'Yes, though in a very different way. I'm a textile artist.'

'Obviously a talented family.'

Turning to him at the bottom of the stairs, I said, 'My father was a passionate gardener and my mother is an artist. I suppose my DNA dictated I'd become someone who dreamed of being a second William Morris.'

'But instead you became the first Ann de Freitas. An original,' he added, with such an engaging smile, I was thrown slightly and led him to the back door in silence.

As I pulled on a raincoat, I said, 'There's only one umbrella, I'm afraid, but it's quite large.'

'Don't worry about me, I'm used to rain,' he said cheerfully.

As we went round, huddled under the umbrella, Mr Grenville's excitement was palpable, but he paid scant attention to the information I gave him, showing more interest in the ancient graffiti carved on the beech trees than the dimensions of the studio. He had a tendency to wander off, his long legs covering the ground quickly, then he'd stand still, apparently impervious to the rain, and stare into space, as if trying to orient himself or imagine something that wasn't actually there. Several times he looked up towards Beechgrave, then back at Garden Lodge, his brow furrowed.

When he joined me again under the umbrella, his spirits seemed as damp as his clothes and hair. 'Thanks for waiting. I hope you aren't getting cold.'

Curiosity finally got the better of good manners. 'You're not actually interested in the house, are you?' He opened his mouth to reply, then thought better of it. To his credit, he met my stern look without flinching. 'Are you just a time-waster? Or checking to see if we're worth burgling? We're not, unless you deal in contemporary portraits.'

'I'm very sorry. I admit I *am* wasting your time. Really I'm just here to see the garden. What's left of it.'

'Why?'

'It's a long story.' He pushed dripping hair back from his forehead and said, 'I don't suppose you'd like to hear it, would you?'

I laughed out loud at his cheek. 'First you admit you're wasting my time, then you ask if I'd like to know *why*?'

'I thought you might. It's a mystery, you see.'

'A *mystery?*'

'Yes. Your mother might enjoy hearing about it. She obviously likes mysteries.'

By now I suspected I was dealing with a patient on the run from Beechgrave's punishing teetotal regime. 'What on earth do you mean?'

'*Murder, She Wrote.* That's what she was watching. My gran used to love that programme.'

I faltered, overcome by curiosity. 'And I suppose if I allow you to tell us this story, you'll want a cup of tea as well?'

His grin was disarming and I suspected he knew it. 'That would be more than I deserve.'

'Dead right,' I said, turning and heading back to the house, leaving him standing in the rain. 'This mystery had better be good,' I called out over my shoulder.

'It is,' he shouted back. 'Completely baffling. Definitely a three-pipe problem.'

I told Phoebe we were having tea with Connor Grenville. Her eyes widened and she zapped the TV with the remote. Turning to him she said, 'Are you going to buy my house then?'

He looked embarrassed and said, 'I'm very sorry, Mrs Flint—'

'It's not Mrs, it's Phoebe.'

'Sorry, Phoebe, but I'm here on false pretences. I *am* looking for a property, but to be honest, this one is a bit outside my price range.'

'So why are you here?' she asked, with a terseness he could hardly fail to notice.

'I suppose I'm here in my capacity as a garden historian and archivist.'

'Really? Is that what you do?'

'Among other things.'

'And you wanted to give our garden the once-over?'

'Well, yes. But only because there's a family connection. With my grandmother, Ivy.'

'Oh? Did she use to live here?'

'She and my great-grandmother were both born here, then later Ivy lived up at the big house, Beechgrave.'

'You don't say!' Phoebe looked up at me and said, 'Get the kettle on, Ann. And crack open a packet of chocolate digestives. I think this is going to be interesting . . .'

When I offered Mr Grenville a towel for his wet hair, he took it saying, 'Please call me Connor.' I reciprocated and said he should call me Ann. The formalities over, I also suggested he remove his sodden jumper so I could dry it in front of the wood-burning stove. As he handed it to me I noted his check shirt had seen better days, but not an iron. Rubbing his hands together to warm them, he thanked me and asked if he could help in the kitchen, an offer I declined.

So it was in a spirit of friendly informality that we gathered round the stove to drink tea. It was dark outside now and the rain had turned to sleet, but Garden Lodge was always a good place to be holed up in bad weather. It wrapped itself around you. Its thick walls and wooden floors felt solid and timeless. They'd last another hundred years or more if left in peace. But, I reflected, the house's new owner might have other, radical ideas. The thought was uncomfortable, so I pushed it to the back of my mind and concentrated on the potential buyer who was now our guest.

When you're an artist, it's hard not to stare at things, including people. You're always looking at the play of light on surfaces, observing shadow and texture. When studied, anything becomes interesting and almost abstract as a collection of shapes and colours. I wondered if Phoebe was already painting Connor's face in her head.

She was certainly paying him a lot of attention, but Phoebe had always had an eye for attractive young men and I supposed Connor could be called attractive. He looked fit and tanned, as if used to an outdoor life. His long, thick hair had darkened with the rain, but when dry, it was a warm mix of blond and toffee shades. He possessed steady grey eyes, a pleasant, open face and a manner that was engaging without being pushy. Nevertheless, I suspected he was used to getting what he wanted. Connor Grenville would be a hard man to ignore.

I passed him the plate of biscuits and, as he took one, he asked, 'Do you happen to know if your family had any connection with the Mordaunts?'

'Who?'

'The Mordaunts. They built Beechgrave and lived there for several generations. The house was sold by Hester Mordaunt in the 1920s, then it was requisitioned during the Second World War. Did you realise this was the Head Gardener's house?'

'Oh, yes,' Phoebe said. 'My husband was interested in the history of the place. He was a keen gardener himself.'

'But he had no connection with the Mordaunts?'

'None that I know of.'

'Nor the Hatherwicks?'

'I've never heard the name. Who were they?'

'Herbert Hatherwick was the Head Gardener before the First World War and he lived here with his family. His son started off as a pot boy in the garden and worked his way up to journeyman gardener before going off to fight in France. Hatherwick's daughter, Violet – that's my great-grandmother – had an illegitimate daughter, Ivy, who was later adopted by Hester Mordaunt, the mistress of Beechgrave. Hester seems to have been quite a remarkable woman. She never married and ran Beechgrave on her own, turning it into a convalescent home for wounded Tommies.'

'Was your great-grandmother impregnated by one of the toffs at the big house?' Phoebe asked with a spectacular lack of delicacy.

'No, not at all,' Connor replied, unperturbed. 'The menfolk were all dead. Killed in the war. That's how Hester came to inherit. There was no one else left.'

'So who was Ivy's father then?'

'Well, that's just it. There are big gaps in the story because the family archive is incomplete. My grandmother and I were investigating when she died.'

'What a shame,' Phoebe said. 'And I suppose a lot of information died with her?'

'More than you might think. Much of the archive was destroyed. There was a fire, you see . . .'

IVY

Ivy Watson threw another log on to the dying fire and replaced the fireguard. She picked her way carefully through the photo albums, letters and postcards strewn on the floor of her small sitting room and settled down again in her armchair. She lifted one of the old albums on to her lap and turned its heavy ornamented pages. Connor had said he needed more photos to scan, partly to preserve them, but also to help him plan the book. He'd asked her to choose her favourites.

It was a pleasant job for a winter's afternoon, but Ivy felt guilty dismantling the family albums Hester had made. Connor had shown her how to keep track of where the photos came from. When she removed a photo, she used two coloured bits of sticky paper, both with the same number written on them. One went on the back of the photo, the other filled the gap in the album. It was a simple system and one that Ivy's old, arthritic fingers could manage. Nowadays writing anything was a trial, so it was kind and clever of Connor to have thought of an easy way to keep the precious albums in order.

She decided he must have a picture of the old beech, the Trysting Tree. Hester had loved that tree and there were many photos of it, taken in all seasons. One of them showed the graffiti in close-up.

Generations of gardeners and housemaids had carved their brief and cryptic declarations of love on its smooth bark, but someone – an educated man, evidently – had carved a Latin inscription: *Crescent illae crescetis amores.* Ivy didn't know what the words meant, but she guessed *amores* was something to do with love. Connor had studied Latin at school and might be interested in deciphering the inscription, so she removed the photo of the beech, making sure she didn't bend it with her clumsy fingers.

As she extracted the corners from the small card triangles holding the photo in place, Ivy saw an envelope had been tucked behind. As she turned it over, she was astonished to see the envelope was addressed to *Ivy Hatherwick.* Until her marriage, Ivy had been known as Ivy Mordaunt. Ivy Hatherwick had been her name before she was adopted as an infant by Hester Mordaunt.

Curious now, she opened the envelope and removed a single sheet of notepaper. At once she recognised her Uncle William's handwriting and noted that the letter had been written the day before he died. Ivy settled back in her armchair, but she'd read no more than a few lines when she suddenly shot forward, her hand covering her mouth. As she continued to read, her eyes widened and she emitted a small whimpering noise. When she'd finished reading, Ivy crumpled the letter into a ball, held it tightly in her fist for a moment, then threw it on the floor. She leaned back, clutching the arms of her chair and wept for a long time.

After she'd composed herself, she bent down, her breathing still unsteady, and retrieved the letter. She spread it out on her lap and read the words again, hoping they might have changed, that she had been dreaming, that her aged brain had simply misunderstood. But the words remained the same and there was no other construction she could put upon them.

Ivy got to her feet and staggered towards the fireplace. Setting the fireguard aside, she threw the letter on to the fire and watched it burn.

When there was nothing left and the flames had died down, she turned and surveyed the family archive spread out on the floor and dining table. Stooping, she grabbed some letters and photographs and hurled them on to the fire. As she gathered up the orderly piles of photos and consigned them to the blaze, she began to weep again, but she stood and watched as the photos buckled, then burst into flames.

As she turned away, Ivy tripped over one of the albums on the hearth rug. She lost her balance and flailed, reaching out for the mantelpiece, but she fell, banging her head on a corner of the table. Stunned, she tried to get up on to her knees, but found she had no strength in her arms or legs. She lay helpless on her sitting room floor, like a felled tree.

Burning letters tumbled from the grate and Ivy watched in horror as they ignited a paper trail of scattered photos leading from the hearthstone to the rug where she lay. She began to shout, calling for help, but her voice was frail and the walls of her cottage were thick. She clutched at her skirt, hoisting it away from the flames. As the rug began to smoulder, Ivy reached up for the corner of the tablecloth and tugged. There was a vase of flowers on the table. Connor had brought a bunch of chrysanthemums and arranged them for her. The water in the vase might be enough to douse the burning rug.

She pulled steadily and felt the tablecloth slide, bringing the vase to the edge of the table. As the cloth travelled, more photographs fell from the table, fluttering into the air before landing on the rug where they curled and smouldered. Coughing, blinded by smoke and tears, Ivy propped herself on one elbow and reached up for the vase. She grasped it and threw the contents at the burning rug. There was a hissing sound and smoke filled the room. Choking now, she dragged herself across the carpet, towards the telephone, thinking of her grandson. The dear boy had taken pity on her ancient eyes and useless fingers and had bought her a special phone with big buttons, saying it would be easier for her to use 'in an emergency'.

When someone answered, Ivy managed to gasp the word 'Fire' and the first line of her address before she passed out.

ANN

Connor earned his tea. It must have been a gruelling story for him to tell, even though he'd gone over the few known facts with the police and in his own mind many times. Ivy had died in hospital of smoke inhalation and although he'd been at her bedside, she'd been unable or unwilling to speak to him.

He'd rescued what he could of the family archive. Some was untouched by the fire, but much of it was burned or damaged by smoke and water from the vase Ivy had emptied in an attempt to put out the fire.

'Do you know for certain that she actually started it?' Phoebe enquired. 'Perhaps it was just a dreadful accident.'

'The firemen said it was clear a considerable amount of paper had been put on to the fire. And the fireguard had been set to one side.'

'I see. That doesn't sound like an accident, does it?'

Connor shook his head. 'There seems little doubt Ivy dumped a load of material on to the fire, most of which burned, but some must have fallen out on to the hearth. The only significant damage was to the rug and Ivy's clothing, but she seems to have doused that pretty effectively when she realised the fire was getting out of hand. But the paper must have continued to smoulder and fill the room with smoke. And at some point she must have fallen.'

'How do they know that?' Phoebe asked, her eyes bright.

'She had a bad bruise on her forehead. She hit something hard, something sharpish. Knowing the layout of that room, I'd say she keeled over and hit the corner of the table.'

'So,' Phoebe said, summing up. 'You're convinced she was trying to destroy the archive.'

'Well, yes, I am, if only because I know my grandmother. If there'd been some kind of accident, if a spark had landed on some photos and they'd started to burn, Ivy would have put out the flames with her bare hands rather than lose them. So it had to be her doing. For some reason she was trying to destroy something that, up till then, had meant all the world to her.'

'Apart from you?' I asked.

Connor looked up, surprised. 'Yes, she was very fond of me. I was like the son she never had. My mother died when I was quite young, so my grandmother stepped in. Dad was in the army and abroad a lot, so it was Ivy who raised me really. She'd always treated that archive with the utmost respect. Reverence, almost. But something must have caused a change of heart. Unless it was some kind of brain storm.'

'Why did she destroy it?' Phoebe asked.

I sighed and wondered if she'd dozed off briefly. 'That's what we don't know, Mum. That's the mystery.'

'No, I mean why did Ivy *destroy* it? Why not just hide it? Put it away in a box on top of the wardrobe. Or in a safe deposit box in a bank. Why did it have to be *destroyed*? And why was she trying to destroy *all* of it?'

Connor and I were silent for a moment or two. I must admit, I was impressed with the clarity of Phoebe's thinking. Years of watching *Murder, She Wrote* had evidently paid off.

'Well,' Connor said, considering, 'if she suddenly wanted to restrict my access to her stuff, it would have been awkward to explain.'

'Was she the type of woman who could lie convincingly?' Phoebe asked. 'Make up some story to fool you?'

Connor laughed. 'Definitely not! Ivy would have been the world's worst poker player.'

'So she didn't want to lie to you *and* she didn't want you to see something.'

'See something?'

'Oh, yes, don't you think so?' Phoebe was well into her stride now. Despite the tragic subject matter, I could tell she was enjoying herself. 'Your grandmother might just have had a change of heart, I suppose, but I think it far more likely she found something – a note, a photograph, something she'd never seen, or never seen in a particular light before. Perhaps it was a letter she'd never read properly. *Something* must have made her change her mind. And then her immediate response must have been, "Destroy the evidence." But why *all* of it? Why not just destroy the offending article?'

'Because she was angry,' I said.

Connor and Phoebe turned to face me. 'Angry?' Phoebe frowned. 'What do you mean?'

'I mean, if Ivy had read something awful or looked at a particular photo and realised something shocking, she might have burned it. Maybe torn it up and hurled the pieces on the fire. That's what you'd do, wouldn't you? But Ivy went on and on, burning stuff, adding fuel to the fire. So I think she must have been very angry. Or in the grip of some other strong emotion.'

Connor frowned. 'So you mean it wasn't just that she didn't want me to know—'

'She didn't want *anyone* to know. Ever. Which makes me think it was something she hadn't known and really didn't want to know.'

'But what?' Phoebe said, gazing into space, her eyes narrowed.

'I don't see how we can ever know. Ivy's dead and most of the archive was destroyed.'

'Well, that's not quite the case,' Connor said, leaning forward in his chair. 'I told you she'd burned a great deal of stuff, but some survived and it's still mostly legible. And there are copies of a lot of photos and documents on my laptop.'

'The trigger can't have been anything that survived though, can it?' I said. 'That would have been the first to go, surely?'

'Oh, yes, of course,' Phoebe said with a groan.

'But whatever it was,' I conceded, 'Connor might still have a copy.'

'I might, but if I do, Ivy had already seen it because she was the one who gave it to me.'

'Damn!' Phoebe exclaimed. 'Just when I thought we were getting somewhere!'

'You see what I mean,' Connor said, looking at me, 'about a three-pipe problem?'

'I certainly do. But you now have my mother on the case and she's not one to give up easily. Nor, I suspect, are you. Perhaps between us we might be able to piece the story together. Or maybe a new piece of evidence will turn up. You never know.'

'I certainly feel encouraged,' Connor said, beaming at Phoebe. 'Some sort of picture is beginning to emerge.'

'If not the one Ivy burned,' Phoebe murmured. She sat back and slapped her palms on her thighs. 'Well, this has been first-rate entertainment, but I can't do any more brainwork on an empty stomach. We need sustenance, Ann.'

'Mum, you've eaten half a packet of chocolate digestives!'

'No, that was mostly Connor.'

'Guilty as charged,' he said, raising his hands in submission. 'I missed lunch, so I'm afraid I put away quite a few.'

'Time for something more substantial then. Will you stay for supper, Connor? I doubt Phoebe will let you go until she's squeezed the last drop of information out of you, so you might as well give in gracefully. It's chicken and leek pie.'

'If it doesn't mean short rations for the ladies, I'd love to join you.'

'Good!' said Phoebe, clearly delighted. 'Now, while Ann is busy in the kitchen, you can make yourself useful with the drinks tray. Help yourself. Mine's a large gin.'

'Is that with tonic?' Connor asked, getting to his feet.

'Just wave the bottle in the general vicinity of my glass.'

'One large gin coming up, madam.'

As he poured her drink, Connor exchanged a conspiratorial look with me. He seemed to be enjoying himself and, as I stood in the doorway, listening to the banter, it occurred to me, he *would* be good with old ladies. He'd been raised by one and perhaps still missed her.

I went to the kitchen to fetch some ice. Taking a lemon from the fruit bowl, I began to slice it. It was touching to see Phoebe so engaged, enjoying her second favourite pursuit: flirting with young men. She was enjoying herself, using her brain, laughing, chatting, being useful to someone. She was in her element and pain was temporarily far from her mind.

Connor's untidy head appeared round the door. 'Phoebe's calling for ice and a slice. Can I help?'

I handed him a tumbler full of ice cubes and a dish of lemon slices. As he took them, I found myself unable to say any more than a heartfelt 'Thank you', but I wasn't thanking him for collecting the ice.

A week later I was in the kitchen preparing lunch when the phone rang. I always left it with Phoebe in case she felt like calling someone for a chat – something she declined to do, even though I was sure she would have loved someone to ring *her*. She'd put Connor's number on the fridge, 'in case anything turns up' and I sensed she'd been brooding about his three-pipe problem.

To judge from the tone of her voice, the call was business rather than pleasure. I wondered if it was another buyer wanting to view the house. I quickly rinsed my hands in case Phoebe handed me the call, but she finished speaking and after a moment, the door opened. She limped into the kitchen with an odd look on her face, something between a grimace and a grin.

'Guess what? We have an offer for Garden Lodge.'

'You're joking! Are they buying blind? No one's viewed it.'

'Connor Grenville has. And he's made an offer.'

'But—' I stared at her, astonished. 'But he can't possibly afford— And he said he wasn't a serious buyer!'

'Well, he's made a serious offer. Four hundred and fifty.'

'That's not a serious offer, it's an insult!'

'Hardly, Ann. No one else has been to view in months. The price is obviously much too high.'

'It's the winter. The agent said there would be little interest until the spring.'

'She was just covering herself. People move all year round, don't they? Disasters happen. Death. Divorce. I suspect four hundred and fifty is much nearer the mark.'

'You're not going to accept?'

Phoebe paused before replying, then, looking very guilty, said, 'I *have* accepted.'

'Mum, that's not how it's done! You say you'll think about it and then you haggle. That won't be his best offer.'

'Oh, I think it probably is. He didn't strike me as the kind of man who plays games. I suspect that's all he can manage. And of course he'd expect me to turn it down. Yet he still put the offer in. He must want it quite badly, don't you think?'

'I suppose so, but that's no reason to accept. I can't think what possessed you . . . Without even consulting me.'

'It's my house,' Phoebe replied, sounding petulant. 'And I knew you'd try to persuade me to reject the offer.'

'I certainly would!'

'Because you want the best for me, don't you?'

'Of course I do.'

'Just as I want the best for you,' Phoebe said, studying a point on the wall over my right shoulder.

'Mum, I don't see what—'

'It's high time you got on with your life, Ann. Stopped worrying about me. I need to get shot of this place and move on.' She looked down and regarded her shabby carpet slippers. 'I wasn't much of a mother to you, but I'm damned if I'll be a burden.'

'You *aren't*, Mum. I've enjoyed spending time with you. I think it's done us both a world of good. I love working in the studio and the garden and I quite enjoy looking after you. It's taken my mind off Jack and the divorce and . . . well, all the past. Please don't feel you have to sell up because you're a *burden*. I do understand how you feel about Garden Lodge. I love it too. I had no idea just how much.'

Phoebe was looking at me, but her expression was hard to read. 'My God,' she said softly. 'You don't actually want me to sell, do you?'

'Of course I do!' It was my turn to avoid her eyes. 'But only at the right price.'

Phoebe pulled out a kitchen chair and sank on to it. 'Come on, Ann. Be honest. When you arrived, you wanted me to get rid of it, didn't you? But now you've settled in. You've spent so much time in the garden . . . worked so hard . . . you've *invested* something in the old place. And I suppose you must feel closer to Sylvester out there too.'

I couldn't speak. Blinking furiously, I said, 'Not just Dad. I feel closer to you now. I just . . . I just didn't think we'd be selling up so *soon*. I was going to carry on renovating the garden, so we could have one last summer here. To say goodbye. Then move on.'

Phoebe nodded. 'That's when Sylvester went . . . You won't remember.' She looked up and searched my face. 'You don't, do you?' I shook my head. 'It was autumn. He always got depressed in the autumn. As soon as the days began to get shorter, he'd panic. It was the thought of winter, you see. It used to get him down every year.' She sighed and said, 'Shall I ring the agent? Tell her I've changed my mind?'

'*Do* you want to sell up, Mum?'

'I don't know now. I thought I did. But I certainly like the idea of one last summer. Time to make our peace with the old place and say goodbye . . . I think perhaps I'll ring back and do my batty old woman act. Tell her I've had second thoughts. But can I ask a favour, Ann?'

'What?'

'If she's already spoken to Connor, would you ring him and apologise? I don't think I can bear to speak to him. I feel bad, messing him about. Would you do that for me?'

'Yes, of course.'

'Right then. You get lunch on the table and I'll be back in a jiffy.' When she got to the door, she turned and said, 'I'm glad we got all that sorted out. After all, there's no need to rush into anything, is there? But we know where we stand now.'

She went back to the sitting room and closed the door. After a few moments I heard the magisterial tones she used when speaking to uncooperative tradesmen. It was an impressive performance and I found myself feeling sorry for the agent.

Phoebe said a curt goodbye, then I heard a whooping noise. She reappeared in the doorway, brandishing her stick. 'The deed is done! Let's have a drink. I've never turned down half a million before. For that matter,' she said, taking a bottle of white wine from the fridge, 'I've never turned down a good-looking young man. Poor old Connor . . . Never mind. We'll raise a glass to him – and his three-pipe problem.'

I felt obliged to ring Connor straight after lunch. It wasn't often Phoebe was conscious of behaving badly, so I wanted to set her mind at rest. I left her with a cup of coffee and took the phone up to my old room.

My mother never had any truck with children's wallpapers. I wasn't allowed ballerinas, ponies or a creature called Holly Hobby. Disney was anathema to her and I grew up understanding that merchandising was exploitation of both parent and child. I knew better than to argue with Phoebe who, as far as I could tell, was always right about everything. She was certainly infallible on the subject of waste-of-space boyfriends, not that I ever admitted it. So I asked her how to decorate my room, avoiding the evils of commercial exploitation. I must have been all of twelve. She said, '*Have nothing in your houses which you do not know to be useful or believe to be beautiful.*'

That was the beginning of my passion for design, textiles and William Morris, though I didn't know then that she was quoting him. She went to the bowed, overloaded shelf where she kept her art books, took down a volume on Morris and handed it to me. Turning the pages, I marvelled at how he turned lilies, chrysanthemums, even humble larkspur and seaweed into repeating designs. It was love at first sight. Phoebe said my enthusiasm showed I had good taste and 'an eye'. I didn't know then that, in artistic terms, having one eye was better than having two.

Phoebe said I could have a William Morris bedroom. I asked how this was possible. Was she offering to paint my walls in Morris style? She explained that you could still buy Morris wallpaper and curtain fabric, but they weren't cheap. They would have to last me until I left home, so I should choose my patterns carefully, but Phoebe assured me Morris designs were timeless and I would never get bored with them.

She was right. I never did. I chose a subdued sea-green wallpaper that featured acorns and oak leaves and paired it with the celebrated Strawberry Thief fabric for my curtains. When they were closed, the birds lined up in rows, staring hungrily at the crop of small wild strawberries. I never tired of looking at those patterns, how they never began and never ended, just repeated over and over until you could no longer see birds, strawberries, acorns or oak leaves, you just saw colour and movement.

I hate to think what my new décor must have cost, but it lasted through my teens and is still in good shape. Phoebe says more than one young artist-assistant has been inspired by his stay in what came to be known as 'the Morris room'.

It was the beginning of something important for me. That room made me happy and allowed me to feel connected to the garden even when I was indoors. It taught me that design – even of something as mundane as wallpaper – could affect how you felt. From the moment the first length of acorn wallpaper went up, I was a convert to the Morris philosophy and tried thereafter to have nothing in my home which I did not know to be useful or believe to be beautiful.

I sat down, contemplated my dancing acorns and rang Connor Grenville.

'Connor, it's Ann de Freitas here. Have the agency spoken to you about your offer for Garden Lodge?'

'Yes, they have. Twice, actually. Once to say my offer had been accepted, then again to say it had been rejected and that the property had been taken off the market.'

'I'm so sorry to mess you around. There's been some confusion, you see.'

'No need to apologise. The agent sounded pretty miffed and so was I to begin with, but after I'd thought about it a bit, I realised I was pleased.'

'*Pleased?* That your offer had been rejected?'

'No, that you'd decided not to sell. I don't think you should. It's a wonderful home and you and Phoebe are obviously happy there.'

'Was your offer never genuine then?'

'Of course it was! I wouldn't waste your time.' He heard himself, then added, 'Well, not *again*.'

'So you did actually want to buy Garden Lodge?'

'Yes, I did, but that was my best offer and I fully expected it to be rejected. It represented all I have – and quite a lot that I don't, to be honest – but I thought if I actually made an offer, it would clarify matters. For me, at least.'

'You must have been very surprised when Phoebe accepted.'

'I thought it might be you, putting pressure on her to move somewhere more practical. But that didn't really add up.'

'Why not?'

'It was obvious you didn't really want to sell. I mean, you didn't try very hard, did you? The business potential of that place is tremendous, but you didn't push it.'

'I didn't think you were a serious buyer.'

'Are you sure that was why?'

I hesitated, then said, 'I was sure at the time, but I realise now neither Phoebe nor I are ready to sell up. She only accepted your offer so I could get her settled elsewhere. In her misguided way, she was trying to be kind. She wanted to relieve me of my responsibilities – I suppose because she so loathed being responsible for me when I was young and she was a single parent.'

'Do you see her as a big responsibility?'

'No, that's what's so silly. I was horrified to discover she felt guilty enough to give up her home. But I've persuaded her to stay put. I think she could with my support. I'd been thinking of selling my flat in Bath, but I hadn't decided what to do. Staying at Garden Lodge has given me a lot of time to think. And remember, I suppose.'

'What do you remember?'

'Oh, just how happy the garden used to make me when I was a child. It sounds ridiculous, but I'd like to make reparation in some way.'

'That's an odd term to use about a garden.'

'I know, but I can't think how else to explain it. And I thought you might understand.'

'Perhaps I will if you tell me more.'

'It was all so . . . *sad*. The garden went to rack and ruin after my father left and now I feel guilty about all the neglect. But I was just a child. There was nothing I could do.'

'When was this?'

'1976. I don't remember much about that time and Phoebe's always refused to discuss it. He just went out one day and never came back.'

'Did he stay in touch?'

'No. We never heard from him again. I don't even know if he's alive.'

'That must have been painful for you.'

'I really don't remember. But I can remember the garden as it used to be. Well, perhaps I don't, maybe it's just that there are photos. Sylvester took lots of the garden.'

'Sylvester?'

'Silvestre Esmeraldo Luis de Freitas.'

Connor laughed. 'Wow! Portuguese?'

'Madeiran.'

'So that's where you get your exotic looks from.'

It was my turn to laugh. 'Yes. And my love of plants.'

'So I'm guessing what you'd really like to do is restore the garden. To how it was in Sylvester's day? Or how it was in its Victorian heyday?'

'I don't think I mind. I'd just like the garden to look *loved*. And I'd like to feel less guilty about it. I also wondered whether a big project would help reconcile Phoebe to her disability. She can't really paint any more, not since she had cancer. The chemo wrecked her nervous system and she's in constant pain.'

'That's why she likes mysteries, isn't it? Something to distract her. Keep her brain occupied.'

'Exactly. I wondered if I could get her involved in planning the restoration of the garden. I mean, it's all about colour and shape, isn't it?'

'Have you heard of Gertrude Jekyll? She was a famous Victorian gardener who had to abandon a career as a painter when her eyesight began to deteriorate. Her designs for flower borders were actually influenced by the Impressionists. I suppose you could say she painted with plants and the garden was her canvas. Maybe Phoebe might like that idea?'

'It could certainly be worth a try. I'd really like to get her outside in the spring, but she'll need some motivating.'

'So now the house is off the market, will you make a start on the walled garden?'

'I'm going to tidy up at least. Find out what's still alive. But it will be a massive clearing job and I'm not sure how much I can achieve on my own. I'll have to discuss with Phoebe what she wants me to do and how much she'll let me spend.'

'Could I make a suggestion?'

'Of course. I'd value your advice.'

'I'm looking for a restoration project. A big one. I want to restore something from a ruin to a garden anyone would be proud to own. And I want to photograph every stage of the process and blog about it.'

'Why?'

'To drum up trade. I want to stop working for other people and set up my own garden business and since Phoebe turned down my insulting offer, I can now revert to Plan A, which was to set up Grenville Garden Landscaping. But I need a flagship project. It needs to be local, interesting and challenging. Restoring Beechgrave's kitchen garden would tick all those boxes and I think there could be a lot of local and media interest, especially as the garden's owned by a famous artist.'

'But Connor, there's no way Phoebe's in the market for all this. She may be famous, but she isn't working. And she hasn't sold a painting in ages.'

'Ah, but that's the beauty of it, you see. You wouldn't have to pay me.'

'We wouldn't?'

'No, not if you allow me to use your garden as a bit of a show home, post photos of it online and maybe use some of them in a book about Beechgrave and the Mordaunts, the one Ivy wanted me to write. I can link *your* project – the garden – with *my* project – the family history. I think I could get an attractive book out of it and carry out my grandmother's wishes. And you have to admit, restoring the garden would make the house easier to sell when the time comes.'

'So you're offering to work for *free?*'

'Yes. But I think I might need some help.'

'What sort of help?'

'Well, if you see yourself as a gardener's boy, I could definitely use another pair of hands. At the moment I'm just a one-man band. And I'd probably need quite a lot of tea and biscuits.'

'I'm sure that could be arranged. Anything else?'

'No, that's all.'

'Connor, I don't know what to say. It's a very generous offer—'

'And naturally you don't think you can trust it. Quite understandable, but there are two things you need to factor into the equation. The first is how much I want to be a part of the Beechgrave story, how much I need to know what Ivy discovered. I don't suppose for one moment the answer lies in the garden, but I just think if I'm on-site, working where she was born, in the shadow of those beeches, I'll be as close as I can get to solving the mystery, short of checking in to the rehab clinic next door.' He paused. 'Does that make any sense?'

'As much sense as me wanting to make reparation to a garden.'

'You see, I have to assume that, in the end, Ivy didn't want me to publish a book about her family, but I don't think she could object to a book about the old garden. Especially if it helped get my business off the ground. So . . . what do you say?'

'Well, it all sounds pretty convincing.'

'And there's absolutely no risk to you. I would run everything by you and Phoebe, from plant lists to the possible intrusion of TV cameras. You'd be the boss.'

'I thought I was the gardener's boy?'

'The chain of command will be complex, but I'm sure we can make it work.'

'Connor, you'll have to come and discuss all this with Phoebe. I think she'll be up for it, but I can't make any promises.'

'Of course. I'd love to talk to her about it. And I'm curious to know if she's had any more thoughts about Ivy's change of heart.'

'She's certainly been thinking about that and I know she'd be delighted to see you again.'

'Okay, talk to Phoebe and let me know when I can visit. Take your time. I'm not going to put pressure on anyone, but the offer's there.'

'Thank you. It's very generous of you.'

'Well, that's the second thing you need to factor in. Remember I said there were two?'

'What's the second?'

'How much I'd enjoy spending time with you and Phoebe, not to mention all the ghosts of Garden Lodge.'

'Ghosts?'

'My grandmother, Ivy. My great-grandmother, Violet. Her brother, William Hatherwick, and the woman who ended up owning Beechgrave, Hester Mordaunt. They're my family, Ann. It would be a privilege to restore their garden. I even thought about buying Garden Lodge so I could do that, but now, if you'll let me, I can do what I'd planned in my capacity as gardener, not owner. It's an arrangement that could suit everyone.'

'Let's hope Phoebe thinks so. I'll get back to you, Connor, as soon as she's made a decision.'

'No hurry. The garden's been waiting since the seventies. A few more days won't make any difference. Those beeches aren't going anywhere . . .'

THE BEECH WOOD

A storm is coming. We sense it. In our roots. In the quivering air. There's a shrieking on the wind and a deep stirring in the earth, as if the numberless dead are tunnelling, like moles, out of their graves, to rail against the heedless living.

A storm is coming, doubtless. There will be destruction. Consternation. We have seen it many times and we shall see it again. We stand, bearing witness to the centuries, impartial, indifferent, offering shelter to any living thing that seeks solace in our shade.

The ancients among us have learned to yield, to sacrifice a bough – sometimes several. There can be strength in weakness. But the ways of wind and weather cannot be learned in a mere hundred years. The young ones stand tall, shallow-rooted. They break when they should bend.

After the storm has passed, some lie fallen – though some of the fallen live yet.

We endure.

ANN

Phoebe had a ringside seat. She said she liked to watch demolition, so I placed a bench against the south-facing wall of the kitchen garden, where, even in January, the weak winter sunshine made its presence felt. Swaddled in a fleece blanket and quilted coat, sporting her tweed cap and gloves, Phoebe sat and watched as we tore up decades of undergrowth and tangles of ivy, honeysuckle and clematis were cut back to expose the mellow Victorian brick.

As Connor hacked and pulled at unyielding brambles, Phoebe called out to him, 'You put me in mind of the Prince in *Sleeping Beauty*.'

He looked up and grinned. Removing a dirty glove, he wiped his forehead with the back of his hand. 'Well, it's high time this beauty woke. She's been asleep for nearly forty years.' He donned his glove again and returned to work, creating heaps of vegetation which I gathered up and put into a barrow, then wheeled out into the lane and emptied into a waiting skip.

As I passed Phoebe, I stopped to ask if she was warm enough and if she still had coffee in the flask beside her on the bench. She seemed touched by my concern and assured me she was thoroughly enjoying herself. 'There's something rather soothing about watching other people exhaust themselves. I've been studying Connor. He has a method, doesn't he?'

'He says he's following the sun as it moves round. The difference in temperature is quite marked. Do you feel it when the sun goes behind a cloud?'

'Oh, yes, though I tend to be more aware of changes in light and shade than temperature. Years of working in that arctic studio.'

'It's not too bad once you've lit the wood burner.'

'I could never be bothered. Just donned my thermals and fingerless mittens and got on with it. But I think I must be getting soft. I can feel the sun's warmth behind me, radiating from the wall and I must say, it's really rather pleasant.'

'Connor says there's fruit on that wall behind you. Peaches and nectarines. The sun lovers. Then on the west wall,' I said, pointing, 'there should be plums and cherries. On the east wall we should find pears and apples. It's hard to tell what's still alive at this time of year.'

'Nothing grows on the north wall, I presume?'

'With luck there could be a Morello cherry.'

'Does Connor know, just by looking at dead twigs?'

'Partly, but there are also a few labels left. Some are the very old metal labels, but some of the newer ones must have been put there by Dad. And we found a notebook in the shed. His gardening notes. It's still legible.'

Phoebe looked taken aback. 'Oh . . . I never thought to clear out the shed. I went through all his other things . . .' Her voice faltered.

'Looking for clues as to why he left us?' I asked gently.

Ignoring the question, she said, 'Do you know, he kept a rosary in there. In the shed! Great long thing. It hung from a beam, coiled, like a snake. Gave me the heebie-jeebies.' Phoebe shivered and rearranged her limbs on the bench. 'We never saw eye to eye about religion. Well, about anything, actually. Lord knows why we married. And as for taking on *this* place . . .' She made a dismissive noise. 'But Sylvester was always happy in the garden. Well, happier. He never learned to live with the British climate, though oddly enough he didn't mind snow. Said it protected the garden while it slept, like a white blanket. Honestly, to listen to him, you'd think he was talking about a child, not a garden! But then he adored children.'

I watched my mother, anxious that she'd waded too far into the past and out of her depth. I was about to change the subject when she said gruffly, 'He loved you, Ann. Don't ever think he didn't. He had no quarrel with *you*. It was me. It was all my doing.'

'Oh, I'm sure there was fault on both sides, Mum. I didn't understand when I was young, but I do now. My marriage failed too, you know.'

'It was *depression*. He loved me. He adored you. But he suffered wretchedly with depression. And I was no use. I didn't even know what depression was then. I thought it was just a question of pulling yourself together. Having a holiday. A change of scenery. So I encouraged him to travel. Thought it would do him good. And it got him out of my hair . . . I hated feeling powerless, you see.' She shook her head. 'That's why I disliked being pregnant. The thought of something growing inside me, something I couldn't control. I loathed the whole damn business. Pity I didn't loathe sex! That would have saved no end of bother.' She raised her stick and pointed. 'I do believe that young man is flagging. Time he was fed. I'll go in and put the soup on. Go and empty your barrow while I make myself useful in the kitchen.'

As she got to her feet, Phoebe raised her cap and shouted to Connor, 'I take my hat off to you, sir! You're a human combine harvester. Tell me, is it satisfying being that destructive?'

'Very!' Connor yelled back. 'But it gives a man an appetite.'

'Duly noted,' Phoebe said. 'Lunch coming up.' She replaced her cap and tottered back towards the house, humming tunelessly.

Following with an overflowing barrow, I watched my mother's feet as they shuffled across the worn, uneven paving stones. When she got to the back door, she clutched at the handle and raised her stick in triumphant salute as I passed.

PHOEBE

Phoebe was thoughtful as she heated the tomato soup. She wondered if it was too late to go through the contents of the shed to see what Sylvester might have left behind. She was curious, but also fearful. It wouldn't do to go stirring things up again after all these years. It was surely best to let sleeping dogs lie. Connor had already roused the sleeping garden. He might wake Ann too . . .

Phoebe heard laughter outside, then the scraping of boots. She ladled soup into three bowls, spilling some as her clumsy hands shook. Matters were beyond her control now. She could only hope for the best, prepare for the worst.

Connor's smiling ruddy face appeared at the door and as soon as he entered, the kitchen felt smaller. Phoebe noted he was a whole head taller than Ann – so like her handsome father, especially when she smiled and she was smiling now. Ann was happy. There was colour in her cheeks and she looked alive. Being outdoors had that effect on her. Or perhaps it was Connor. The man's energy and good humour were infectious.

'Lunch is served,' Phoebe announced. 'Tomato soup. Campbell's best. Campbell is my cook,' she added with a wink to Connor. 'Help yourselves to cheese and ham. I've cut plenty of bread, but it's doorsteps, I'm afraid. That's all my gammy hands can manage these days.'

'The only way to eat bread,' Connor replied, removing his boots and leaving them on the doormat. He went over to the sink and began to wash his hands. 'After this I'll be ready to go another ten rounds with Sleeping Beauty out there. I do believe she's beginning to stir . . .'

On an impulse, Ann put an arm round her mother's waist and kissed her on the cheek. 'Thanks for doing all this, Mum. I'm looking forward to it!'

Thrown by the show of affection, Phoebe bent and grasped her stick. Moving cautiously through the kitchen, she called out over her shoulder, her voice slightly querulous, 'Would one of you be kind enough to bring my soup through? Oh, and there's beer and cider in the pantry. Just help yourselves. You've earned it.'

ANN

When Connor had finished for the day, cleaned up and gone home, Phoebe and I collapsed for the evening in front of the stove. The wind had freshened and was whining now in the chimney. I must have been dozing when Phoebe suddenly announced, 'Nice boy, Connor.'

'Mmm . . . ? Oh, yes, he's very kind, isn't he? I hope he manages to make a go of his garden business.'

'I'm sure he will. All that energy, plus a capacity for hard work. He seems to know what he's about.'

'Yes, he trained at horticultural college.'

'Is he married?'

'I don't know. He's never mentioned a wife.'

'Girlfriend?'

'I've no idea. He's got a flatmate. Male. Maybe he's gay.'

Phoebe shook her head. 'Don't think so. My antennae – which have never failed me yet, I'll have you know – indicate he's straight. There's probably a girlfriend somewhere.'

'Maybe. But when you're setting up your own business, there's not a lot of time left for socialising. And the older you get, the pickier you get.'

'That sounds like the voice of bitter experience.'

'Well, it's not easy to find someone who'll put up with you being married to a business. Jack and I worked really hard at separate careers and we were both very successful, but the marriage went to the wall. Isn't that what happened with you and Dad?'

Phoebe shrugged. 'It just wasn't in my nature to be domestic. Or faithful, I'm afraid. But you mustn't give up looking, Ann. You're too young and far too attractive.'

'I haven't given up,' I replied, without much conviction.

'After all, you're only forty-three.'

'Forty-four, actually.'

'Really?' Phoebe looked confused as she calculated. 'Damn. You've had another birthday, haven't you? Sorry, I lose track of time. I suppose I should get a calendar, but really, what *for*? One day is much like another for me.'

'Mum, you've remembered my birthday once in the last ten years,' I said, laughing. 'It's really not an issue. I've got to the age where I prefer to forget about birthdays.'

'Me too. Shall we have a birthday amnesty? No more until further notice?'

'What a good idea.'

'But we'll have to find other reasons to drink champagne.'

'We need a reason?'

'That's my girl!' Phoebe said, slapping the arm of her chair. 'Let's have some the next time Connor's here. I need him to be in a good mood.'

'Why?'

'I'm thinking of asking him to sit for me. Just a few sketches. I have an idea for a portrait, if I ever feel up to tackling it. Do you think he'd do it?'

'I'm sure he'd feel very flattered to be asked.'

'Good! We'll ply him with champagne first though, then catch him off-guard.'

'You really like him, don't you?'

'I do, and for some unknown reason, he likes *me*, so I think he might do it. He has an interesting face, I think. A lot of conflict there. And he's still grieving for poor old Ivy, isn't he?'

'I suppose so. I haven't really given it much thought.'

'You don't have to *think* about it, Ann,' Phoebe said, sounding tetchy. 'You can see it in his face.'

'Well, *you* can.'

'So could you if you looked properly. But I don't suppose you've seen past the pleasing exterior. Can't say I blame you. Six foot, broad shoulders and a nice arse. He's very easy on the eye.'

Shocked that my mother's assessment of Connor so closely resembled my own, I squirmed with guilty embarrassment. 'I wish you wouldn't talk about men as if they were *specimens*. Connor is our friend.'

'It's my job. I study faces and bodies, but I see past the surface of things. Connor's a nice-looking chap. Regular features, apart from that long nose. And he smiles a lot, doesn't he? Makes an effort to be pleasant. There's almost something angelic about him – all that unruly fair hair and those high cheekbones. Like a Burne-Jones angel. But a *fallen* angel . . . If you ask me, Connor's angry. He's suffered loss. And rejection. I can see it in his face.'

'You can really see all that?'

'Oh yes, plain as a pikestaff. Anyone who smiles that much has to be pretty miserable, don't you think? Perhaps some champagne will cheer him up.'

Large amounts of fresh air and exercise ensured I was sleeping better than I'd done for years, but that night I was woken by the sound of screaming. I lay in bed, struggling to make sense of the eerie sound that had woken me.

It was the wind. A gale was tearing round the house, ripping off slates, flinging flowerpots from one side of the garden to the other. I recalled the so-called hurricane of 1987. A teenager then, I'd slept through it all and got up the next morning to find trees lying on the ground, like fallen soldiers on a battlefield.

This storm sounded bad. I got up and went to the window, drawing back a curtain to look outside. I didn't recognise the moonlit landscape. Trees were leaning at a crazy angle but when the wind relented, they sprang back, swaying until the impact of the next powerful gust sent them keeling over again. As I watched, there was a cracking sound like a gun shot and a branch sailed past the window, its smaller twigs scraping the glass. Startled, I stepped back, then leaned forward again to rearrange the curtains, so that if the window broke, the glass couldn't travel far into the room.

As I drew the curtain, I took a last look at the garden, casting an anxious eye towards the studio. If one of the closer beeches came down, the studio could receive a direct hit. The thought of Phoebe's unfinished canvases buried under brick dust and rubble made me consider going out to rescue them, but I dismissed the idea as too dangerous. With my eye I measured the distance between the nearest beech and the studio and was estimating its length when, to my horror, I saw the studio door open and a large canvas appear. It appeared to be wrapped in a blanket and was moving very slowly on carpet-slippered feet.

I threw open the window, whereupon the wind tried to wrench it from my hand, almost dragging me over the sill. I yelled 'Mum!', even though I knew Phoebe wouldn't hear me above the din which had now reached a frenzied crescendo. Unable to shut the window, I had to let it go and winced as the draught slammed the bedroom door behind me. Grabbing my dressing gown, I pushed my feet into some shoes and ran downstairs, tearing through the hall and into the kitchen where I found the back door open and swinging. I hurled myself into the wind and headed for the studio.

When I reached Phoebe, I put an arm round her in an attempt to keep her upright and yelled, 'Mum, what on earth are you *doing*? Get indoors! A tree could fall any minute.'

'I needed to move the canvases,' she wailed. 'Just in case.'

'Give it to me, I'll bring it in. Get indoors now. Go *on*! It's not worth getting killed for a painting – even one of yours. Get inside, *please*.'

She staggered towards the back door, mounted the step with difficulty, then turned to watch as I struggled across the garden. The canvas resisted the wind like a sail and a sudden vicious gust wrapped my dressing gown round my legs, almost lifting me off my feet. I stumbled, but got as far as the step where Phoebe was waiting, arms outstretched to take the canvas from me.

'Oh, well done!' she gasped as we both fell into the kitchen. 'I couldn't sleep for worrying about it and I had *such* a bad feeling.' She sank down on to a chair. 'Thank you, Ann.'

I turned away, intending to shut the back door, but froze as I heard a long, loud groan, punctuated with cracking sounds, like a volley of shots being fired. Alarmed, Phoebe got to her feet. We stood side by side in the open doorway, clutching each other, speechless with terror as we watched the descent of a beech as it described an impossibly slow arc across our field of vision. It just missed the studio but flattened the shed as if it had been a Wendy house. The tree's crown, a massive tangle of branches, filled the garden where, moments ago, Phoebe and I had been arguing.

We stood gaping at the fallen tree, which looked twice as big now it was horizontal. Stunned, tearful, I reached for my mother's hand and squeezed it, unable to speak. She managed a wheezy little chuckle and said, 'Well, that was lucky, wasn't it?'

The clear-up took days. When they found the rusty tin in a hollow in the trunk, I set it aside for Connor who I thought might like to see the seed packets. When he came back at the weekend to work in the walled garden, the fallen beech was gone apart from its massive stump, as big as a dining table. Delighted by the hundreds of concentric rings revealed on the cut surface, Phoebe had decided to keep it.

'It reminds me of Op Art from the sixties. The circles are dazzling, aren't they? You feel drawn into the very centre.' She touched the cut wood with reverence. 'If my hands were any good, I'd have a go at carving something on that surface. A face, perhaps . . . A Green Man, something like that.' She looked up at me. 'Don't you think so? That's what it should become. A piece of sculpture. A monument to . . . something. Don't know what exactly. But something that old shouldn't just cease to be, should it, like a mere human being?'

Connor said the beech would continue to live on as a piece of living sculpture because it still had roots in the ground, enough to ensure it would cling on to life. He took a commemorative photo of Phoebe and me, posing in front of the stump, then we all went indoors for tea.

Connor offered to help in the kitchen, so I asked him to set out crockery on a tray. As I reached for the tea caddy, I remembered the old tin and its seed packets. I opened a cupboard, took out the tin and handed it to him.

'What do you make of this? It was found in a hollow in the tree. Someone must have climbed up to put it there.'

'You're kidding.'

'The men found it when they were disposing of the trunk. There are old seed packets inside.'

'Really? Well, the seeds could still be viable,' he said, prising open the lid.

'Don't get too excited,' I said, filling the kettle. 'The packets are all empty.'

He'd taken several out and was turning them over. 'How do you know they're empty? They're all sealed.'

'You can feel. And if you hold them up to the light, you can see there's nothing in them.'

'Yet they've all been glued shut.'

'Yes. I suppose someone wanted to preserve them as art work. A collector of some kind, perhaps.'

'But why put them outdoors – and in a *tree* – if you wanted to preserve them?'

'Yes, it's odd, isn't it? It seems more likely they were trying to hide them.'

'Why would anyone want to hide seed packets?'

'Search me. I thought you might have some ideas.'

He turned a packet over and examined the printed text closely, then looking up, he said, 'Do you mind if I open one? I'll do it carefully with a knife, so I don't tear it.'

'Go ahead. But I think you'll find it's empty.'

As I made the tea, Connor took a knife from the kitchen drawer and slid it under the glued paper flap. He ran the knife gently back and forth until the glue cracked, then he upended the packet over a plate and tapped. Nothing came out. Still refusing to believe it was empty, he looked inside.

'My God . . .'

'What?'

'Look!'

He handed me the packet and I peered inside. The interior was completely covered with tiny words written in pencil in a copperplate hand. I looked up at Connor, who was grinning now and wielding the knife with a determined gleam in his eye.

'May I?'

'Please do.'

He slit open the seed packet along its glued edges and smoothed it flat on the kitchen worktop. 'It's a letter!' He pointed to the top left-hand corner of the yellowed paper oblong where someone had written *My dearest*. 'There's no date though. And no signature. No name anyway. Just a letter. Is that a W? It's very ornate.'

I bent over the packet and examined where he was pointing. 'Yes, I think that's a W.'

Connor was already opening another packet. 'This one's the same. Every inch is covered with tiny writing. These are love letters!'

'How do you know?'

'Read them,' Connor said, thrusting one into my hand. He was working his way through the packets now, opening them carefully and spreading them flat. 'They're all from W.'

'How maddening that they aren't signed or dated. I'd love to know who wrote them.'

'Not to mention why they had to be hidden in a tree. Wait a minute . . .' Connor peered closely at one of the packets. Without looking up he said, 'You wouldn't have a magnifying glass by any chance?'

'Phoebe has a magnifying bookmark. She uses it to read newspapers. It'll be on the table somewhere . . . Here it is,' I said, handing him the piece of transparent plastic.

'I just want to see this handwriting normal size . . . Yes, I thought so. I recognise this hand.'

'Really?'

He looked up and nodded. 'Well, I've seen it before, definitely. Somewhere in my grandmother's archive, but I can't remember where.'

'Connor, look – that's an H, isn't it? "My dearest H". Isn't that what it says?'

'Yes, I think so . . . Maybe these were love letters written to Hester Mordaunt. These packets could be a hundred years old. Easily.'

'Hester? The unmarried daughter?'

'The one who inherited Beechgrave. The woman who adopted my grandmother and gave her a name.'

I poured three mugs of tea, preoccupied, then remembered something. 'Didn't you say Hester wrote a diary?'

'Volumes. Some were destroyed in the fire though.'

'But you still have some of them?'

'Yes, and photocopies of some pages which were subsequently destroyed.'

'So if we read the diaries—'

'We might find out who W was. And why his letters had to be hidden in a tree.'

'And more importantly, why she never married him.'

Connor lifted the tea tray, shook his shaggy head and grinned. 'Phoebe's going to *love* this.'

PART TWO

PART TWO

HESTER

June 5th, 1914

Walter has proposed.

Mother is thrilled. Father seems very pleased too. I was too astonished to respond when Walter finally made his intentions clear. Eventually, I said I needed time to consider. Mother says that was quite proper, but I should accept soon if we are to organise a wedding before Christmas. There is talk of war, though Father says nothing will come of it, it is just the Kaiser sabre-rattling.

I suppose I should record the details of this momentous event! Walter proposed in the rose garden. No doubt he thought that would be romantic. He was not to know roses irritate me rather. They are very beautiful, but they do not last. Perhaps that is why they are so admired. They enjoy a short season, like asparagus. But you can at least eat asparagus.

Sitting in the rose garden, I felt as if I were at a summer ball, surrounded by young ladies got up in yards of pale silk and satin, the air heavy with their suffocating scent. I had far rather sit in the kitchen garden than the rose garden. How comical, if Walter had proposed in the kitchen garden! Yet how much more appropriate, since the purpose of marriage is to be fruitful and multiply.

I suppose if I marry, Mother will have to tell me what multiplying entails. I once asked Arthur and Eddie, but they refused to tell me. They smirked and said I should find out soon enough. Then Arthur winked at Eddie, which was perfectly horrid of him. I have no desire to be fruitful if it means inflicting brothers on a daughter of mine.

When I was sitting in the rose garden with Walter I noticed something interesting. The bees prefer single roses. The double blooms, though much showier, seem to hold little attraction for them. I sat observing this phenomenon for some minutes and confess I might not have taken in all that Walter had to say about the happy future he intends to offer me.

I wonder why bees prefer single blooms? My brothers would not know. All they have retained of their excellent and largely wasted education is the rules of various sports.

I should have liked to be a scientist. A botanist, perhaps. Or a plant collector who travelled to China, like Mr E. H. Wilson, though I should prefer not to have my leg crushed in an avalanche of boulders and have to set it using a camera tripod for a splint. If I could not be a botanist or an explorer, I think I should have liked to be a gardener. When I mentioned this to Mother, she laughed. Sadly, I am a source of constant and unintentional amusement to my family. Mother explained that ladies paint flowers and wear them, they do not grow them.

The rules of life seem to me as unfathomable as the rules of cricket, yet I feel sure the bees know what they are doing. There has to be a reason why they go only to the single flowers, why they are never distracted by the opulence of 'Souvenir de la Malmaison'.

I wish now that I had paid more attention to Walter when he was proposing. Perhaps I might feel more enthusiastic about marriage if I had. The truth is, I have never really thought about it much, but I know I should. Mother says time is running out. I am twenty-two.

June 12th

I have been considering Walter's proposal and have come to the conclusion that I wish I were a man. To be female is to be second-rate, or rather to be regarded as second-rate.

To console myself, I shall record the disadvantages of being male, but I fear the list will be very short.

I should detest having to smoke cigars.

I think it unlikely I should be able to drink port in any quantity.

I doubt I could ever be reconciled to whiskers or shaving.

I have no interest whatever in horse-racing or shooting things with guns.

After this, the issues are less clear. Men talk of the financial obligation to provide for a family, but it seems to me, if they would refrain from producing such large families, they would surely manage better. A man does at least have a choice. He can choose not to marry. He does not become a burden on his family in the way that I, if I do not marry, will become a burden to Arthur or Eddie. My greatest inducement to marry is the thought that, if I do not, I will inevitably become nurse and companion to whichever of my parents survives longest, after which I shall have no choice but to cast myself on the mercy of my brothers, who will be obliged to house, feed and clothe me.

It comes as no surprise, therefore, that Arthur and Eddie are all in favour of my marriage to Walter – or indeed anybody. Eddie even had the effrontery to suggest this might be my last chance to make a good match.

For that reason alone, I was tempted to decline Walter's proposal, but he is a good, kind man and confident we are well suited. This surprises me as we have spent little time together, almost none of it alone, but I scarcely know what 'well suited' means. My parents have no interests in common, but have been married for nearly thirty years. Perhaps sharing a home and children are sufficient bond.

I am, in any case, discouraged from pursuing a wider range of interests. Whenever I demonstrate that I have more intelligence and initiative than a lap dog, Father looks shocked and accuses me of displaying 'unfeminine tendencies'.

I wish I could work. I stand at my bedroom window and watch the garden staff digging, raking, planting, pruning, cutting the grass – all of it in the fresh air, often in sunshine. I long to be busy, to be *doing*, to smell the damp earth as I turn it. How glorious that would be! To crumble a handful of it in my hands and see it teeming with life: seeds, roots and tiny insects. And, oh, how I should love a bonfire! I am sure I should not mind the smoke at all. Can it be any worse than the stench emanating from the billiard room? To stand burning rubbish on a cold November day, tending the flames and feeding the fire with a pitchfork – the thought makes me quite dizzy.

I watch our gardeners at work and long to know what they know, do what they do. Mother will not even let me arrange the flowers. She says the Head Gardener must do it. It is his responsibility, she says, as if these things are set down on tablets of stone.

It has often struck me that if an activity is enjoyable, satisfying or lucrative, it will be the province of men. What have they left us to do other than supervise the people who supervise the servants? Bear children, of course, but nothing I have observed or heard about motherhood suggests it is enjoyable or satisfying work, nor is it lucrative.

I suppose if I marry him, Walter will insist on a family. He did not mention this when he proposed. At least, I do not think he did. He made mention of 'duty', but I am not sure now if it referred to his or mine. I have to conclude that he might have hinted at the need for children.

When I am married, I shall insist on arranging my own flowers. Walter can hardly begrudge me that, surely? But I despair of ever being allowed to dig, or build a bonfire.

I have quite forgotten what I was going to write next. When I looked up from my window seat, out at the garden, I saw young Hatherwick, the Head Gardener's son, watering the bedding plants. It is a pleasure to watch these simple, repetitive tasks, performed with the experience of years and an economy of effort that confers a sort of physical grace. Hatherwick appears to me to be a man who knows what he is doing. And why.

I *ache* with envy.

ANN

'So it looks as if the unknown lover was Walter,' Phoebe said, handing Connor her empty wine glass, which he duly refilled.

'Why do you say that?'

We were gathered in the sitting room, listening to Connor read from Hester Mordaunt's diary. The book was a hundred years old and badly charred. Some pages were spoiled where the ink had run and only the second half was legible.

Listening to Connor – who was enjoying himself impersonating Hester – was like tuning into a radio play halfway through. We were trying to identify characters and their motives. Phoebe was entranced. When we showed her the inside of the seed packets, she was consumed with curiosity, then, when Connor told her he thought he recognised the handwriting, she insisted he bring Hester's diary to show us. He'd turned up with the diary and two bottles of red wine, ready to sing for his supper.

'Well, it *must* be Walter,' Phoebe insisted. 'The packets are signed "W".'

Connor's smile was infuriatingly enigmatic. He had the advantage over us. He'd already read some of the diary, but not wanting to pre-empt Phoebe's detective work, he turned to me and said, 'You're very quiet, Ann. Any theories?'

'I don't think it can be Walter.'

'Why not?'

'Well, she's obviously not very keen on him. And she never did marry him, did she?'

'No. Hester never married anyone.'

'And Walter doesn't sound the type who'd keep seed packets.'

'He chose the rose garden for his proposal,' Phoebe offered in Walter's defence.

'Yes, but I don't think he was a nature lover. Hester didn't think she could ask him about the bees.'

'Or the *birds* and the bees,' Connor added.

'Perhaps the packets belonged to Hester,' Phoebe said. 'Maybe it was a little game they played. Like writing messages on fans. People did some weird things as a substitute for snogging.'

'They certainly did,' Connor said, refilling my glass but not his own. 'Shall I read on?'

'Yes, please!' Phoebe said eagerly. 'Let's make a night of it. But, *your* glass is empty, Connor. That lamentable state of affairs must be rectified.'

'No, I'm driving later.'

'Rubbish!' Phoebe snorted and looked at me. 'He can stay over in the studio, can't he?'

'Of course – that is, if you'd like to,' I said, turning to Connor. 'Don't let yourself be browbeaten by my mother. I'm sure she'll let you go home if you promise to leave us Hester's journal.'

'Until I've photocopied it, I'm sleeping with it under my pillow.'

'Well, that settles it then!' Phoebe said, grabbing the bottle and filling Connor's glass. 'Bolt the doors, Ann. Now, are we all sitting comfortably . . . ? When you're ready, Connor. You have a captive audience.'

He cleared his throat, sat back and resumed his reading.

HESTER

Mother says I must give Walter his answer. She assumes my answer will be 'Yes' and faced with her certainty, I have been unable to initiate a discussion. I am not at all sure what there is to discuss, but feel I should consider all the implications of marriage, in particular marriage to Walter Dowding, for the fact is, I do not love him.

I am not so naïve as to assume that love is necessary for marriage to be a success. Respect, loyalty and compatibility are as important as love – or so I must assume. I know few married women and they do not discuss marriage. They discuss their husbands' and children's achievements and occasionally the achievements of their cook. All I know about marriage is what I have observed at home and what I have gleaned from my reading. Sadly, the novels of Thomas Hardy, of which I am inordinately fond, give me no grounds for optimism.

I should have liked very much to fall in love, for the experience. I cannot imagine what it must feel like. Not altogether comfortable, I fear. Perhaps this is why I like reading Hardy. His books are full of feelings I have never had – and some I hope never to have – but I do want to know about them.

I should give Walter his reply, but I am too hot and tired to think about it any more. How can I be tired when I never do anything more strenuous than write this journal and read to Mother?

June 14th

There was a terrible scene today. Mother was very upset. So was I, but I managed not to cry until I reached the seclusion of the beech wood, where I finally gave vent to my feelings.

I had simply asked for more time. Mother said I cannot possibly need more time since there is really nothing to consider. Apparently I have no right to become a burden and that is what I shall be if I decline Walter's offer. Mother made it quite clear she thinks I am unlikely to receive another, so I shall be beholden to my brothers for the rest of my life.

I had rather be dead. Or married.

Walter shall have his answer tomorrow.

June 15th

It is done. I am to become 'Mrs Walter Dowding'. It sounds very distinguished, but I was rather attached to 'Miss Hester Mordaunt'.

Walter says I have made him very happy. He did not mention the word love. Neither did I.

Afterwards, I went down to the wood and sat beneath the Trysting Tree, the old beech with tangled roots like a giant's ball of knitting wool. I cried for a long time and missed dinner.

I must have fallen asleep for when I opened my eyes I found I was being watched. I was frightened until I realised it was young Hatherwick. I believe his name is William. He explained that he had come upon me, asleep in the wood and was concerned for my safety, so he had waited until I woke. I was confused, still muddle-headed with sleep and said nothing. The light was fading and I felt nervous, alone in the wood at dusk.

Hatherwick had already taken his leave and turned away when I called him back. Mother would have been horrified, but I did not care. At that moment I did not care about anything, least of all Mother. I needed to talk to someone, so I talked to Hatherwick for a little while. I told him I was to be married. When he congratulated me, I said I should much rather travel the world and collect plants, like Mr Ernest Wilson. He did not laugh, nor did he look surprised. He suggested I might have many opportunities to travel as a married woman. I told him that unless I made an enormous fuss, I should not even be permitted to arrange my own flowers. He smiled then, but it was a sad sort of smile, as if he understood.

There was a long, uncomfortable silence, then he asked if I should like to borrow a book about plant collecting in China. I said I should, very much. He told me his sister, Violet, would deliver it and I could keep the book as long as I liked.

I am very tired now, but cannot sleep. The conversation with Hatherwick runs through my head, over and over. His act of kindness has made a great impression on me and I am eager to read his book. I do hope he will remember to send it.

THE BEECH WOOD

We bore witness at the beginning. We stood, as we have always stood, observing merely, while she watered our roots with her tears.

Her body shuddered with sobs as she rested her dark head on her arms. Her fine clothes absorbed moisture from the soil and the cool evening air. Finally, she slept, her limbs awry, her body twisted, like one who lay dead.

When he came upon her in the clearing, he stood still, fearful until he saw she breathed. He looked back the way he had come, then stood guard at a distance, his strong, rough hands in his pockets, watching her.

As soon as she opened her eyes, she saw him and got to her feet, alarmed, shaking out her long skirts. She reached out and placed a hand on one of us to steady herself while she gathered the strength to run. He stepped back, his palms raised towards her in a gesture of submission. As he removed his hat, she recognised him and said his name. He inclined his head, trying not to stare as she lifted a hand to an errant strand of hair and tucked it behind her ear.

She was dressed in green, tall, slender, like a young sapling, bending easily at the waist to brush leaves from the soiled hem of her skirt. He noted the silky brown of her hair, like horse chestnuts, the hazel of her unhappy eyes. She seemed to him the very spirit of this dark, green place.

His heart was full and he wanted to touch her. Instead, he sought a way to help. He had his reward. When she smiled, her long, troubled face was transfigured. It was as if the sun's rays had suddenly penetrated the woodland gloom. He could not prevent himself from smiling in answer.

Thus it began.

WILLIAM

June 15th, 1914

When William Hatherwick returned home to Garden Lodge his sister, Violet, set aside the sock she was darning and chided him for missing supper. As he cut himself a thick slice of bread, she set a bowl of soup before him.

'Eat it before it gets cold.'

'It was such a fine evening, I went for a walk. I forgot the time.' He swallowed some soup, then said, 'Do we have any brown paper and string?'

Violet went to the wooden dresser and pulled open a drawer. She withdrew several pieces of used string and a creased sheet of brown paper, smoothed flat and neatly folded. 'Are you sending a parcel then?' As she deposited the paper and string on the table, she bent and whispered in his ear, 'Who's the lucky lady then?'

William ignored his sister's nudge and said, 'Would you deliver a book to Beechgrave for me? I'm lending it.'

'I didn't think Mr Mordaunt took much interest in the garden,' Violet said as she settled down again in her chair. 'Doesn't he leave everything up to Father?'

'Yes, he does. The book isn't for him. It's for Miss Mordaunt. She's interested in horticulture. Unlike her father.'

Violet looked up from her mending, wide-eyed. 'You've spoken to Miss Mordaunt?'

Scraping up the last of the soup from his bowl, William avoided her eye. 'We discussed plant collecting. I was able to satisfy her curiosity on a point and suggested she should read one of my books. I propose to lend it to her. It's very informative,' William added, finishing the last of his bread and butter. 'And entertaining. I think she'll enjoy it. So would you take the parcel up to the house for me? Tomorrow. Miss Mordaunt's expecting it.'

'Very well, if you've promised it to her. But William—'

'And I don't see any need to mention this to Father. The book's mine. There's no harm in lending it to an interested party, is there?'

'I suppose not,' Violet answered cautiously.

He rose from the table and said, 'The soup was very good, Vi. Thank you.'

'I baked jam tarts. Strawberry. Your favourite. Will you have one with a cup of tea?'

'Not now. I'm going upstairs to read.'

'You'll wear out your eyes with all your studying! On a fine night like this a young man should be walking out with his sweetheart.'

The criticism was familiar, but William knew his sister spoke with affection. She was also expressing her own frustrations. Since the death of their mother, Violet had had little opportunity for leisure.

'As you're well aware, Vi, I cannot marry until I'm appointed to the position of Head Gardener. The path to advancement is study and the increase of scientific knowledge. I must make my own way in the world. No one else can do it for me. Goodnight.'

In the spartan seclusion of his room, William gazed out of the window towards the beech wood. There was not enough light to read, but he postponed the lighting of his candle by taking a volume from his bookcase, which he proceeded to wrap. He made a neat parcel, taking care with the corners, then tied it up with string. He took a pencil and wrote

Miss H. Mordaunt

Beechgrave

Setting the book aside, he lit his candle and placed it on the table. Overwhelmed suddenly with exhaustion – his twelve-hour working day had started at six in the morning – William yawned, then dragged a callused hand through his thick dark hair, greasy now with sweat. He opened the window wide and leaned out, inhaling the scents rising from the garden below: lilac, honeysuckle and night-scented stocks. He closed his eyes and almost reeled. A man could get drunk on their perfume.

As he removed his waistcoat and shirt, he looked again at the dark outline of the beech trees against the night sky. Ignoring the promptings of conscience and common sense, William reached for his sketchbook and picked up the pencil again. He sat down at the table by the window and placed the open sketchbook so it took advantage of the candle and the rising moon. He began to draw quickly and as he drew, he forgot his aching limbs and the nagging pain in the small of his back, aggravated by hours spent scything long grass. He forgot everything. All he remembered was the face he now drew: the silky hair in disarray; the thick, arched brows; the curve of dark lashes on her pale cheek. He hesitated to draw her mouth, not because it was challenging, nor because he'd forgotten it. To draw her mouth accurately, as he had seen it, her lips parted slightly as she slept, the upper lip drawn up so he could see her small white teeth, to record such a thing seemed intimate and intrusive, so he hesitated for a moment, then, grasping the pencil firmly, he completed his sketch.

He put the pencil down and rubbed his eyes. When he opened them again he examined his drawing by the light of the guttering candle. It was a good likeness. Very good. It was a knack he had, not just to draw, but to be able to draw from memory. Once he'd seen something, he could always remember it. A list of Latin plant names, a building, a face. As a boy he'd seen a child crushed by barrels falling from an overturned dray. He could see it still – the small, twisted limbs and the blood running in the gutter. Having a good memory could be a curse.

William's sketchbooks were repositories for his memories. He didn't draw to record. His brain did that. He drew for the pleasure of reliving an experience. It was over now, but while he'd been drawing her, with the breeze from the window cooling his damp skin, he had felt almost as if he were with her again, in the wood, standing guard, watching and keeping her safe, as if she were a sleeping princess in a fairy tale and he her faithful servant.

He dated the sketch but didn't sign it, nor did he write her name, but he said it softly before he fell asleep: 'Miss Hester Mordaunt.'

HESTER

June 16th, 1914

William Hatherwick has been as good as his word! I have by my side a copy of Mr Wilson's book, *A Naturalist in Western China, with Vasculum, Camera, and Gun: Being Some Account of Eleven Years' Travel, Exploration, and Observation in the More Remote Parts of the Flowery Kingdom.*

I do believe I was more thrilled to receive this book than Walter's proposal.

June 21st

Our musical evenings are now augmented by another fiddle player and Mother is delighted that we can expand our repertoire. Walter plays the violin and so our piano quartet occasionally becomes a quintet. Mother plays piano, Arthur the cello and Eddie the violin, very badly. Although I play the viola, I am more comfortable physically with the violin. However, I much prefer the sound of the viola. Years of listening to Eddie torture his E string dulled my enthusiasm for the fiddle.

Mother has insisted we learn some new music to play together. This has annoyed my wretched brothers. They have welcomed Walter into the family, but would rather he play billiards than music. I for one am grateful for our *soirées*. They relieve me of the obligation to make small talk. Walter is a dear, kind man, but inclined to be taciturn. I believe he is aware of the defect because he smiles and nods eagerly when others speak, but this only serves to make him look slightly foolish. I suspect Walter finds Mother intimidating. She does little to put him at his ease, even though she admires his playing.

Undoubtedly Mother is the best musician in the family and undoubtedly Mother knows it. As she plays, she affects a martyred expression, as if conscious she casts musical pearls before swine. Father does not play and Mother claims, when out of his hearing, that he is tone deaf. This might be true. He attends our musical gatherings with little enthusiasm and often falls asleep. Perhaps this is the cause of Mother's martyred expression. Music is her great love – I sometimes think her *only* love – and in that respect, she failed to marry a kindred spirit. But that is surely one of the virtues of the married state: it unites those with disparate tastes. Life would be deadly dull if we all shared the same enthusiasms, the same passions. How should we ever learn anything new?

Mother said an odd thing this evening. After we had finished playing *The Trout*, she sighed and said, 'Such a tragedy that Schubert died so young. Only thirty-one. I shall never reconcile myself to the loss of so much great music.'

I doubt she expected a response, but Walter, still flushed and smiling from his musical exertions, announced, 'Whom the gods love, die young.' Mother must have thought his reply a little glib, for she turned to him and said, 'Then I must assume, Walter, that they are not at all partial to *me*.'

He stopped smiling and went very red. Arthur managed to control himself, but Eddie choked and had to leave the room, coughing. As the door closed, Father woke up and began to applaud. I avoided Arthur's eye. He, Walter and I studied our music intently until the sound of Eddie's paroxysms died away.

June 29th

I called at Garden Lodge to return *A Naturalist in Western China*. I was loath to part with it, but I had had it in my possession for over a week. I read the whole book and copied out some of my favourite passages.

Violet answered the door to me, her father and brother being at work. She looked very surprised, but offered me a glass of lemonade. As the day was hot and I was thirsty, I accepted her kind offer.

I sat on a bench outside, sipping the deliciously cool lemonade and inhaling the scent of climbing sweet peas. Violet was busy in the garden with a pair of scissors and I paid her little heed. I was studying the delightful informality of their cottage garden. I decided I preferred it to our extravagant massed bedding.

When I stood up and handed her my empty glass, Violet presented me with a bunch of sweet peas. She had bound them with a piece of garden twine and apologised for the rough nature of the posy. 'But the scent is just heaven,' she said. I was very touched. I asked her to be sure to thank her brother for the loan of his book. She assured me she would and thus we parted on cordial terms.

I took great delight in arranging my flowers in a small jug. They sit on my bedroom mantelpiece and the room is full of their glorious scent.

I confess, I have done a foolish thing, but not, I hope, a wrong one. When I returned the book, I wrapped it in the same brown paper in which it was delivered, but I did not return the seed packet that someone – William Hatherwick, I presume – had used as a bookmark. The packet was empty and had contained lettuce seeds, nothing out of the ordinary. I hardly think William or Mr Hatherwick will need to refer to the packet.

I did not realise I had left it out until after the parcel was made up. I considered undoing the string and inserting the packet, but it hardly seemed worth the trouble. In any case, I found myself strangely unwilling to part with it. I wished to retain it as a memento of the happy hours I spent reading Mr Wilson's thrilling book.

I shall use the packet as a marker in my journal. I can always return it at some later date, but I doubt it will be missed. It is just an empty seed packet.

July 5th

Yesterday I told Mother I was going into Bristol to attend a lecture with my friend, Charlotte Reid and her brother, Laurence. Unfortunately, this was a lie, but I prefer to think of it as a ruse, one with a certain risk attached as Mother occasionally sees members of Charlotte's family and might enquire about our excursion. I took the precaution of telling Mother the lecture was being given under the auspices of the Royal Geographical Society, so I think it unlikely she will show any further interest. Mother's idea of a voyage of exploration would be a stroll along the pier at Clevedon, and then only in fine weather.

It would have been quite out of the question to tell her I wished to attend a meeting of the Women's Social and Political Union. The prospect of women's suffrage fills Mother with horror. I appear to be the only person in my family who does not subscribe to the idea that women are not only the weaker sex, but also an inferior sex.

The meeting was held at the Victoria Rooms and was apparently a more orderly affair than usual. The newspapers have reported with relish that WSPU meetings have been frequently disrupted by male hecklers throwing missiles: vegetables, rotten fruit, even stones. Surely no one who hurls objects at defenceless women deserves the right to vote?

Yesterday the women of the WSPU were not quite defenceless. I was told the orderly tenor of the meeting could be attributed to the presence of half a dozen professional boxers, hired to protect the speakers. These redoubtable gentlemen were easy to identify by their fearsome expressions and misshapen noses. For this information I'm indebted to Violet Hatherwick, who attended the meeting with her brother, William.

Shortly before the meeting began, we found ourselves side by side on the steps of the Victoria Rooms. It seemed contrary to the spirit of the gathering to ignore Violet, who was Mother's maid until her own mother died and she had to leave us to keep house for her father and brother. So I nodded and smiled and she nodded back. Courting the disapproval of my companions, I struck up a conversation with Violet, who always seemed to me an intelligent girl, wasted, as so many are, in the mindless drudgery of domestic service. It was then she informed me, with a mischievous smile, that the boxers had been engaged. She said William had insisted on accompanying her, though Violet had assured him she was quite capable of looking after herself. Indeed, her lively and combative expression suggested that if a rotten cabbage had sailed in Violet's direction, she might have caught it and hurled it back.

William spoke up to say he was eager to hear the speakers and would have attended on his own account in the interests of furthering his education and the cause of universal suffrage. I believe this was the longest sentence I had heard him utter and the first that was not of a horticultural nature. I must have looked surprised, for when he finished speaking, he cast down his eyes and looked uncomfortable.

I hastened to rescue the conversation by informing them that I had resorted to subterfuge to attend, telling my parents I was attending a Royal Geographical Society meeting. When I mentioned my anticipated difficulty, should anyone enquire about the content of the lecture, William reached inside his jacket and pulled out a carefully folded leaflet. He opened it up, then tore off a corner and handed it to me, saying, 'I attended this lecture last week. The speaker's credentials and the subject of his talk are summarised.' He then indicated the torn corner. 'I've removed the date. I'm sure a cursory study will enable you to answer any awkward enquiries.' He smiled and I was struck then by his resemblance to his sister, though William is darker and usually of a more solemn countenance.

The WSPU meeting was splendid! Laurence fell asleep and snored until Charlotte prodded him with her umbrella, but when I left the Victoria Rooms, my mind was teeming with new ideas. I wished I could offer places in the car to the Hatherwicks, but of course it would never do. In any case, I'm sure they would not have accepted.

As Johnson drove us back to Beechgrave, Charlotte and I studied the Geographical Society leaflet and agreed our story. I remarked that I should have liked to attend both events and Charlotte said, when women achieve full independence, we shall be able to go where we want and do what we want; that the doors of higher education and even the professions will be open to us, when once we have a say in the governing of our country. Charlotte is a passionate and convincing speaker. She could have gone on the stage. Listening to her, my spirits never fail to rally. Laurence, however, remained unmoved and dozed most of the way home.

Charlotte is right. The future will be challenging for women, but it cannot fail to be exciting, unless, of course, this wretched war happens. But how, in this enlightened age, can war be necessary? The Germans are our friends and the Kaiser is King George's cousin. I asked Arthur to explain, but he just said it was all talk, there would be no war, but when I asked Father, he said he thought there *would* be a war. He declined to explain why, assuring me I would not understand.

I suppose if we live in a world where grown men throw bricks at intelligent, articulate women, anything is possible.

ANN

Phoebe was asleep. Impervious to booze, she'd always been a night owl, partying like someone half her age, but nowadays pain exhausted her. She sat slumped in her chair, her head falling forward, a heap of bony limbs. Connor and I regarded her in companionable silence, then he looked at me and whispered, 'Perhaps I'd better stop reading.'

'Yes. She'd hate to miss anything.'

He closed Hester's diary. 'Call it a day then?'

'I think so. You must be tired of reading in any case.'

'Not really. It's nice to have such an appreciative audience.' He stood up and stretched his long limbs. 'Ann, I really don't need to stay over. I can ring for a taxi.'

'No, of course you must stay,' I said, collecting our wine glasses and placing them quietly on a tray, so as not to wake Phoebe.

'I don't want to put you to any trouble.'

'It's no trouble at all, but I can't promise you'll be very comfortable. It's just an old Z-bed. Your feet will probably stick out the end.'

'Oh, I'm used to that.' Connor opened the door for me and followed me into the kitchen. 'You're sure? I mean, you didn't really get to vote, did you? It was Phoebe's invitation.'

'She's your number one fan, you know. If she were ten years younger—'

'And I was ten years older,' he answered with a grin.

'Oh, no, she'd take you as you are. And younger.' The glasses slid as I set down the tray and one almost toppled over. As I caught it, I was aware I must have drunk more than I thought. The conversation felt slightly out of control, even indiscreet, but I found I didn't care. It was nice to have someone to talk to.

Leaning against the worktop, I said, 'Age has never really meant much to Phoebe – physically or morally. When I was young, I used to be very shocked, but now I rather admire her attitude.'

'So do I,' Connor replied. 'And I'm flattered you think if I played my cards right, I could be in with a chance.' His face was deadpan, but I must have stared, because he cracked eventually and laughed. 'Don't worry, I have no designs on your mother. But I *am* very fond of her.' He continued to look at me and said, 'I've grown fond of you both.'

I smiled, feeling pleased but also awkward. 'Phoebe's a person who's easy to admire, but not, I think, easy to love. There have been times – difficult times – when I've asked myself if I actually love my mother, but I've never doubted how much I respect her.'

'As an artist or a person?'

'Both.'

'But I shouldn't think it's been easy being her daughter.'

I looked at him, surprised. 'No, it hasn't.' Once again I had that vertiginous feeling. It might have been the red wine or the apprehension that I was saying – and thinking – too much. 'I've always thought I fell short in various ways. She's never actually *said* I've been a disappointment to her, but . . .'

'You think you have.'

'Yes . . . Well, *no*, not really. I mean what did she expect? That an artist of her calibre would produce another? That just doesn't happen. And I hardly think she can be disappointed my marriage ended. It lasted fifteen years – a lot longer than hers. She's never expressed the slightest interest in grandchildren, so I don't think she holds that against me.'

Connor folded his arms and regarded me thoughtfully. 'So maybe Phoebe *isn't* disappointed in you.'

'You mean, I'm just paranoid?'

'Possibly.'

I laughed, delighted. 'Come on. Let's get you settled in the studio.' I picked up the key to the studio and opened the back door.

I led Connor out into the darkness. I heard him inhale the night air and I did likewise, glad of the bracing cold after the smoky wine-and-wood-burner fug indoors. I stopped and glanced up at the stars, to check they were still there. They were. 'Perhaps you're right, maybe I *am* paranoid. After all, my five-year-old brain had to find some reason for my father running away.'

I unlocked the studio door and switched on the light. 'You're in luck. I always leave the stove ready to light so I don't have to start my working day laying a fire.' I knelt down in front of the stove, opened the door, struck a match and lit the firelighters. As I watched them burn, I sat back on my heels and said, 'I must have thought Dad left because I'd done something very, very bad.'

Connor was standing behind me and didn't speak. I imagine he was hypnotised by the flames too, or just tired. It was late and he'd worked hard in the garden. Eventually he said, 'Did your five-year-old brain come up with anything?'

'No. I was always a very well-behaved child. I didn't even do much in the way of teenage rebellion. My mother was an embarrassment to me with her bohemian friends and young lovers, so I was rigidly conventional. That was how I rebelled.'

Connor sat down on the shabby chaise longue. 'But you thought you must have driven your father away.'

'Something like that. I remember it as a bad time, but I don't recall any details. I can remember Phoebe shouting. Going ballistic. And there was a lot of crying – hers and mine. But I don't remember what it was all about. I don't think anyone actually explained things to me.

Dagmar – Phoebe's agent – came down from London and whisked me away. She took me to her flat where I ate lots of sweets and ice cream. I can remember throwing up. And she bought me a new doll. I'd never owned anything so lovely. I was almost scared to play with her, she was so beautiful. Dagmar read to me at bedtime, which was a real treat. She tucked me up in a little box room with an old patchwork quilt on the bed and I can remember thinking, "I don't ever want to go home." I wanted Dagmar to be my mum.'

'So in fact,' Connor said carefully, 'it's you who's disappointed in Phoebe, not the other way round.'

I looked up, shocked by his words, but unable to deny the truth of them. 'I was very young. I could be bought with dolls and bedtime stories. Speaking of which,' I said, getting to my feet, 'this one's gone on long enough. I should let you get some sleep. I'm being a very boring hostess.'

'Not boring at all. In fact, a lot of what you say strikes a chord with me.'

'Really? Well, that makes me feel slightly better.'

'Phoebe never actually told you she was disappointed in you. My father said little else from my teens onwards. He wanted a clone, not a son and I . . . well, I wanted to do something different with my life.'

The stove was burning nicely now, so I went over and sat beside Connor. 'Didn't you say your dad was in the army?'

'Yes. He assumed I'd follow in his footsteps. That's often the case. You get army families. Ours was one until I let the side down. So I know what it feels like to think you don't measure up, how tough it can be to go your own way without any support or even encouragement.'

'How old were you when you lost your mother?'

'Four. I don't remember anything about her. She's just a photo album. I sometimes wonder if that's why I grew up so interested in archive stuff. Letters, diaries, photos . . . Those people all seem real to me. Well, as real as my mother.'

'Do you have any brothers and sisters?'

'I had one brother, much older. He went into the army and got himself killed.'

'Oh, I'm sorry.'

'Ivy was like a life force. She was the one who shared my interest in growing things. She was the one who taught me to garden, much to Dad's disgust. Then when he realised I wanted to make a *career* out of it . . .'

'He wasn't happy?'

'He was angry. He talked about horticulture as if it was hairdressing and about as useful. Dad was an army surgeon, so I could see where he was coming from.'

'Oh dear. Medicine *and* the army. That was a lot of pressure.'

Connor shot me a grateful look. 'Yes, it was. But Dad wasn't just angry, he was ill. He'd seen a lot of appalling things on active service. Not just mates dying. Civilians. Children. It affected him deeply. Permanently. He thought the world was a terrible place and he only saw the bad. So he drank a lot. Said it helped him relax, but I can't say I ever saw it mellow his mood. He had a vile temper. And he lost control a few times.' Connor paused and I noticed his big hands were clenched as they lay on his thighs.

'Did he ever hit you?'

'Occasionally. Then I got to be taller than him and hit back. He left me alone after that, but it was shame, not fear. Dad didn't do fear. It was a point of honour with him.'

'How horrible for you. For *both* of you.'

'Yes, it was all pretty undignified. Ivy was always trying to patch things up between us, but Dad insisted on seeing my rejection of the army as a rejection of him and my brother's sacrifice. That's what Dad always called it. Kieran didn't just die, he made the ultimate sacrifice. When I rejected the army, Dad said I was rejecting generations of Grenvilles, even rejecting being a man. He just didn't get it. But his head was a mess, poor sod. Combat didn't ever stop for him. He was always looking for a fight.'

'He's dead, I take it?'

'Yes. His battle ended some years ago.' Connor gazed at the flames dancing behind the glass door of the stove. 'But the guilt . . . and the disappointment . . . Well, you would know. They go on and on, don't they?'

I felt an impulse to put an arm round this sad young man, to offer some sort of indeterminate comfort, but there seemed to be no context in which to touch him and I began to doubt my motives for wanting to do it.

Connor leaned forward and clasped his hands loosely between his thighs. Staring at the floor he said, 'At Dad's funeral all his army mates told me what a great bloke he was. Fearless. A natural leader. One of the best. They said I must have been very proud of him.' He sat back and sighed. 'I suppose I would have been if we'd ever really known each other, if he'd ever talked – really *talked* about his work, instead of giving me all the understated, stiff upper lip crap. I tried to feel proud of him at the funeral but I was just . . . angry.'

'Do you know why?'

'Oh, yes. I was angry because he was gone and he'd never, ever been proud of me. And now he never would.' Connor looked up, his eyes moist, beseeching. 'But how can you be angry with the *dead*?'

'Very easily. For a start there's no chance of them ever coming back to apologise. And it's all over, isn't it? Finally. You're lumbered with a bad ending. Or just not knowing what was really going on.'

His smile was lopsided and uncertain. 'So . . . I'm not just paranoid then?'

'I don't think so. But what do I know? You said *I* was paranoid.'

He tilted his head to one side and looked at me. 'In the nicest possible way.'

'Thank you. I *think*.'

'You know what I'm talking about then? The anger?'

'Oh, yes. Sylvester hardly knew me. He never saw what I became or what I did. Okay, I haven't done anything important, but I would have liked him to know me. And of course I would have liked to know him.' I hesitated, shot Connor a sidelong glance, then said, 'For what it's worth, I'd just like to say, that . . . well, that *I'm* proud of you.'

He turned and stared. 'Whatever for?'

'The way you've worked in the garden, giving it all you've got. The way you've befriended Phoebe. She's really not the easiest of people, but you've given her a new lease of life. She looks forward to seeing you. We both do. And I admire what you're doing for Ivy. In her memory. Trying to understand what went wrong.'

He frowned. 'Is that what I'm doing? I suppose it is. To begin with, I was just curious, but it's become a bit of an obsession now. I mean, what could be so bad, you actually want to destroy your past? Your *memories*? I just don't get it.'

'Me neither, but I'm sure you're doing the right thing. I think it's important to understand where we've come from. To make sense of things and try to make the best of them.'

'Have you forgiven him?'

'Sylvester? For leaving?' I got up, opened the stove door and threw in another log. 'No, I don't think so. Not really. My own marriage failed, so I can understand what he did. But I don't think I've forgiven him. Not yet.'

'That's the hard bit. Still work in progress for me.'

'And me . . . Look, I think I'd better go back and check on Phoebe. The loo's through that door,' I said, pointing, 'and you'll find towels and probably a new toothbrush in the cupboard. Oh, and there's milk in the fridge. Make yourself tea or coffee in the morning, then come over for breakfast when you're ready.'

He stood up. 'Thank you. And thanks for listening – to Hester's story and mine.'

'It's been a pleasure. Truly. I can't wait for the next instalment.' As I looked up at him, I realised, had I been taller, I would have kissed him on the cheek. In the few seconds' hiatus, I sensed Connor having the same thought and wasn't surprised when he bowed his untidy head and brushed my cheek with his lips.

'Good night, Ann. Sleep well.'

'You too. Good night.'

When I got back indoors, I found Phoebe had not only put herself to bed, she'd attempted to tidy the kitchen. There was a scrawled note under a dirty wine glass saying, *Cracked. Sorry.*

I preferred Phoebe to leave loading and unloading the dishwasher to me, but she liked to demonstrate she was still capable of living independently. When she tackled jobs, there were sometimes casualties. To protect her hands, I'd forbidden her to deal with broken glass and crockery.

I wrapped up the cracked glass, put on my coat and headed for the recycling bin, taking some empty bottles. On my way, I saw the light was still on in the studio. Connor hadn't pulled the blinds down and was sitting on the chaise longue staring at the wood burner. I hurried through the garden and disposed of the bottles. On my way back, I glanced at the studio again. He was sitting with his head in his hands.

I stood in the shadows, rooted to the spot despite the cold. If I went in and asked if he was all right, it would look as if I'd been spying on him. Obviously, I should ignore him, go indoors and get to bed. But his head was still in his hands . . . I resolved to go indoors. And didn't.

Connor suddenly got to his feet. In one smooth movement, he removed his sweater and tossed it on to the chaise longue. Kicking off his shoes, he started to unbutton his shirt. It was now quite clear I had no business standing in the garden watching a man undress, but if I crossed the garden now, I'd be moving into the light and Connor might see me. Even if he didn't think I'd been watching him, he'd feel embarrassed. He'd removed his shirt and was unzipping his jeans before I turned and fled to the garage where I waited for several minutes, feeling a complete idiot – and a lot more besides.

When I felt sure he must have gone to bed, I emerged and set off for the house, keeping my head down. The only light came from the kitchen window now and I scurried towards it. Shivering convulsively, I shut the back door behind me, remembering to leave it unlocked for Connor in the morning. I turned out the lights and went up to my room. Too tired to clean my teeth, I undressed quickly and got into bed where I continued to shiver and think about what I'd seen and what I'd felt.

I must have dozed off, because I had no idea how much time had passed or what had happened when I found myself sitting up in bed, clammy with sweat, my heart pounding. I stared into the darkness, trying to interpret the rapidly fading vision I could see in my mind's eye.

I was outside. In the wood. It was very early in the morning. And I was watching someone . . .

Then I remembered Connor standing in the studio. As I started to cry, my vision evaporated so completely, I thought I must have imagined it. Overwhelmed by fear and self-pity, I wept for the things I'd wanted and never had. A father. A child. And I cried for what I wanted now and didn't have. A man. A man like Connor. Kind, intelligent, sensitive, with – as Phoebe had noted – broad shoulders and a nice arse.

Disgusted with myself, I lay down, hauled the duvet up round my shoulders and closed my eyes. I shivered and snivelled and eventually I slept.

With the approach of spring, we settled into a comfortable routine. Connor came over at weekends and worked in the garden. I fed him and photographed him for his blog, then in the evenings the three of us would pore over the Mordaunt archive and Connor would read from Hester's diary. It was like doing a gigantic jigsaw, one we knew was incomplete, but which we nevertheless felt compelled to try and finish.

There was a standing invitation for Connor to stay over on Friday and Saturday nights so he could drink and make an early start in the garden after the breakfast I insisted on cooking for all three of us. Phoebe enjoyed these weekends so much, she counted the days, anticipating Connor's return and her next fix of what she liked to call 'The Mystery of the Mordaunts'.

I was pleased for her. It was heartening to see her engage with both projects. I was less happy about the fact that I too found myself counting the days. I looked forward to Connor's visits, for all the same reasons as Phoebe and another I could not have shared with her. Or Connor.

'Things are hotting up,' Connor announced as he filled our glasses. 'War breaks out tonight.'

'Jolly good!' Phoebe said cheerfully. 'I've been looking forward to that.' She settled back in her armchair and lifted her feet on to a worn leather pouffe. 'But I do hope you haven't been cheating, Connor.'

'*Cheating?*' His face was a picture of mock outrage. 'Phoebe, what *do* you mean?'

'You know. Reading ahead. To see what happens.'

'I've dipped in here and there, but I haven't read everything. I was fairly sure what upset Ivy couldn't have been in the diaries. She'd had them for years.'

'But they're quite hard to read, aren't they?' I said, handing round the now customary plate of chocolate biscuits. 'Hester had tiny writing and it's very elaborate. What was Ivy's sight like?'

'That's a good point. She was ninety-seven when she died and her sight wasn't brilliant for the last decade. But she *could* have read the diaries years before, when Hester died. That's when they would have come into her possession.'

Phoebe clapped her hands. 'Come on, let's get on with the story. Don't keep us waiting for this week's thrilling instalment. *The lamps are going out all over Europe* . . . Isn't that what someone said?'

'That's right.' Connor picked up the diary and opened it where he'd left a bookmark. 'Sir Edward Grey, Foreign Secretary, the night before war was declared. *The lamps are going out all over Europe. We shall not see them lit again in our lifetime.* So let's see what Hester Mordaunt had to say about it . . .'

HESTER

August 5th, 1914

We are at war. Germany has declared war on Serbia, Russia and France and now we have declared war on Germany. Mobilisation has already begun. How has this happened? Only days ago the papers were full of civil war in Ireland and now we are at war with Germany.

We had to respond to the invasion of Belgium, of course. Neutrality was unthinkable. We were honour-bound to come to their assistance, but was there really no alternative to war? If that is indeed the case, why are men so eager to fight? To die? Arthur and Eddie are as excited as schoolboys, full of plans to enlist immediately. To listen to them whoop, you would think they had received an invitation to join a particularly good shooting party.

Father is calm, but subdued. So is Mother. Neither has said much, but it is clear they view the current situation with dismay and apprehension. I overheard Mother discussing food shortages with Cook. Father has already mentioned digging up some of the lawns to increase food production at Beechgrave.

The fate of Europe now depends on decisions women have no power to influence. We can only watch helplessly as husbands, brothers, sons and sweethearts go off to fight. But we must show ourselves worthy of citizenship, even if our claim to it is not yet recognised.

August 6th

Arthur and Eddie are still determined to enlist. Father says Eddie is too young and cannot enlist without his consent, but I fear Eddie will soon wear him down.

I heard Mother weeping in the music room, so I went in to try to comfort her. I put my arm around her but could think of nothing reassuring to say. I am not so naïve as to assume my brothers lead charmed lives and will walk through the fire unharmed. Millions of young men will engage in this conflict and many thousands must die. So I simply held Mother's hand, feeling quite helpless.

When she had regained her composure, she began to sort through her sheet music, appearing to cast some aside. Her eyes were red, but her expression was determined. She hesitated only once, when she came to an album of her beloved Beethoven sonatas, but after a moment, she dropped it on to the discarded pile on the carpet.

'We have no use for German music now, Hester,' she said. 'It would be unpatriotic to play or even listen to it. Germany is our enemy. Their music is forever tainted by their wickedness!'

Mother did not wait for me to respond, but swept out of the room, her back very straight.

The sight of so much Beethoven and Brahms lying in a disorderly heap distressed me. I knelt down, gathered the music into my arms and took it away to my bedroom where I hid it at the back of my wardrobe. If the newspapers are right and this dreadful war is over by Christmas, Mother might be glad I put her music by for her. Until then, she will miss Beethoven dreadfully. So shall I.

August 10th

Walter has now declared his intention to enlist. He said he hoped to make me very proud of him. I told him I was already proud of him and his patriotic fervour.

I think I am proud, but my feelings are not at all clear. I fear for my brothers' safety and wish they could either be spared the coming ordeal or that I could somehow share it with them. I am also afraid for Walter, but at the same time I have to admit – to myself at least – that I am not sorry the wedding has been postponed. Mother says a spring wedding will be much nicer and we shall have more time to plan and shop. The guest list would have been sadly depleted with so many of our young men away fighting, so it is best that we wait until the war is over.

August 16th

This evening Mother insisted we play some music together in honour of Walter's decision to enlist. We could only play a trio since Arthur and Eddie have already left for their training camp. The sound we made seemed very thin. I never thought I should miss poor Eddie's contribution to family music-making. The sight of Arthur's cello case standing in the corner like a naughty child lowered my spirits. Mother's too, I suspect. We played two short pieces, *con brio*, then she seemed to lose heart. She closed the piano lid and, quite disconsolate, said, 'We shall be reduced to duets soon, Hester. I wonder, is there anything for piano and viola?' I reminded her I could always play Eddie's violin. Still she would not rally, but made her excuses and left the room, dabbing at her eyes with a handkerchief.

Walter left soon afterwards and I went for a walk in the wood, then wandered back by way of the kitchen garden, just for the exercise. As I passed Garden Lodge, Violet Hatherwick ran out to speak to me. She must have been looking out of the kitchen window. After a few polite exchanges, she informed me that her brother wanted to enlist, but felt torn between his duty to his country and his duty to the Mordaunt family. Apparently he has firm ideas about how the garden could be made more productive with the use of fertilisers, but his father is convinced the fighting will be over by Christmas and considers talk of food shortages alarmist. William disagrees. Violet said he has been drawing up plans for the best use of the garden in the event of the war continuing next year.

I did not know how to respond to this dismal thought. In the silence that ensued, Violet said she had remembered something important and disappeared indoors. After a moment, she emerged with a book, saying, 'William said I was to offer you this, Miss.' I examined the spine briefly, then opened the book at the title page. It was a copy of *Land of the Blue Poppy: Travels of a Naturalist in Eastern Tibet* by Francis Kingdon-Ward. Once again a seed packet had been used to mark a place, but this time it had been slit and opened out so that someone – William presumably – could write on the blank side, *For the attention of Miss H. Mordaunt.*

Violet explained that, if I found it of interest, William wished to lend me the book. I said I should very much like to read it. We exchanged a few more pleasantries, then I set off back to the house, hugging the book with excitement.

I went up to my room to study my new acquisition. The packet on which my name was inscribed had once held sweet pea seeds. Why this fact should seem worthy of recording, I do not know, except that I am very fond of sweet peas, both their colours and their scent. William Hatherwick cannot have known this, of course, but the coincidence pleases me. I shall keep this seed packet, together with the other one, inside my journal.

September 3rd

The de-population of Beechgrave continues. William Hatherwick has enlisted, along with several other staff. The tactical retreat following the Battle of Mons, where our heroic British Expeditionary Force was greatly outnumbered, has spurred many more men to enlist, as has the news that the German army is only thirty miles from Paris.

I feel utterly useless. There must be something more I can do apart from knit socks and mittens for our soldiers! To distract myself, I have taken to walking in the wood most evenings, when it is fine. Yesterday I met a tearful Violet walking with her brother. Apparently Father has promised all the men that their jobs will be held open for them, so they are free to answer the call to arms. Mr Hatherwick Snr. will have to manage with the pot boys and the few garden staff who are left.

William asked if I should like to borrow any of his books while he is away at the Front. He said Violet could bring them up to the house for me to peruse and that I should keep any that interested me 'for the duration'. I thanked him for his kind offer and said I should be delighted to act as custodian of his library. He and Violet then set off back towards Garden Lodge. I was about to continue on my walk when William stopped and turned back. He indicated to Violet that she could go on ahead, then he hurried over towards me. He looked anxious, rotating the brim of his hat in his hands, as if possessed by some strong emotion. He cleared his throat, then said something very odd. I am still trying to digest its significance.

He said, in the event of his failing to return, I should keep his books – all of them. Violet had no use for them and his father's sight was beginning to fail, but William said he wanted to know his books would be read. I was taken aback and suggested a collection of fine books could be sold, but he shook his head. He then cast a glance over his shoulder at his sister who had ambled on ahead and said he wanted me to have the books because he knew I would appreciate them and because (this was the strange part I did not understand) he owned nothing else of value, save his pocket watch and he wanted to give that to Violet.

I am sitting now at my writing table, surrounded by several piles of books that Violet kindly brought up to the house. I think she must have used the donkey cart to transport them! I have browsed through some of the books already, noting the places William has marked with old seed packets and I have read many of his neat marginal notes made in pencil.

I feel as if I have been entrusted with a great treasure. Safeguarding such a collection is an honour and I am so very glad of the opportunity to study. It will, I am sure, prove an excellent distraction from the war and will prevent me from worrying excessively about the fate of our menfolk.

I know Mother would not approve, but I have added William Hatherwick to my nightly prayers. He has been so very kind, I wish to pray for his safety, together with Walter's and my brothers'. It is my fervent hope they will all return home safely.

September 13th

There is talk of the Kaiser suing for peace! But there have been so many rumours, I hardly dare hope this one is true.

September 29th

My diary has been much neglected of late. I write to Arthur, Eddie or Walter every day and by the time I have concocted something out of nothing by way of news, I am too low in spirits to record the tedium of my days. My brothers' cheerful but infrequent letters describe their training, which consists of exercises to develop physical fitness, drill, marching, field craft and so on. It sounds dreary, but they seem to be enjoying themselves. Eddie in particular appears to think it all a great lark.

I pray they remain in good spirits if they are eventually sent abroad. But surely the war cannot continue for much longer?

October 10th

It does not seem at all likely the war will be over by Christmas. Mr Kitchener has said it could last years.

I am knitting furiously. Poor Mother can manage little more than winding wool into balls, but she likes me to sit with her while I knit. I wish I could describe the silence as 'companionable', but it is not. It is not even comfortable. Knitting gives one far too much time to think.

October 21st

Mother has lost her appetite and seems quite melancholy. After the postman has been, she has no interest in the rest of the day, nor does she follow the progress of the war. I think perhaps she is trying to ignore it.

At times her mind seems to wander and she has started to play Beethoven again, from memory. I have not reminded her of what she said. Fortunately, Father does not recognise it as German music. Nor, I imagine, do the servants.

November 15th

Like Mother, I now live for letters, though Walter's are so brief and inconsequential, they offer little food for thought. They are affectionate, however, if somewhat repetitive.

While reading my last letter from Walter, I realised I can no longer recall what he looks like. I have a photographic portrait, but when I think of him and try to bring his face and person to mind, I see only his head and shoulders, as they appear in the portrait, floating like the Cheshire Cat's grin. Try as I might, I cannot remember Walter himself. His photograph is not even a good likeness. Walter generally looks cheerful and often smiles. In this, the only picture I have of him, he looks stiff and uncomfortable, as if his collar is troubling him. That is not at all how I remember Walter.

Though the truth is, I do not remember Walter.

December 6th

Scarborough, Whitby and Hartlepool have been bombarded by the German navy. There have been many casualties. Mother is hysterical, but I am too angry to be frightened.

I have decided to abandon this wretched journal. It seems pointless to chronicle such a futile and unhappy life, especially as I have no right to be unhappy. After all, what sacrifices have I been called upon to make? Nothing more than postponing my wedding! In Hartlepool people have died horribly.

This diary has become a repository for self-pity and cowardly thoughts. I am ashamed of it and ashamed of myself.

I shall waste no more ink and paper.

April 13th, 1915

After an interval of several months, I take up my pen again. I can no longer bear to keep all my thoughts and feelings to myself, but there is no one to whom I can talk, so I have resumed this journal.

I fear I shall go mad. So many men of our acquaintance have been wounded, are missing or known to be dead, that ordinary life has become impossible. I dread leaving the house in case I encounter someone I know who has been bereaved. I live in daily expectation of a telegram that will confirm my worst fears. Only letters and postcards from loved ones bring peace of mind – and that short-lived. Poor Charlotte's family had a letter from Laurence after they had received the telegram to say he was dead. Imagine the agony, reading a letter from a dead man!

I must try to order my thoughts. It would be all too easy to give in to despair, as Mother has done, but that would be unpatriotic. The writing of this journal must serve as a mental discipline. I shall record here the thoughts I cannot share with my brothers or Walter, or even my parents.

May God forgive me if I commit unloving or disloyal words to paper.

April 18th

I am very concerned about Mother. She has become even more demanding, perhaps because she is unwell. She often asks me to read to her, but she will not listen to a newspaper. She prefers light novels and old letters from Arthur and Eddie, which I have read so many times, I now know them by heart.

I have tried to rouse Mother from her lassitude by asking for help making up parcels for 'the boys', as we call them. They write that they need sundry provisions: books, candles, matches, soap, cakes, tins of milk and butter, etc. They have promised us more letters if we can supply them with writing paper and envelopes, which are in short supply.

I have started to attend First Aid lectures and I continue to knit. My main recreation is reading, particularly William Hatherwick's books. I have copied out many favourite passages into a notebook. I refuse to countenance the idea that these volumes might one day be mine. Our boys *will* return. All of them. The alternative is unthinkable.

I keep myself occupied – frenetically so at times – so that when I retire, I fall asleep almost immediately. I have taken to going on long walks around the estate as Mother does not like me to go very far from her. The highlight of a long and mostly tedious day is my walk to the beech wood and back. On the way I make notes of what is happening in the garden. I am not sure why I do this, other than to have something to tell Violet Hatherwick when I see her, which I do most days. I believe she looks out for me now.

Violet is in the habit of asking me, 'What looks well in the garden today?' and she includes my answers in letters to William. She says she is 'not much of a letter writer' and is glad of any news with which to supplement hers, so I have taken to giving her a piece of paper with my garden notes scribbled on it. I believe she copies them out for William.

Evidently he enjoys hearing about Beechgrave's gardens. Violet has several times read out excerpts from his letters in which he thanks me for sending a little piece of England to war-ravaged France. So when I walk through the garden – or the wood, which Violet says is one of William's favourite places – I try to see what he would see, so that I (or rather Violet) can reassure him that, despite this cataclysmic war, life goes on. Things still grow, bloom and set seed.

Thank God – oh, thank God! – for the dear bees.

April 20th

If only Walter wrote longer letters. He has even less to say on paper than he did in person. I struggle to reply because he tells me so little about his life at the Front. It is much easier to write to Arthur and Eddie who tell me about their friends, the parcels they receive, what it is like to be shelled for hours. They never complain, though Eddie said the horses have a very hard time of it. How typical of dear Eddie to consider the animals!

Walter's letters are all much the same: warm thanks for my last letter, a brief description of his state of health, enquiries after mine, concluding with fond regards for my parents and assurances that he is 'as ever', my 'most devoted Walter'. Am I unreasonable to want to know more? He mentions that he reads, but not what he reads. He commends the courage of his fellow officers, but tells me nothing of what sort of men they are. He says the destruction in France is 'indescribable', but I do so wish he would try.

I must be content. Walter's letters tell me he is still alive. I cannot, *must* not ask for more.

April 23rd

I am too tired to write this evening. The keeping of this journal was once a pleasure, or at least a pastime, then it became an outlet for my overburdened emotions, but now I can hardly bear to live this life, let alone record it.

But how dare I complain? I am warm and dry and I have plenty to eat. I even have a good supply of paper and envelopes. The same cannot be said for Walter and my poor brothers.

I can hear Mother playing in the music room. Music is her great consolation, but now there are only the two of us, she insists I play Eddie's violin to widen our repertoire. I feel uncomfortable doing so. I cannot explain why, except to say, I feel as if it tempts fate, to rehearse a future I hope will never come to pass.

I *must* put a stop to this endless brooding! What is the point of recording so much sadness, anxiety and loneliness? I cannot imagine that my descendants – if I have any – will show any curiosity about my little life. Momentous things are happening beyond the English Channel, but here at Beechgrave life merely staggers on, a pale imitation of what it once was.

The garden too. It is unkempt and neglected because so few staff remain and, as Mr Hatherwick our Head Gardener put it, 'The abundance of work presses hard on the smallness of time.' Nevertheless, our oaks have been felled. Father gave the order in response to an appeal from the Admiralty for donations of wood for shipbuilding.

How I hate, hate, *hate* this war! And how hateful it is to be a woman in time of war. Mother refuses to let me look for any sort of voluntary work and claims she cannot spare me. Father is no more sympathetic. He says my duty is to look after Mother while he works long hours managing the saw mill and an estate crippled by a shortage of manpower.

May 2nd

Some good news at last. When I saw Violet today, she invited me into her little parlour to listen to the latest news from William. He has started to create a garden! He and some of the other men found some tulips and wallflowers in the ruined gardens of a French village that had been destroyed by shells. They dug them up and transplanted them to make a little garden behind a wall of sandbags. William had sent a charming little sketch. I had no idea he was such an accomplished artist, but Violet said he has filled many sketchbooks over the years.

William has asked Violet to send him some seeds. I begged her to give me the list as I should like to buy the seeds myself and send them. She did so willingly.

I shall venture into Bristol to find a seed merchant where I shall buy William all the seeds he needs, then I shall make up a parcel and enclose a little letter.

I could weep with happiness to think that somewhere, someone is trying to grow something; that in the midst of unimaginable slaughter and destruction, something new will live!

May 6th

Arthur is dead. He was killed in action at Ypres.

Father collapsed when he heard the news. Dr Maguire has told Mother we should prepare for the worst. She is beside herself with grief. I can hear her calling for me now, shrieking.

Shall I have no leisure to mourn my dear, brave brother?

May 7th

Father is holding on. Mother seems convinced all will be well, but Dr Maguire is not optimistic. Neither am I, but I continue to pray for Father's recovery.

May 8th

Father passed away this evening. I was at his bedside, but I spared him the news that Eddie has been wounded.

Even if Eddie should survive, I fear Mother will not bear up. The balance of her mind is disturbed now and she is incapable of making arrangements for the funeral. Dr Maguire gave her something to make her sleep and when he left, a blessed silence descended, a silence in which I felt altogether numb. I have cried so many tears for Arthur, I am quite exhausted, but now Father is dead and I must mourn his loss too. If Eddie dies, I fear I shall go mad with grief, like Mother.

When I was certain she was sound asleep, I went out and walked down to Garden Lodge. Violet opened the door to me and as soon as she saw me, she took me by the hand and led me into the little parlour where, to my surprise, I cried and cried. I was convinced I had no more tears left to shed.

Violet asked no questions. She must have heard what had happened. Bad news travels fast these days, even though there is so much of it. She made tea and asked if I should like to hear more about William's trench garden. I said I should, very much.

As she read, I gazed about me, stunned with grief, and noticed for the first time how red Violet's hands are. The skin was very dry and cracked in places. I suddenly remembered her brother's square brown hands as he turned his cap nervously, speaking to me in the woods.

The thought of him planting flowers with those hands in the mud of a foreign field furnished me with some queer sort of comfort.

Violet's hands shook a little as she read William's letter. She is fearful, afraid she will lose him. Or perhaps there is someone else at the Front, a man who means even more to her than her brother. There is so much I should like to know, but cannot ask. There is so much I should like to tell, but cannot say.

When Violet had finished reading, I took her rough hand in mine and held it. We sat for a while, in silence, staring into the fire. Waiting.

May 12th

There is no news of Eddie, who is being cared for in a Belgian field hospital. I long to go and visit him but I doubt Mother would manage without me, nor can I readily ask her permission to travel since she does not acknowledge that Father and Arthur are dead, nor that Eddie is wounded. She is at least calm nowadays, unless I cross her. Calm, but unhinged. Her conversation is directed not towards me, but to her absent husband and sons. This is how Mother's poor shattered mind copes with unspeakable loss: she does not speak of it.

Instead she plays the music we all used to play together – trios, quartets, quintets – but she plays only the piano part, so the music makes little sense. I cannot bear it and refuse to enter the music room now, but occasionally I stand outside and listen. It is pitiful to hear her accompany music only she can hear. Sometimes she even stops to admonish Eddie for not keeping time, as if he were in the room.

I have tried in earnest to pray for Eddie, but I am losing faith in the power of prayer and derive no comfort now from the exercise. I feel rather like Mother, talking to myself, rambling on irrationally, but there are days when I envy Mother the solace of her madness. Is that very wicked of me?

May 16th

My dear brother Edwin is dead. They say he did not suffer. I wish I could believe it. I have not told Mother yet. I dare not.

No more.

I have no more words.

ANN

Connor closed the journal slowly and said, 'Poor Hester.'

Phoebe blew her nose. 'Very affecting. It's extraordinary how involved you can get with people you've never met and never will. I mean, it's not even *fiction*, it's just a diary. But it really brings it home to you, doesn't it? The personal cost of the war. Such a pointless war too.'

'All war is pointless,' Connor said firmly, setting the diary aside.

'You think so?' I asked, refilling our glasses.

He leaned back on the sofa. 'Well, this one was called "the war to end wars", but it just set the stage for the next. And I don't think anyone disputes that the Treaty of Versailles contributed to the rise of Nazism. How can any problem ever be resolved by fighting? Right won't necessarily prevail. *Might* will. Haig said, "Victory will belong to the side which holds out the longest." What a pathetic admission!'

'But surely,' I said, 'some things are worth fighting for?'

'Oh, yes, things are *worth* fighting for, but the fighting itself is pointless unless you're on the winning side. Might – or sheer endurance – will carry the day. Haig was absolutely right. The Allies didn't win because we occupied the moral high ground, we won because the Germans lost.'

'I imagine you and your father didn't exactly see eye to eye over this issue,' Phoebe said, with a mischievous twinkle.

Connor laughed and shook his head. 'Dad and I nearly came to blows over my pacifism. It was an embarrassment to him. He thought it was unmanly and un-British and he would never accept that my views in no way dishonoured the fallen, even though my brother was one of them, as was my grandfather. You can acknowledge bravery and self-sacrifice, but still see war as a terrible waste of lives and resources. Dad thought that was a betrayal. It was bad enough I wasn't prepared to follow in his footsteps, but being a *pacifist* as well . . . I used to quote Churchill back at him,' Connor said with a wry smile.

'Churchill?'

'When Siegfried Sassoon spoke out against the war in 1918, Churchill responded with, "War is the normal occupation of man. War – and gardening."'

'Oh, *touché*!' Phoebe exclaimed, delighted.

Connor leaned forward and picked up Hester's journal again and leafed through the pages. 'Would you like me to carry on? Or have you had enough for tonight?'

'More please!' Phoebe said, settling back in her armchair and hoisting her feet on to the leather pouffe.

Connor shot me a look of enquiry.

'Can you bear to indulge us a little more?' I asked.

'Happy to.'

And so he resumed his reading.

HESTER

September 26th, 1915

It is many weeks since I wrote in this journal. My father is buried in the shade of the village church, but my dear brothers lie in foreign soil. They died protecting a country I have never visited. When I do go, it will be to tend their graves.

With no bodies to bury it is still hard to believe they are dead. I have created a little shrine in my room to my brothers' memory, with photographs, fresh flowers and the last letters they sent home. It occurred to me that many of the Beechgrave staff are in the same unfortunate position, mourning loved ones buried or lost on foreign soil, so I have let it be known that flowers, pot plants and any kind of personal memorial can be left in front of the summer house. There is a paved area that is suitable and easily accessible to all. It is my intention that this will become a Garden of Remembrance, open to all and at all times of day. I think it is important that Beechgrave should honour and mourn *all* its dead and that we should do that together.

I wear deep mourning still and am glad of it. What to wear is one decision I do not have to make each morning – and there are so many now. At twenty-three I am effectively head of the household. Mother is incapable of making any decision, however small. Even menus are beyond her, so Cook comes to me now. Nothing was actually said, but the Beechgrave staff – the few men who have not enlisted and the women who did not desert us for more lucrative work in factories – have, with palpable relief, shifted their allegiance to me. I run the house and I am also nominally responsible for the gardens and the saw mill. If I stopped to think about any of this, I should be terrified. Before Father died my only responsibilities were reading to Mother and tidying her music. The only things I organised were the dried flowers in my herbarium.

Mr Hatherwick Snr. can be left to his own devices in the garden, although he is so short of men, drastic changes are called for. Food production must be our priority next year and he has agreed to employ some women for the menial tasks.

Fortunately for us and for him, Mr Evans was too old to enlist and he continues to manage the saw mill as he did when Father was alive. He has fewer men, but they are prepared to work longer hours and I am prepared to pay them. The mill is a source of income and the gardens a source of food, but the house itself is a drain. Heating it, cleaning it, maintaining its aged fabric costs a great deal of money. Since there is only Mother to consider, I wonder about selling the house or leasing it, but who would want a great big house – and a very old-fashioned one – in wartime?

I have no uncles to advise me, only two widowed aunts, so I have written to Walter to ask what he thinks I should do. After we are married things will surely be easier. His family business is importing tea and I am sure trade will flourish once again after the war. I doubt Walter would wish to live at Beechgrave. He can never have expected I should inherit, nor do I think we could afford to live here, but I fear Mother will not survive removal to a new home. She leaves her room only to play the piano. All meals are taken up to her and some days she does not even dress. Her friends ceased to call once they realised she was no longer capable of lucid conversation. Some continued to write, but Mother does not open her letters, let alone reply. She has immured herself in a solitary world of grief and madness, but I have saved all her correspondence in case she should recover one day and wish to read it.

Yet Mother is not, I believe, as lonely as I, for she conducts animated conversations with Father, Arthur and Eddie. She does this even when I am in the room. In the intermittent silences, I find myself straining to hear the words my dead loved ones are supposed to utter. Sometimes it is all I can do to refrain from asking, 'What did Eddie say?'

I have shut up many of the rooms. They sleep under dust sheets and behind closed shutters. I long to join them. More than once I have considered hiding beneath a dust sheet in one of those distant rooms to make myself invisible, unavailable to Cook, Mr Hatherwick and Mr Evans. I wonder how long it would be before I was found?

I have made a provisional inventory of articles that could be sold. If we owned less silver, there would be less of it to clean. However, I can do nothing without Mother's consent unless I act independently and therefore improperly. Since Mother does not even know half the house is closed, how could she miss its contents? I wish to do the right thing, but these days it is not at all clear what *is* the right thing.

I wander round the house, gazing at artefacts I was never meant to own. All this should have been Arthur's, or in the event of his early demise, Eddie's, never mine. How I should like to sell Eddie's gun collection, or even just give it away! I cannot bear to see any agent of death in this house, so his guns have been packed away, along with all the fishing rods and tackle. I cannot even bear to see mousetraps laid.

Sometimes I fear my mind is no more robust than my mother's. There has been so much death. I spend every spare moment in the garden now, even when it rains. I do not care. I simply stand under an umbrella and watch things grow.

October 1st

The garden is dying. I cannot bear it. I can smell autumn on the wind and know winter cannot be far behind. I have gathered dahlias, chrysanthemums and seed heads to arrange indoors. The colours are welcome, but scarcely lift my spirits.

I have seen some terrible sights in the streets. Broken boys in wheelchairs, men with faces so disfigured, one cannot help but flinch at the sight. I am ashamed of my weakness, ashamed of this war. How can anything be worth this sacrifice?

January 1st, 1916

I have decided to begin the New Year by resuming my journal. The days are long and dark and my lethargy is such that I find it hard to move away from the fireside. I should knit, I suppose, but I prefer to write, though increasingly the activity seems pointless. Nevertheless, I derive an odd sort of comfort from it. Writing imposes order on my chaotic thoughts and feelings. Without this, I fear I might resort to conversing with the dead, like Mother.

Mr Hatherwick is ill. His bronchitis is no better and for several days he has been unable to leave his bed. Fortunately, there is not a great deal to do in the garden at this time of year and the staff need little guidance.

When I visited him I took some of Cook's excellent beef broth and some stems of flowering witch hazel that I had gathered from the garden. We came to an understanding after Father died that I should be allowed to pick flowers whenever I wanted and arrange them myself. I was dismayed to see his deterioration and insisted on sending for Dr Maguire. Mr Hatherwick protested and said he would soon be on his feet again.

The look in Violet's eyes told me she was as anxious as I. Apart from natural concern for her father, she must be concerned for her future.

Garden Lodge is allocated to the Head Gardener, so in the event of their father's demise, she and William would lose their home.

While Mr Hatherwick was preoccupied with one of his many coughing fits, I asked Violet to send one of the boys with a message to Dr Maguire. When she returned, her father and I were discussing William's eligibility for promotion to Head Gardener. I proposed a new, less demanding post for Mr Hatherwick which was to plant and maintain new woodland which, we both agreed, was a job that has been neglected for many years.

Mr Hatherwick's mind was thus happily engaged with plans for the future. He said he was relieved to know his children would continue to have a home, though he said he was sure a pretty girl like Violet would soon find herself a husband 'when all the lads come home'. Violet blushed so furiously, I wondered if she already had a candidate in mind.

Mr Hatherwick expressed pride in his son's achievements and pointed out that, as Head Gardener, William would then be able to marry. He shook his head and said, 'He's lost his heart to some lass, I'm certain of it, but he's not saying who. He's a close one is our Will!' His wheezy chuckles led to yet another coughing fit, so I made my excuses and left.

It had of course occurred to me that an intelligent and personable young woman like Violet must have a sweetheart. Since I took over the household, I have perforce become acquainted with the romantic entanglements of Beechgrave's female staff. Cook insisted I dismiss one girl who had apparently brought the household into disrepute. I was not altogether clear what she meant. Cook, though outraged, was vague in her denunciation.

When I interviewed Sarah, matters were no clearer. She told me between sobs that her young man had promised to marry her and that she had just wanted to send him off to the Front happy. This seemed to me an admirable goal. I asked if he lived still and she said, yes, as far as she knew. I enquired whether it was still his intention to marry her on his return and she assured me it was and that he was 'very pleased about the baby'.

Light dawned and I finally understood why Cook was so affronted. However, even she admits Sarah is a good, reliable worker and replacement kitchen staff are hard to come by nowadays. I told Sarah I would have a word with Cook and see if we could come to some arrangement. The poor girl almost prostrated herself at my feet. It was most embarrassing.

Cook threatened to give notice, which I had expected. I countered by saying my mother's only remaining interest in life was food; that she looked forward to the tempting trays that were delivered to her bedside several times a day and that I thought it likely Mother would choose to starve to death rather than partake of inferior fare. While Cook preened, I pleaded with her to stay and – the *coup de grâce* – I offered to increase her wages. The combination of flattery and bribery proved effective and Cook returned to work, grumbling, but mollified.

I suppose somewhere in the village or even at Beechgrave, a young woman must be praying fervently that William Hatherwick will return home safely. When I left Violet and her father this morning, I took the liberty of asking her if she knew to whom Mr Hatherwick had referred. Violet looked a little confused and said she had no idea.

'A close one' indeed, if even his sister knows nothing of his affairs of the heart.

January 27th

Thanks to Dr Maguire's ministrations and a strong constitution, Mr Hatherwick is much better, but by no means fit for work. Full recovery might take some time, especially at his age and so today I wrote to William Hatherwick to tell him that I should like to appoint him Head Gardener on his return. What began in earnest as a business letter took a more sentimental turn when I decided to thank him for the loan of his books which have been such a source of comfort and distraction in these dark days of grief. I also told him I had come to depend on Violet, whom I now regard as a friend. There was a great deal more I wanted to say, but I did not know how to express it, so I closed my letter by saying I had been delighted to hear about his trench garden and admired his enterprising spirit.

After I had sealed the letter, I laid my head down on my arms and, still seated at my desk, wept for several minutes. Why, I do not know. I enjoyed writing the letter and was sure it would bring comfort and peace of mind to its recipient. Exhausted and perplexed, I wiped my eyes, took up my pen again and inscribed William Hatherwick's name on the envelope. As I did so, it occurred to me that however cheerful the letter, however much good news one includes, it is hard not to wonder if the addressee will ever read it. One might be writing to a dead man.

When I went downstairs, I found a new letter from Walter. It was short, as his letters always are. It told me little more than that he was still alive. I suppose that is all that matters.

January 30th

Violet is so happy! William is coming home on leave. She almost danced round the parlour in her excitement. I know how much she loves her brother, but something about her manner suggested to me that someone else might also be coming home, someone who perhaps means as much to Violet as William.

It is a pity she cannot confide in me as perhaps a sister would. How I have longed for a sister to help me shoulder the burden at Beechgrave! I would not wish for another brother. That would seem disloyal and I should not wish to sacrifice another brother to this interminable war, but a sister who would confide in me and in whom I could confide would be a blessing indeed.

Violet said William had received my letter but had had no leisure to reply and now he is on his way home. She says I must visit while he is at Garden Lodge.

I shall like that very much.

February 13th

I attended church today, alone as usual. Mother rarely leaves her room now. The rest of the house might have burned down and she would not know.

William Hatherwick is much changed. I did not recognise him this morning. I assumed the tall young man in uniform escorting Violet must be her sweetheart, but when he removed his cap, I realised who it was. He looks years older.

I think I must have changed too, for when our eyes met there was a moment of blankness in his before he nodded. I really should not have stared so, but I could not believe a man would change so much in so short a time. One hears stories of the horrors our men experience and the casualty lists reveal how much death they see, but until I saw William's face today, I had not the faintest notion what the war does to the men who survive. I had only considered what happened to the dead. Indeed, I have been much preoccupied with thoughts of dead men: my brothers, Father, Charlotte's brother Laurence and the staff we have lost at Beechgrave. Today, when I met the Hatherwicks, I almost felt as if I were addressing a dead man. William talked and smiled occasionally, but with such reserve, such an air of detachment that I was put in mind of a quotation from *Romeo and Juliet*, the scene where the mortally wounded Mercutio jokes with Romeo. He says, 'Ask for me tomorrow and you shall find me a grave man.' That is how William Hatherwick seemed to me. A grave man.

When I arrived home, I sat at my dressing table and studied myself in the looking glass. Were the deaths of my father and brothers graven on my face? I cannot say. I can hardly recall a time before the war, let alone what I looked like then. I know I am thinner, for grief is a great killer of appetites, but I am not as pale as I used to be. Hours spent walking in the woods and garden have banished my ladylike pallor. If he were alive, Father would complain that I have become a hoyden. How I miss his grumbling and the way his bushy brows used to shoot up in shocked disapproval.

I wonder what Walter will think when he sees me again? And what shall I think of him? Will the war have changed him? It surely must. Shall we even recognise each other?

February 15th

This morning I called on the Hatherwicks. It made me so happy to see the three of them together, a family again, but it also reminded me how much Mother and I have lost. I think perhaps I have lost even more than Mother since she is almost unreachable now, lost to me, shut away in a world of her own.

The Hatherwicks left their father dozing by the fireside with a pot of tea and went for a bracing walk in the woods. William wanted to see the snowdrops. Violet clung shivering to his arm and I walked on his other side. I felt sure he would not want to discuss the war, so I asked him about his trench garden. Inevitably the conversation drifted on to the need for something cheerful, something living to compensate for the terrible conditions the men live under and the horrors they are forced to witness.

I am sorry to say I became upset at the thought of what my brothers had endured and what William must return to all too soon. Violet rushed to my side and put an arm round my waist. She tried to comfort me, but I could not stem the flow of tears. The Hatherwicks offered to accompany me back to Beechgrave, but I said I preferred to go alone.

I hurried off, ashamed of myself for having spoiled their walk with my useless grief.

Before we parted, William said something extraordinary to me about my brothers. It was meant to comfort and I think, in a way, it did, but I cannot bring myself to record it here. Not yet. Because I fear what William said might be true.

WILLIAM

February 15th, 1916

The beech wood was still dark in winter. Leaves clung on until spring, but as Hester and her friends entered the wood, they sensed, as always, a benign presence. The wood, with its ancient trees engraved by men long since deceased, had more to do with the dead than the living, but here, William thought, death would be peaceful, even companionable. A man would not feel alone, abandoned, like those left groaning in No Man's Land.

William wished fervently that he could be permitted to decide the moment of his death. Granted this privilege, he would choose to leave the world now, here, in this wood, whole in body if not in mind, walking between his sister, Violet, and his employer, Miss Mordaunt. If he were still capable of feeling happiness, William would die content, but he had lost the habit of happiness. The numbness never seemed to abate, yet as they strolled along the familiar path, dotted with clumps of snowdrops, his heart was full – of what he wasn't sure, but he remembered happiness used to feel something like this.

Hester had insisted he use her Christian name. He kept forgetting and the women laughed together comfortably as William tried to adjust to the new friendship. He didn't laugh, but smiled shyly at his own awkwardness, saying little that was not an answer to a question. He listed the names of flowers he had grown in his trench garden, but when he tried to explain what the garden meant to him and what it meant to the men, Hester started to weep.

Mortified, William looked on helplessly as Violet took her weeping friend's hand and tried to comfort her. Hester stuttered her apologies and spoke of her dead brothers who had died as officers, though William still thought of them as boys, young lads who used to climb the very trees that now surrounded them.

He wanted to help. He wanted to restore the calm, bright happiness he had seen on Hester's face as she took tea in the parlour, seated beside his father who, though in good spirits, had the look of death in his face. William had seen too much of it to be mistaken.

Now Hester shuddered in an agony of grief and spoke of losing her family, everyone, even her crazed mother. She clutched at Violet's hands, telling her how much her 'second family' meant to her.

William turned away and bowed his head. He longed to take Hester's soft little fingers in his callused hands. He wanted to brush the curling lock of hair from her damp cheek, but he stood aloof, his mute suffering a companion to hers. When he looked up, he saw his sister gazing at him in silent appeal, so William spoke.

His voice was deep, authoritative and Violet hardly recognised it. It was the voice he sometimes used with the boys who'd signed up for death and glory and saw only death. They needed a father, an older brother, someone who understood the ways of a wicked world. William had been all these and more. He'd learned what to do when men went to pieces, but he'd never seen a woman so distressed, not even Vi. He couldn't just stand by and watch and so he spoke.

'Miss Mordaunt . . . Hester . . . It might be better this way. Believe me, they're better off dead than wounded.'

At the sound of his voice, Hester lifted her head, her eyes wide with horror. 'Better off *dead*?'

'Better dead than wounded.' She stared at him, uncomprehending, but he met her eyes. 'If you knew the things I have seen! I cannot speak of them, but no man would wish to survive some of the wounds this war inflicts. Your brothers are at peace now. It's over for them, but for some of the living, even some of the whole, it will never be over. Their bodies will heal, but their minds have been destroyed. I've witnessed that. Men driven mad by the noise. The mud. The blood . . . Better dead than insane, surely?'

Hester stared at him, supported still by Violet. 'Better *dead*?'

'Better still that this war had never begun, but your brothers are out of it now. They died as proud young men. They won't come home blind or crippled. They won't have to see women turn their faces away from hideous disfigurement. They won't have to bear the weight of anyone's pity.'

Hester straightened up and wiped her eyes. 'No. They would have hated that.'

'Your grief cannot bring them back, but if it could, your brothers would only be sent back to the Front – to die again! So let them rest now. *You* must rest too. They're at peace and I'm sure, wherever they are, they know how much they were loved. How very much they are missed.'

Hester blinked at him and stammered her thanks, then turned to Violet. Summoning a wan smile, she said she would like to go home. Declining an offer of company, Hester apologised once more for her outburst and turned back to William. She gazed into his solemn brown eyes and tried for a moment to imagine what those eyes had seen, then she extended her hand. It seemed to Hester that William swayed slightly before taking it, but she assumed the unsteadiness was hers.

'If what you say is true, William – and I'm sure it must be – how can you face going back?' She didn't withdraw her hand and he could not let it go.

'I haven't left. Not entirely. Only part of me has come home. Most of my mind is still in France. Tending my garden. Tending men's wounds. I'm here, in this wood with you and Vi, but I'm thinking about the lads. Wondering how they're managing. How many have been wounded in my absence. How many are now dead. Even here . . .' He looked up at the tree canopy sheltering them. 'In this earthly Paradise, I can still hear the guns. The screams of the wounded. The moans of the dying . . . My body is here with you at Beechgrave, but my mind is with them. In Hell.'

Speechless with horror, Hester clutched at William's hand and bowed her head. She swallowed and said, 'May God take good care of you, William. You will be in my thoughts and prayers.'

After a moment, he said, 'I could not wish for more, Miss Mordaunt.'

'*Hester*,' she insisted, looking up into his face, still holding his hand. 'Hester.'

She turned away quickly, threw an arm round Violet's neck and kissed her on the cheek, then set off in the direction of the house, walking briskly. For no reason she could fathom, Hester felt as if she'd been released from some kind of captivity. Her heart soared, like a bird set free from a cage.

HESTER

February 17th, 1916

William has returned to France. We did not say goodbye. I avoided visiting yesterday so he should have a last day with his family, uninterrupted by a visit from an outsider. But Violet delivered a letter from him this afternoon. In it he thanked me formally for offering him the post of Head Gardener, which he intends to take up after the war is over. He said the thought of returning to work at Beechgrave will sustain him in the conflict to come.

I am glad that is settled.

February 28th

When I saw Violet today, she said Mr Hatherwick has taken William's departure badly. Apparently he is quite cast down again and has lost all appetite, convinced he will not see his son again.

This news led to a disturbing realisation. If Mr Hatherwick should die and if William does not return, I shall have no choice but to turn Violet out of Garden Lodge as I shall need the house for a new Head Gardener. So I have considered offering Violet the position of lady's maid to my mother. Agnes gave notice yesterday, which was not unexpected. Looking after Mother is like caring for a child now and more than I can ask of a lady's maid. I doubt I shall be able to find a replacement for Agnes, so for now I shall have to look after Mother myself, but it is a position that Violet might fill competently. Mother knew her well before she left us to look after the Hatherwick men, but I wonder if she will remember her now?

I can hardly ask Violet to live in servants' quarters after she has had so much independence and responsibility at Garden Lodge, but I could perhaps open up the small room next to Mother's for Violet's use, then Mother would have both of us to hand, one on either side. That would suit her very well.

I do believe my plan might work. At least I would not have to think of making Violet homeless. There is an alternative if William does not come home, but I hope and pray that he will and that Mr Hatherwick will make a full recovery.

March 13th

Many of Beechgrave's flowerbeds and some of the lawns have been turned over to food production. Huge quantities of seed have been sown and, from his sickbed, Mr Hatherwick has suggested many heavy-cropping varieties.

He grows weaker every day. Violet says he eats very little, so I asked Cook to send over some tasty morsels to tempt him. I report to him daily to keep him informed of progress being made in the garden. It appears to cheer him a little.

April 10th

I have neglected my journal of late in favour of working in the garden, but I must write now in an attempt to calm my mind. I have not heard from Walter in almost a week, which is most unlike him. His letters are short, but they are regular. His mother has not heard from him either.

April 13th

Now poor Violet is unwell. She has tried to disguise the fact, but she looks pale and ill and she is not her usual cheerful self. When I paid a call today, Mr Hatherwick waited until she was out of the room, then he asked me to keep an eye on her. He said she was very poorly and could not keep food down.

Nursing her father must be taking its toll and then there are her fears for William at the Front. Violet has literally worried herself sick.

April 15th

I received a communication from William today. There was no message other than the date and his signature. It was a pencil sketch of his trench garden. In the picture the flower beds and shelter are surrounded by a devastated wood. The trees are just skeletons, bare, broken trunks, with all their branches gone. The beds are edged with stones and William has drawn a soldier standing on the boardwalk, leaning over watering his plants. Behind him is a sign nailed to a dead tree. It says, 'Regent Street'!

This simple little missive has raised my spirits. William's sketch conveys the bleak horror of the battlefield, but it is not without hope. It celebrates the indomitable human spirit.

Still no word from Walter.

April 18th

Walter Dowding is dead. He died in France at St Eloi. Mr Dowding called to bring me the news in person. Apparently Walter did not suffer. It was a sniper's bullet to the head.

I received the news yesterday with a composure Mr Dowding no doubt attributed to shock, but I felt nothing. Searching my heart for grief, I found it empty. Today letters of condolence began to arrive, including one from Walter's mother.

After I read it, I had to get out into the fresh air. I ran through the garden until I reached the wood and found the beech tree, the one known as the Trysting Tree. I sank down and leaned back against the tree, then I spread Mrs Dowding's crumpled letter on my knees and smoothed the page. I read the words again, mouthing them silently, trying to feel what I knew I should feel. There was anger and an immense sadness, but nothing more, or nothing I dared own.

In her grief, Walter's poor mother had thought of me and penned a few hasty, heartfelt words. Deprived now of a close family tie, Ursula Dowding hoped we should be united by our grief. She assured me that, bereft of her only child, she would continue to think of me as the daughter she had hoped to welcome into her family when this dreadful war was over. Towards the end of the letter, her bold hand began to falter. The final lines sloped steeply. She wrote, 'Walter is at peace, of this we can be certain. It is only for ourselves that we must be sorry. But let us not be sorry, Hester! Let us rejoice that, as women, we have been allowed to play our part, making this great sacrifice for our King and country.'

I stared at the letter for some time. To my horror, I found I was not sorry. Grieved, certainly, at the manner of Walter's death and its utter futility, but the thought of his absence made my heart beat faster – not with rage or despair, but with hope, an emotion long-forgotten which

I quashed immediately, appalled. But alone beneath the old beech tree, I could acknowledge the truth. Walter's death means I am free. For that terrible mercy, I shall rejoice. Secretly. Shamefully.

May 20th

I have neither the will nor the energy to record anything more than the bare details of another death.

Herbert Hatherwick passed away last night. Pneumonia. Violet hopes William will be permitted to come home for the funeral. She is exhausted with nursing her father and looks quite ill herself.

If I lose Violet, I do not know how I shall be able to carry on.

May 22nd

William has been granted leave. It is doubtful whether he will be home in time for his father's funeral, but he will at least be able to comfort Violet, who is prostrated with grief. Mr Hatherwick's death was not unexpected, but she seems inconsolable. She will no doubt rally when William returns.

May 23rd

As the war drags on, I have been considering how I might be more useful. My brothers and Walter Dowding made the ultimate sacrifice for their country. And I? I have done nothing. I do nothing. I wait. Wait for news, wait for the war to end. And then? When it is all over? Does life hold anything more for me than looking after Mother?

I remember seeing an extraordinary notice in *The Times*. It said something to this effect: 'Lady, fiancé killed, will gladly marry officer totally blinded or otherwise incapacitated by the War.' I could not decide if it was one of the saddest or one of the bravest things I had ever read. Perhaps it was both. I have seen several such notices since.

I am neither so desperate nor so selfless that I could enter into a practical arrangement of this sort. Not now. The war has changed me, changed everything. Before the war, my family expected me to marry without love and I was ready to do it. But now I cannot. The war has taken so much from me, but it has given me freedom of a sort. I am prepared to live for another, to dedicate my life to his, but there must be love – and more than the love I feel for Mother and my dear friend Violet.

But freedom brings responsibility and so I have been thinking how I might put Beechgrave to better use. I should like to make a real contribution to the war effort. In particular, I should like to do something to help the men who survived the slaughter, but are now broken in body and mind. I am of the opinion that Beechgrave would make an excellent convalescent hospital. I am sure patients would derive benefit from the garden produce and exercise taken in the garden. Those unable to exercise would surely be strengthened and comforted by fresh air and the fine views afforded by the house.

Since I can do nothing to bring back my dead, I shall honour their memory by turning my attention to the living and those who are struggling to rebuild their shattered lives.

May 24th

William arrived today, too late for his father's funeral. I have not paid a call yet. I thought it best to leave brother and sister to grieve together.

I hope while he is at home William will be able to spare some time to advise me about increasing food production from the garden. In the absence of Mr Hatherwick, it is now my responsibility. I must instruct the staff or leave matters in the uncertain hands of Dawson, a journeyman gardener who is now the most experienced of the staff who remain.

May 27th

Something has happened that never should have happened. Something terrible.

I am lost, quite lost.

Dear God, help me.

ANN

'Aha!' Phoebe said, jabbing at Hester's diary with a bony forefinger. '*That* must be what sent Ivy over the edge. "Something terrible." What can it have been, I wonder? Read on, Connor. Don't leave us dangling.'

As Phoebe settled back in her armchair, Connor shook his head. 'That's it.'

'What do you mean?'

'She doesn't say any more.' Connor leafed quickly through the journal. 'There's a gap of about six weeks before the next entry.'

'Oh, how maddening!' Phoebe grumbled.

'Looks as if Violet's pregnant by then, but I don't think that can have been the disaster, do you? Hester seems more concerned about what to do with Beechgrave.'

It was late. The wine bottle and coffee cups were empty. The room was warm and stuffy. Before Hester dropped her bombshell, I thought Phoebe was in danger of dozing off, but she sat upright now, awake and alert, watching Connor. I got up to put another log in the stove. 'Perhaps the "something terrible" refers to William's death,' I suggested. 'Did he die in the war?'

'No. There are photos of him taken years later. He was alive when Ivy went off to horticultural college in her teens – that would have been in the early 1930s – but he died not long after. So it wasn't that.'

Connor set the diary aside, leaving it open on the sofa. 'But I've had a quick look at the next volume of Hester's journal and—'

'Cheat!' Phoebe exclaimed, launching a cushion at Connor who caught it neatly and grinned. 'That's strictly against the rules!'

'It was just a *little* peek. William seems to go off the radar for about a year. Missing in action, I suppose.'

'Did Ivy ever mention the missing year?' Phoebe asked.

'No, other than to say William refused to talk about the war. Actually, what she said was, he *couldn't* talk about the war. She said he didn't remember a thing about it. Shell shock, I suppose.' Connor turned to me. 'You're looking thoughtful, Ann.'

'Am I? Puzzled is what I feel. I don't think the "something terrible" can be what drove Ivy to destroy the archive. Don't you think in ninety-odd years she'd have found the time to read her adoptive mother's diaries? And even if she didn't, what is there in that entry to make a nice old lady do what she did? Her action was extreme, but the journal entry is vague. And if Ivy already knew what it referred to, why did she suddenly decide the evidence had to be destroyed? It doesn't add up. I think this was something awful for Hester, but not Ivy.'

'It must refer to something pretty dire though,' Connor said. 'I mean, Hester kept going despite the loss of most of her family and her fiancé. But *this* – whatever it was – made her shut up the house.'

'We don't actually know the two were connected,' Phoebe pointed out.

'That's true. It could just have been staff shortages, I suppose.' Connor looked at me again and leaned forward. 'You've got a theory, haven't you?'

'Possibly.'

'Ooh, don't be a tease!' Phoebe rapped on the tea tray with a spoon. 'Spill the beans, Ann.'

'Well, it's only a hunch, but my guess is, Hester wasn't referring to death. By this time she was an old hand at death, wasn't she? No, it had to be something bigger . . .'

'*Bigger?*' Phoebe exclaimed. 'What could be bigger than death?'

'For Hester? Sex. I think sex could have been bigger than death.'

Connor looked at me, then let out a low whistle. I reached over, picked up the diary and read aloud.

> '*Something has happened that never should have happened. Something terrible.*
>
> '*I am lost, quite lost.*
>
> '*Dear God help me.*'

'Oh my Lord . . .' Phoebe murmured. 'Poor old Hester!'

THE BEECH WOOD

He came at dawn to say farewell. Certain he would never return, he touched us, many of us, with strong, hard hands that had nurtured seedlings and killed men. He stroked our grey bark – a placatory gesture – then took out a knife. One by one, he gouged letters to form a sentence few would understand.

He stepped back, regarded his handiwork and murmured, 'As these words grow, so may our love.' Turning his head slowly, he looked about him, trying to fix the images in his tortured mind. He heaved a shuddering sigh and, as the air left his body, he began to shiver, though the day was mild.

His downcast eyes saw something small and bright lying on the ground. Her brooch. The ornament that had lain upon her breast.

He closed his knife and put it in his pocket, then stooped to pick up the brooch. Turning it over in his fingers, he saw the catch was broken, but not beyond repair. He would mend it for her.

As he dropped the brooch into his pocket, his hand trembled. He looked up at the smooth bark he had desecrated, removed his cap and said, 'Forgive me.' Whether it was to us he spoke, whether to her or to his God, we did not know.

He replaced his cap, turned and strode away to war, her brooch clinking against the knife in his pocket.

PART THREE

VIOLET

July 13th, 1916

Georgie Flynn was dead. Violet heard the news from Mrs Ellis, Cook up at the big house. She had it from her sister, George's mother, who'd had a telegram, so Violet knew it must be true. With her father dead and William away in France there was no one in whom Violet could confide. Miss Hester had said, if William should die, a position would be found for her up at the house, but that generous offer had been made before Violet realised her predicament. She hadn't even written to George to tell him the news because she wasn't sure, or rather she hoped very much that she was wrong. Now she was certain.

Violet sat down at the kitchen table and considered her future. While William lived, she need not despair. He would be angry certainly, but he would stand by her. He was a good man. He knew George and liked him. They'd been at school together. But might William lose his position if he allowed a disgraced sister to keep house for him? And how easily would he find a new position? What if he didn't return . . . ?

As she fought down a wave of nausea, Violet thought briefly of swallowing rat poison, then considered drowning herself. She concluded hanging would be quicker and less painful, but she had no idea how to tie a noose. Undaunted, she trudged upstairs to search through William's book collection for a volume that might enlighten her. Something nautical perhaps.

As she struggled to read the books' spines, Violet's resolve gave way. Sinking to the floor beside the bookcase, she wept and wished she'd never been born, or at least never set eyes on that luckless charmer, Georgie Flynn. The smell of burning bread brought her to her feet again. Wiping her eyes on her apron, she hurried downstairs.

She would have to tell Miss Hester. Better she should hear the news from Violet herself, rather than gossip from the servants' hall. Miss Hester had always been kind. She was fond of Violet, fond of William too. She would doubtless do what she could. In any case, thought Violet, as she took a scorched loaf from the oven, the baby might die. Babies died all the time. All might yet be well.

There was a knock at the door. As Violet set the loaf down, she craned to see out of the window.

It was a boy with a telegram.

So convinced was she that her brother must be dead, it was with something like elation that Violet learned he was missing in action. He might yet live. He *must* live! For if William were to die . . . Well, there was no other remedy. She would just have to find a good strong piece of rope and hang herself from the Trysting Tree.

Hester received Violet in the morning room. At the sight of the telegram, Hester turned pale, but her face remained impassive. After she'd read it, she handed it back to Violet, then went over to the window where she stood and looked out on to the garden. Vegetable beds now sub-divided the vast lawn of which her father had once been so proud. Hester no longer felt guilty or even sad that cabbages had replaced cabbage roses. Of what earthly use was beauty now? And was there anything more pointless than a lawn? People needed food, not flowers. Families were losing their menfolk and their livelihoods. The war was like a plague, except it didn't carry off the weak and elderly. Those it left behind. This plague took the young and the strong, those who would be missed most.

Hester remembered Violet and turned away from the window. She went back to her seat, where she listened in silence to Violet's assurances that William would eventually return home. As the girl prattled on, Hester tried to think. Glancing up, she saw Violet sitting with her head bent, her hands clasped tight in her lap.

'What is it, Violet? Is there something else? Something you haven't told me?'

Violet had prepared her speech and delivered it without raising her eyes from the floor. When she'd finished, the poor girl looked so miserable, Hester wanted to tell her all would be well, but, on the face of it, things looked bad, very bad indeed. Violet needed hope though. So did Hester. Hope that the war would end soon; hope that William would eventually come home; hope that Violet and her baby would thrive. How could they carry on without hope?

Hester had already considered the possibility that she might become responsible for Violet's welfare, but she hadn't expected to support a child. Thinking quickly now, she decided to set her plans before Violet, but first she had to settle her own mind. She needed to think that what had happened was not just what Violet had called 'a few moments of madness'. Hester needed to believe in love, in passion, in something bigger than death. She thought if she understood exactly what had happened, she'd be able to help Violet and sympathise with her sorry plight, but the reasons for her curiosity were complex. It seemed to her lamentable, almost shameful that a young girl who'd worked as a maid for the Mordaunts should understand the momentous thing that had happened to her, when Hester did not.

Hester realised she was angry – not with Violet, nor even George Flynn, but with herself, with her own ignorance. She just wanted to *know* – and damn the social niceties. She jumped as if she'd said the words aloud. Recovering, she smoothed the folds of her skirt over her knees. When she looked up, she found Violet watching her anxiously with William's dark, troubled eyes. Hester's nerve almost failed her, but she cleared her throat and said, 'I'd like to ask a question, Violet, if I may. A very personal question. Would you mind telling me *how* you came to be . . . in this unfortunate position?'

Violet blinked, astonished. She opened her mouth to reply, then shut it again, unsure whether Hester required circumstantial detail or – this surely could not be the case? – whether the mistress of Beechgrave sought enlightenment.

'I'm afraid I don't understand, Miss.'

'When did . . . the incident take place? Some time ago, I should imagine?'

'Three months ago, near enough. When Georgie was home on leave.'

'I see.' Hester nodded encouragement. 'Go on.'

Violet looked uncomfortable and her eyes roamed around the room until they settled again on her clasped hands. 'We went to the woods. That was where we used to go . . . Courting. It was almost dark. But there was a moon.'

Hester waited a moment, then spoke again with a gentle smile. 'It was not, I think, the *moon* that led to your predicament.'

'No, Miss.'

'He kissed you, I suppose? George Flynn?'

'Oh, yes, there was a good deal of kissing.'

Hester blushed but persevered. 'And . . . ?'

'We held each other tight. For a long time.'

'I see. But there must have been more . . . I should imagine?'

'Yes, Miss.' Violet took a deep breath and said, 'Georgie – *George*, I should say – took me up in his arms and carried me to a part of the wood that's known for . . .' Violet broke off and began to wring her hands.

'For . . . ?' Hester prompted.

'For being *comfortable*, Miss. If you take my meaning. It's where courting couples go. They meet under the Trysting Tree.'

'The one with all the carvings of names and dates?'

'Yes. That's where young people go to declare their love.'

'And . . . consummate it?' Violet failed to meet Hester's eye, but nodded. 'It's secluded there, I take it?'

'And there's a mossy bank,' Violet said with a significant look.

'Rather damp, I should imagine.'

Violet looked surprised, then said, 'I'm afraid I don't recall.'

'No, of course not. You would remember only George. George and his ardour. You would forget everything else, I'm sure.'

Violet nodded eagerly. 'Yes, Miss. That's *just* how it was!'

'So you and he, you . . . lay down together? On the mossy bank? And that would be when it happened?' Hester cleared her throat. 'A sort of embrace? Passionate?'

'*Very* passionate.'

'One that effected a . . . physical union.' Violet nodded. 'And that was *enough*?'

'More than enough, Miss.'

'I see. To think it takes so little . . . to produce a child.'

'I told Georgie we shouldn't, but he knew I didn't really mean it, with him off to war in the morning.' Violet lifted her chin. 'Any girl would have done the same, I'm sure, if she loved her man.'

'Any girl?' Hester's eyes widened. 'You think so?'

'Well, yes, if she was made of flesh and blood! Anyway, it was all over before I knew it and Georgie left for France the very next day. At least he went off happy,' Violet added with a sniff.

'Did he ever know? About his child?'

'No, I never told him. I wasn't sure and it didn't seem right to worry him until I was. Then by the time I *was* sure—' Tears started into Violet's eyes.

Hester glanced up at the window and watched as the sky darkened. There would be rain soon. But the gardens needed it. That's what Mr Hatherwick used to say. William too.

She turned back to Violet who was wiping her eyes. 'I'm so sorry, Violet. We live in such very difficult times. How is one supposed to know what is right and what is wrong?'

'I just followed my heart, Miss Hester. I can't believe that was wrong. Foolish maybe, but not wrong, surely?'

'No, I don't think it was wrong of you, Violet. Not at all. It's the war that's wrong. Thank you for answering my questions so honestly. I hope you'll forgive my curiosity and not think it very strange. I had only the vaguest notions about . . . love. And I didn't marry, so my mother never had occasion to—' Hester ground to a halt.

'Did your brothers never tell you?' Violet asked with a pitying look.

'No. I asked them once, but they seemed to think the subject unsuitable for a young woman, even though ignorance has such far-reaching consequences. Did *you* know?' Hester asked earnestly. 'Did you understand that what you and George were doing might lead to . . . new life?'

'Yes, Miss. I hoped it wouldn't, but I knew it might. I've seen it happen to other girls.' She shrugged. 'Some are lucky, some aren't. But if your man's going off to fight for King and country—'

'And if you fear you might never see him again . . . Yes, I can quite see how something like that might happen. In the heat of the moment . . .' Hester looked up as the first heavy drops of rain thudded against the window panes, beating an irregular tattoo. 'I don't blame you, Violet, and I certainly won't judge you, but we must address the issue of your future. If William fails to return and if, as you say, no other family member is prepared to take you in, you will, as I understand it, become homeless, with no means of support.' Violet stared at the floor again and nodded, disconsolate. 'Your situation is serious then. So serious, I imagine you would raise no objection if I appointed you lady's maid to Mrs Mordaunt.' Violet looked up sharply. Unable to speak, she shook her head. 'Good. Then that's what I shall do. You will no doubt remember from your previous service in this household that Mrs Mordaunt was a particular and demanding mistress. Well, you will find her much changed. I have to inform you that an excess of grief has overturned my mother's mind.'

'I'm very sorry to hear that.'

'So if you accept this position, you will find it . . . *challenging*.'

'I shan't mind, Miss. Not a bit.'

'I shall also require you to disguise your . . . predicament for as long as possible. My mother is not naturally observant, but she is censorious. I cannot and will not confide in her,' Hester said firmly.

Violet grinned. 'You can conceal a good deal behind a well-starched apron and a large tea tray, Miss!'

'Indeed.' Hester smiled. 'I fear we might have to become rather resourceful in the coming months. I trust I can rely on your discretion.'

'Silent as the tomb, that's me,' said Violet, laying a finger on her lips.

'I shall require you to live in, of course, and, for a variety of reasons, it's my intention to shut up most of the house. I'll need your help with that. You might also have to cook for us. I doubt Mrs Ellis will be persuaded to stay on once she hears I'm going to dismiss most of the staff.'

'I'm a good plain cook,' Violet announced. 'Mrs Ellis herself said I have a light hand with pastry.'

'Then I think we shall manage very well. The position I'm offering you is unusual, but you will be well remunerated. In the meantime, I shall shut up Garden Lodge. The Lodge and the position of Head Gardener will remain vacant until we're quite convinced that William . . . that your brother will not be coming home.'

'Oh, thank you, Miss Hester!'

'As for your child, we shall accommodate it at some distance from my mother's room. I'm sure we can create a pleasant nursery in one of the other rooms.'

'Oh, Miss, you're so very kind!'

'Every child should be welcomed into the world, whatever its provenance. A new life is a very precious thing, especially these days.'

'And especially when the father's already dead,' Violet added, laying a protective hand on her belly. 'This baby might be all the family I have now.'

'Let us hope and pray that isn't so. If the poor mite has been deprived of its father and possibly its uncle, it will nevertheless have a loving and capable mother and a true friend in me.' Hester rose and took both Violet's hands in hers. 'Beechgrave welcomes you and your child. In exchange, I expect loyalty, discretion and unquestioning obedience. *Unquestioning*, Violet. Do I make myself clear?'

'Yes, Miss.'

Hester squeezed the girl's hands. 'But let us still be friends, we who have lost so much! Let us not lose each other in the hard times to come. I promise to stand by you in your hour of need and I trust you will stand by me.'

'Ask anything of me. If it's in my power and doesn't harm William or my child, I shall perform it.'

'I could ask no more of the dearest of friends,' Hester said, her voice unsteady. 'You can have no idea, Violet, how much I shall depend upon your support.'

'I'll never be able to repay you, Miss Hester, but a more loyal friend and servant you shall not have – not till the day I die.'

'Oh, do please call me Hester! We're sisters now. Sisters in misfortune.'

When, finally, she was able to speak, Violet's reply was a soundless whisper. 'Thank you. *Hester*.'

HESTER

July 13th, 1916

A distressing and difficult day. If I can set it all down, perhaps I shall feel better able to cope. There are times – and today was one of them – when I long to lie down, go to sleep and never wake up. I used to think Mother had lost her reason. Now I wonder if hers was a sane response to a world gone mad.

Violet came to see me this morning. She had two pieces of news, both of them very bad. I regret to say she has received a telegram informing her that her brother is reported missing in action on the Somme. She delivered the customary platitudes one employs under these sad circumstances. She assured me William might still be alive, that he is missing, not dead, then repeated the now-familiar anecdotes about men who turn up on their own doorsteps long after their families have abandoned hope. I do not believe either of us was convinced. It requires energy to hope, energy and faith, both of which are in short supply these days. But we both owe it to William to continue to hope and so I shall.

Violet's second piece of news was just as disturbing and she suffered wretchedly in the telling of it. Some minutes passed before I realised what, in her euphemistic way, she was struggling to say. It concerned yet another death in action: George Flynn's, a name unknown to me, though when Violet referred to 'Georgie', I recalled she had mentioned him before in connection with William's leave. The nature of their relationship was unclear, but I assumed Violet was grieving over the death of a sweetheart. In a somewhat confused account, she mentioned marriage several times, though it appeared Flynn had not actually married her.

This, it transpired, was the source of her anxiety. Incoherent with grief and shame, Violet described to me her gradual realisation that 'a few moments of madness', as she put it, were to have lasting consequences. By the time she had recited her litany of sickness and discomfort, I was convinced the poor girl had cause to be concerned for her future – and the future of another. There were moments during this painful and embarrassing dialogue, in which Violet referred repeatedly to her 'predicament', when I feared I might laugh or burst into tears. By dint of concentrating on my interrogation, I did neither.

I had already concluded that, if William should fail to return, I must employ Violet at Beechgrave. This morning's conversation confirmed that I have arrived at a crossroads in my life where there are no signposts, so I have taken inventory of my life. I find I no longer wish to receive visitors, nor do I want to venture farther than Beechgrave's beloved gardens, filled as they are now with potatoes, leeks and marrows, like a market garden. I am too exhausted to manage Beechgrave with the few staff who remain and they are insufficient in number to keep the house in good order. Mother still waits for her dead sons to come home and believes Father is away on business, so I must act alone.

I believe I must shut up Beechgrave. I have asked Violet to help me pack away the valuables I wish to keep and make a list of those I wish to sell. We shall leave Mother's wing alone and I believe she will be none the wiser. Violet can have the room adjacent to Mother's. I shall also be on hand, along the corridor. I think it might work very well.

Despite all that has happened in the last year, despite all I have lost, it is still possible to number many blessings. Chief among them, I count my friend, Violet Hatherwick and her 'predicament' for it has forced my hand. I must and will act. I shall also pray – without much conviction, sadly – for William Hatherwick's safe return and, together with Violet, I shall prepare for new life at Beechgrave.

It will be a blessed relief to rest and talk no more of death.

PHOEBE

Phoebe had persuaded Connor to sit for her. He posed, perched on a stool in the studio, looking out into the garden where heavy rain bounced off the paths. It drummed on the roof and filled the silence in which Phoebe usually preferred to work, but her curiosity about this young man prompted her to ask, 'What's with all the hair, Connor? It's fun to draw and would be lovely to paint, but isn't it rather a bother?'

Connor laughed his deep laugh, the one that reminded Phoebe of a teddy bear Ann had as a child. It had an amiable growl and, until its fur had worn away, the bear had been the same golden colour as Connor's hair. But Connor wasn't cuddly. There was something animal about him though, Phoebe thought. Nothing threatening or predatory, just something vital, instinctive. Connor relished life.

'I just don't have time to get it cut, Phoebe. I keep meaning to buy some sharp scissors to hack some of it off, but I never get around to it.'

'It's not an act of rebellion then?'

'Against what?' Connor asked mildly.

'Your military antecedents. I wondered if being unkempt was a statement. Long hair. Un-ironed shirts. Muddy shoes. I imagine your father would have had forty thousand fits.'

Connor was silent for a moment and it crossed Phoebe's mind she might have overstepped the mark, but she felt she knew Connor quite well now. Theirs was a frank and easy relationship, a friendship that was – unusually for Phoebe – uncomplicated by sex.

'A statement? No, that never occurred to me,' Connor replied, with a hint of awe. 'You could be right, I suppose, but it's not conscious. I suppose I just feel more comfortable being a slob.'

It was Phoebe's turn to laugh. 'Alternatively, perhaps you have an undiagnosed Samson complex.'

'Samson?'

'You know, the Bible story. Does your formidable strength depend on the length of your hair?'

'Not as far as I know. It keeps my head warm in winter though.'

'Well, if you ever want a trim, Ann's a dab hand at cutting hair now. She does mine. Saves me a fortune and I don't have to listen to all that "Where did you go on your holiday?" crap.'

'I'm sure Ann's got much better things to do with her time.'

'Oh, it wouldn't take her long. She'd say you have very "forgiving" hair, like hers. Thick and wavy. I'm deeply envious,' Phoebe grumbled. 'I had perfectly good hair until I lost it all to cancer, then when it grew back it was sparse and *white*. I was horrified! Hadn't seen my natural colour in *years*.' Connor turned his head, as if about to speak. 'Don't move! I'm doing something difficult . . . To judge from the quantity of hair you currently possess, I doubt you'll ever go bald, but take it from me, there are few things more dispiriting than having a freezing bald head in the depths of winter. I used to wear fleece hats in bed, but they slid off, so some well-meaning soul knitted me a big baby's bonnet with a chin-strap. I told her I'd rather die of hypothermia.' Connor smiled but didn't move or speak. 'To begin with you're grateful for *any* hair, even white stubble,' Phoebe admitted grudgingly. 'But disenchantment soon sets in. You'd think the fear of death would drive out all personal vanity, wouldn't you? Strangely, it doesn't, despite the fact that when you have no hair, no eyelashes, no eyebrows and no pubic hair, you scarcely feel human.'

'Didn't you have a wig?' Connor asked.

'Oh, yes. Couldn't bear the damn thing. It was so tight, I felt as if my head was in a vice. It gave me headaches, so I mostly wore scarves and hats. I've always been a hat person. Still am,' Phoebe said, adjusting her denim cap.

'You've had a tough time, Phoebe, that's for sure. I admire your indomitable spirit.'

'Indomitable, my arse! It's sheer bloody-mindedness. In any case, there's always someone worse off than yourself.' She put down her sketchbook, removed her cap and scratched her head, ruffling her sparse, red hair. 'You can relax for a moment. I'm about to rant, but you don't actually need to listen.'

Connor turned to face her. 'I'm all ears.'

Phoebe replaced her cap and folded her arms. 'Do you know what kept me going? When they put that bloody great darning needle into me and pumped me full of cherry-coloured poison? Thinking about the *children*. Kids who suffered even more than me, because at least I understood what was being done to me. And then I used to think about the nurses whose job it was to make those poor kids suffer, in order to save their lives. What a terrible way to earn a living! Finally, I would think about the parents of those children, who had to watch their babies suffer. *That's* what kept me going. Or at least it saved me from self-pity. Because it was one thing to go completely bald and have to wear a rubber tit, but I was damned if I was going to feel sorry for myself. I spared myself *that* indignity,' Phoebe said with a haughty sniff.

Connor said nothing, but a grin spread slowly across his open face.

'Did I say something funny?' Phoebe snapped.

'No. I'm smiling because you're heroic, Phoebe. You just don't give a damn, do you?'

'No, I don't. Never have. And cancer did nothing to mellow me, I'm pleased to say.' She pointed through the window. 'Looks as if the rain's easing up now. I dare say you're eager to get outdoors again.'

'I could certainly do with a bit of fresh air. But finish off your sketch. I'm in no hurry.'

He resumed his pose and Phoebe picked up her pad again. She drew in silence, observing how shafts of sunlight now brought out tawny shades in Connor's hair and tanned skin. She sighed and said, 'You know, I should have done this in pastel. The colours are very interesting now. You'll have to sit for me again.'

'I take it that's an order, not a request?'

Phoebe didn't look up but smiled despite herself. Once again, curiosity got the better of her. 'Do you have a girlfriend, Connor?'

'No.'

'Boyfriend?'

'No.'

There was a short silence, broken only by the sound of Phoebe's charcoal stick scratching at the cartridge paper.

'Do you, Phoebe?'

'Do I what?'

'Have a boyfriend?'

'No, I don't . . . Neither does Ann.'

Phoebe paused to observe him carefully, but saw no reaction apart from a slight twitch at the corner of his mouth which might have been the beginning of a smile. He continued to stare through the studio window and said, 'Duly noted.'

Phoebe tore the finished sketch from her pad and took it over to a table where she sprayed it with fixative. Connor got to his feet, stretched his arms and arched his back. She returned and handed him the drawing. As he examined it, she noted he turned a little pale, but Phoebe was unperturbed. When confronted with her vision of them, people were often shocked.

Connor shook his head, at a loss for words. Finally, he said, 'I love it!'

'Good. You have excellent taste,' Phoebe announced, wiping her hands on a grubby cloth.

'But I see what you mean about the hair. Definitely in need of a hard prune,' he said, handing back the sketch.

She waved it away. 'It's yours. That was just a preliminary scribble, so I can get to know your face.'

'You mean I can *keep* this?'

'Of course. Sell it when I'm dead. It might make you a bob or two.'

'You're joking!' he said, outraged. 'I shall get it framed. Just in case I *do* go bald.'

Phoebe chuckled. 'Well, I'm glad you like it. Some people hate how I see them. I'm fearfully honest, you see. But I suspect you can handle it.'

'Could you handle a kiss?'

'I thought you'd never ask!' said Phoebe, opening her arms wide.

Still holding his sketch, Connor hugged her with his spare arm and kissed her on the cheek. 'Thank you, Phoebe.'

She ruffled his hair. 'Have a word with Ann. I'm sure you'll find she'd be happy to oblige.'

They regarded each other for a moment, then Phoebe winked. Connor laughed his booming laugh and went off in search of Ann, to show her his portrait.

After he'd gone, Phoebe finally acknowledged the pain in her hands. Wincing, she massaged her fingers, one by one. It had been a good morning's work. Painful, but productive.

The rain set in again before lunch and Connor abandoned any idea of working in the waterlogged garden. Phoebe suggested they have what she called 'an archive day' and Connor was prevailed upon to drive home to fetch several cardboard boxes of photos, diaries, letters, even a family Bible for Phoebe and Ann to sift through in the quest to solve the Mystery of the Mordaunts. After lunch they gathered in the dining room to unpack the boxes.

Even though the content was unexceptional and the authors were long dead, Ann felt something like an illicit thrill as she removed old letters from their envelopes and perused them. She soon recognised the handwriting and style of each family member, especially Ivy's. She had sent many lively letters home from horticultural college in the 1930s, but one letter in particular caught Ann's eye.

'Connor, this is very odd.'

'What's that?'

'It's a letter from Ivy to Uncle William. It appears to be the first one she sent from college. Have you ever seen it?'

'Not sure.' He moved round the table to look at the letter. 'What's it about?'

'The content isn't what's odd. It's the condition of the letter.'

As he took it from Ann's hand, Connor saw that the large clear handwriting was blotched where liquid had made the ink run. The blots were irregular in shape, but roughly circular, as if drops of water had fallen on to the paper.

Phoebe hobbled over to join them and peered at the letter. 'Looks like Ivy was crying when she wrote it.'

'Yes, that's what I thought to begin with,' Ann replied. 'But then I thought, Ivy wouldn't have sent a tear-stained letter home, surely? She wouldn't have wanted them to know she was homesick. And in any case, if you read the letter, it's clear she's having a great time. Or *says* she is. So I don't think these can be Ivy's tears.'

'But there's nothing in the letter to make anyone cry,' Connor said. 'Let alone William.'

'Well, Hester might also have read it.'

'And maybe Violet,' Phoebe added. 'Perhaps she was missing her daughter badly.'

Connor took the letter and examined the paper closely. 'Maybe the marks aren't tear stains. Perhaps someone was watering a plant or arranging some flowers and the letter got splashed.'

'That seems more likely,' Ann conceded. 'It's a lovely letter. Anyone would have been delighted to receive it.'

'Yes, she was a good correspondent,' Connor said, his face darkened by sadness. 'Great fun. Her letters and postcards got me through some bad days at boarding school. I used to keep them and read them over and over.'

'And thus was the young archivist born,' Phoebe said, laying a hand on Connor's shoulder.

'Yes, I suppose you're right.' He bent down and heaved another box on to the table. 'Here's something to interest you, Phoebe.'

'Ooh, what?'

'Old sketchbooks.'

She pounced and started to turn the thick pages, declaring, 'The artist has some skill. Were these Hester's?'

'No, I don't think so,' Connor replied. 'The drawings are nearly all houses and gardens. Mostly Beechgrave. But there's something that looks like it was once a French château, in ruins. As far as I know, Hester didn't go abroad during the period these books cover. The artist dated the sketches but gave no clue as to their location. But many of the drawings are obviously Beechgrave. Except . . .' Connor paused in his unpacking.

Phoebe looked up from her perusal of one of the sketchbooks, sensing another clue. 'What? There's something odd about them?'

Connor took the lid off a shoebox containing photographs and extracted a handful. 'This is what Beechgrave looked like around 1916. They're all dated on the back. As you can see, the lawns and ornamental gardens have been dug up and replanted with vegetables. Now compare *those* with the sketches done by our unknown artist.'

'I see what you mean. Then these must have been drawn before they turned the gardens over to food production.'

'But that's just it, they weren't. Look at the date.' Connor pointed to some figures in the corner of a page. 'Tenth February, 1917. Well, in the first place rose bushes wouldn't have been in flower in February and, secondly, these photos indicate the rose gardens had been dug up by 1916. So that means—'

'These were drawn from memory!' Phoebe exclaimed. 'If so, they're even better than I thought. The artist has quite an eye for detail.'

'So they were probably drawn by Hester then,' Ann said, taking the sketchbook from Phoebe. 'Perhaps she was feeling nostalgic about the good old days before the war.'

'But what about the château?' Connor persisted. 'It's obviously been drawn by the same artist. Could it be imaginary? Would Hester while away her time drawing picturesque ruins, buildings destroyed in a war that killed both her brothers and her fiancé? And why would she keep drawing Beechgrave – obsessively, almost – when she lived there?'

Phoebe looked at Connor and narrowed her eyes. 'You've got a theory, haven't you?'

'Well, it's more of a hunch,' he said, tipping the contents of another shoebox on to the table. He retrieved some envelopes bound together with a black ribbon. 'These telegrams announced the deaths of the Mordaunt brothers and the news that William Hatherwick was missing in action in 1916, but he was back home again by the spring of 1917. I think these could be *his* sketchbooks. Maybe he saw this château in France and drew it from memory. Beechgrave too, perhaps, when he was in hospital.'

'What about this building?' Ann asked, showing him another page. 'It's not Beechgrave and it's not ruined. It looks like a stately home.'

'Could have been a military hospital. That's what they did with a lot of the big houses. Hester eventually turned Beechgrave into a convalescent home for Tommies.'

'Did Ivy never say who the sketchbooks belonged to?'

'I never asked. I didn't find them until after her death.'

'It's odd that all the sketches are dated meticulously but not signed,' Ann said as she flipped through the pages. 'No name at the beginning either. The work is strangely anonymous.'

'Yes, that's what struck me. And if you compare the sketchbooks with the diaries, you'll see Hester has her name and address at the front of each of them and every entry is carefully dated.'

'So you're saying, if these sketches were Hester's, she would have recorded what the buildings were, or where they were. She was methodical, wasn't she?'

'Exactly.' He beamed at Ann with frank admiration.

She smiled back uncertainly. She wanted to help Connor, who had done so much for Phoebe and Garden Lodge, but the quantity and variety of archive material seemed almost overwhelming. Ann turned her attention to the photographs, her thoughts disordered.

'Connor, this envelope's empty,' Phoebe announced. 'Where are the contents?'

'Search me.'

'So why have you kept an empty envelope?'

'Because it seemed like a significant empty envelope.'

'How so?'

'Well, look who it's addressed to.'

Phoebe read out the name. '*Ivy Hatherwick.* What's remarkable about that?'

'That wasn't her name. I mean, that was her birth name, but by the time she could read, she'd been adopted and was known as Ivy Mordaunt.'

'But why on earth would she have saved an empty envelope,' Phoebe asked, 'however it was addressed?'

'I doubt she did. She could have destroyed the *contents* in the fire.'

'Ah, the plot thickens!' Phoebe said gleefully. She looked up from the empty envelope to see Connor looking past her. He appeared to be watching Ann, but his brow was contracted into a frown. Turning, Phoebe saw Ann staring, white-faced, at a photograph she held between her fingers. As Phoebe watched, it fluttered to the floor as Ann gripped the back of a dining chair for support.

'Ann? Are you all right?' Phoebe bent to retrieve the photo, but Connor ducked and got there first. It was a photo of his great-grandmother, Violet, pictured with her infant daughter, Ivy. They were sitting on a swing, which hung from a branch of a large beech tree.

'Are you feeling unwell?' Phoebe asked. 'Sit down for a bit. You're looking quite peaky.'

'No, I'm fine. I just felt a bit . . . peculiar, that's all. I don't know what came over me.'

'Was it something to do with this?' As Connor held out the photo, Ann shrank back.

'I don't know. I think it might have been.'

'Here, let me see,' Phoebe said tersely. Connor handed over the photograph without taking his eyes off Ann.

Phoebe examined the photo. 'Ah, this is the old beech! The one that came down in the storm. Do you remember that night, Ann? It was terrifying! I expect that's what upset you. Remembering all that. It would give anyone a nasty turn. Delayed shock, that's what it is,' Phoebe said emphatically. 'And I dare say you could use some lunch. We all could. Connor, be a love – go and put the kettle on. I'm gasping.'

Surprised by the endearment, Connor turned to look at Phoebe but she avoided his eye. As he left the room, she quickly shoved the photo under a pile of letters, then turned to Ann, inviting her to admire another sketchbook.

ANN

I ate very little while Connor and Phoebe tucked into quiche and salad. She was more voluble than usual, compensating perhaps for my silence. I didn't mean to be the spectre at the feast, but my brain couldn't process their chatter. Connor would throw back his head and laugh and I'd realise I had no idea what Phoebe had said. Everything seemed distant somehow. Or maybe it was just me. Connor and Phoebe got on so well now, I felt like a spare part – a mere baker of quiches and dresser of salads.

The morning's archive session had depressed me and I didn't know why, but these days I wandered round in a state of tired confusion. I worked hard during the day, designing, gardening, cooking and cleaning, but I wasn't sleeping well at night.

Jack's girlfriend had given birth to a baby girl and he'd emailed me a photo of her. I appreciated his tact in sparing me a portrait of mother and baby doing well and was genuinely very happy for them all, but their bliss seemed only to increase my sense of isolation. I put this down to loneliness, months spent looking after an elderly parent, adapting my life to fit in with hers. I'd become a carer and knew I should make more effort to get out and see my friends. They sometimes invited me to do things at weekends, but I always declined. Weekends were when I helped Connor with the garden, when I took photos and helped him design his website. My days were full.

On the face of it, we were all having a very pleasant time and Phoebe was flourishing under the new regime, yet persistent nightmares and insomnia made me wonder at times if I was losing it. I seemed to have become two different people. With a comfortable life, a thriving business, friends, freedom, I had almost everything a woman could want. But there was another me, an alter ego who felt frightened, almost desolate at times, as if I'd lost everything that ever mattered. But I hadn't. My marriage had failed and I was childless, but I'd come to terms with those sad facts years ago. I'd filled my life with other things, determined not to want what I couldn't have.

Sometimes I got up in the middle of the night and poured myself a glass of wine, hoping it would send me off to sleep. I would sit at the kitchen table, brooding. After the second glass, I'd ask myself whether the problem was really quite simple, simple and insoluble. I asked myself if the problem was Connor.

When he was around, I felt awkward, confused as to the footing on which we stood. When he wasn't around, I felt as if I was waiting until he was. He was a friend, a quasi-employee, my project manager, a tonic and companion for my aged mother. Connor had become many things to us, but not what I wanted him to be, which meant he'd been added to the list of things I was determined not to want.

It seemed determination was not enough.

After lunch I declined Connor's customary offer of help and loaded the dishwasher myself while he and Phoebe returned to sifting through photos and letters. I tidied the kitchen, then wiped down all the worktops. It was when I found myself sweeping the floor – very thoroughly – that I realised I didn't want to go back into the sitting room.

I put my head round the door to ask if anyone wanted tea. There were no takers, so I said I was popping out for a breath of fresh air and shut the door without waiting for a reply.

As I headed for the beech wood, I resolved to keep Connor at a professional distance, whilst doing all I could to help with the restoration of the garden and solving the Mordaunt mystery. I thought I might even take on a little project of my own: researching shell shock and memory loss, to see if I could account for the anonymity and subject matter of the sketchbooks, which intrigued me. The artist had drawn Beechgrave many times. It was clearly an obsession. Would William Hatherwick have missed his old home and job to this extent? If so, what prevented him from returning after he'd gone missing? Was Beechgrave more to him than his job, his home, his sister? Did it represent something he wanted, but couldn't have? Happier times? Lost memories . . . ? Or did Beechgrave represent a *person* William wanted, but couldn't have? And was that perhaps why he'd stayed away?

I came to a halt beside the upended stump of the fallen beech. I studied the knotted root plate and marvelled at the complexity of a tree's life support system. How tenaciously those roots had clung to the soil, burrowing down, wider and deeper, grounding the massive trunk and canopy above. Nevertheless, it had been felled, not by man, but by the wind. Age and weather had weakened the ancient beech until one day its strength gave out.

I couldn't help thinking of Phoebe. My mother could still walk, but she had to lean on a stick. She still worked, but cancer, trauma and pain had worn her down. Even before that, she'd struggled as a single working mother. As far as I knew, Sylvester had never sent us any money. We never even got a Christmas card from him, but at least he hadn't laid claim to his half of the marital home.

As I wandered on through the wood, I tried to think what I could actually remember of my father, as opposed to what I'd been told, or what I'd gleaned from looking at old photos. It wasn't much. I thought I could remember standing on a swing, like the young Ivy Hatherwick, with Sylvester standing behind me, pushing the seat gently, as I swung back and forth. I remembered feeling quite safe, even though I was standing up on the swing, because I knew my father was right behind me.

'I've brought you some tea.'

I spun round, my heart pounding, to see Connor holding two mugs, one of them extended towards me.

'Oh! You startled me.'

'Sorry. Thought you'd have heard me coming.' He handed me a mug and I drank gratefully, comforted by the heat of the tea.

'I was miles away. Thinking about when I was young and used to play here.'

'Your very own wood. Lucky girl.'

'I suppose so. I had no one to play with though.'

'Did you talk to the trees?'

I looked up surprised. 'Yes, I did, actually. I'd forgotten until you said that, but now I remember, I did. I think I even had names for some of them. I used to sing to them too,' I added, rather embarrassed. 'And dance sometimes.'

'I bet they enjoyed that.' He looked round, surveying the trees, but I saw no hint of mockery on his face.

'There used to be a swing.'

Connor turned to look at me. 'Like the one in the photo?'

'Yes. I can hardly remember it now. It wasn't there when I was older. I remember climbing trees, but I don't remember sitting on a swing.'

'Rope rots eventually. Maybe someone thought it was dangerous and took it down.'

We drank our tea in silence until Connor said, 'Something's bugging you, Ann. Is it me?'

'*You?*' Tea spilled from my mug and scalded my hand.

'Well, our project. The garden. Or is it all my family stuff? You must be getting fed up with it by now. And it's not as if we're actually getting anywhere.' He waited for me to reply but I didn't know what to say. 'The garden's almost finished, so we can call it a day soon. Then if you wouldn't mind letting me come back to take a few seasonal photos . . .' He paused and searched my face again. 'Or you could take them yourself and email them to me if you prefer. I can be out of your hair in a few weeks' time if the weather's kind. Then you'll get your life back,' he added with one of his wide smiles, but it looked pasted on. Above, his eyes looked disappointed.

'Phoebe won't know what to do with herself at weekends. She keeps talking about painting you. Don't be surprised if she asks you to come back and sit for her.'

Connor's face brightened. 'I'd be happy to. If that's all right with you.'

'Why wouldn't it be?'

He shrugged. 'Just checking. I don't like to presume. And you're pretty hard to read.'

'Am I?'

'Well, *I* find you hard to read.' He raised his mug and swallowed some tea. 'Quite confusing, in fact.'

'Really . . . ? Maybe that's because *I'm* confused.'

'What about?'

'Oh, everything . . . What to do about Phoebe. Selling the house. Getting a divorce. Getting older. You name it, I'm confused about it.'

'Do you still have feelings for your husband?'

'Only friendly ones. We split up years ago but we didn't bother with divorce. Neither of us was a big fan of marriage and we didn't expect to marry again. No, it's just . . . well, I suppose it's a watershed, isn't it? I've arrived at a point in my life where some things have come to an end. Youth. Marriage. My childbearing years. And now I have to decide whether to become a carer for my mother or whether to farm the job out to someone else.'

'I think Phoebe wants you to have your own life. And she'd never forgive you if you gave up your work. She could probably manage on her own with some help, couldn't she? I'd be happy to look in now and again.'

'Thank you, Connor, you're very kind, but I think I'd still worry about her living alone.'

He gave me a stern look. 'We both know how much Phoebe would hate to hear you say that.'

'You're right. She'd be furious.' His smile seemed genuine this time, but I looked away and said, 'Sometimes I wonder if it's not so much that Phoebe needs looking after, as I need someone to care for.'

'I think you need someone to care for *you*, Ann. Care *about* you.'

'Do you?'

'Do I *care*?'

'No, I mean, is that what you think? About me? That I— I'm sorry, I'm not explaining myself very well.' I glared at the ground. 'Oh, what is the *matter* with me?'

Connor put down his mug, then took mine. He set it down and said, 'May I?' and took hold of one of my hands. I felt rooted to the spot, as if I was being pulled down into the earth, like one of the trees that encircled us.

'May I?' he asked again. Lifting one of his big, strong hands, he placed it behind my head, cradling my neck and threading his warm fingers through my curling hair. I managed to raise my eyes as far as his chest and stared at a moth hole in his Fair Isle sweater. I noted the colours – dove grey, moss green, burnt umber – and resolved to look for them in my work basket. Mending. That's what you did when you looked after people. You mended things. Toys. Sweaters. Broken hearts. You made them whole again. I wanted to do that. Mend things between me and Phoebe. Between me and my father. But I'd never be able to do that because I didn't know where he was. Nor did Phoebe. There was just a gaping hole, a hole where my father had been. A hole in my life, even a hole in my memory.

Connor was kissing me and I didn't know what to do other than kiss him back, so that's what I did. I don't know how long that might have gone on if it hadn't started to rain.

He pulled away and said, 'Let's get you inside before you get soaked.'

'Connor—'

'It's okay. I'm not going to assume anything. I'm just glad you weren't angry. Or offended.'

'No. I was . . . pleased.'

'You don't look it,' he said with a laugh.

'Don't I? How *do* I look?'

'Confused.' He raised a finger to my mouth and touched it. 'But beautiful as ever.' He looked up. 'It's really coming down now. Let's get back to that stove.'

He took my hand again and pulled me through the wood, back towards the house. As we ran I called out, 'Connor, wait!' I let go of his hand and turned, looking back the way we'd come.

'What is it?'

'I don't know. Something . . .' I looked round at the trees, searching. I'd no idea what for.

'Did you leave something behind?'

'No. But I remember that I *did* leave something here, a long time ago . . . And I remember coming to look for it.'

'You didn't find it?'

'I don't remember. I just have an awful feeling . . .'

'About the thing you lost?'

'No. About something that happened.'

'Here?'

'I think so.'

'Something bad?'

'Yes.'

'So bad, you don't remember what it was?'

'So bad, I don't *want* to remember what it was.'

Connor stared at me, then threw an arm round my shoulders. 'Come on. Let's get out of here. This place is giving me the creeps.'

HESTER

February 10th, 1917

Ivy Hester Hatherwick was born yesterday. She is so very small, but she seems strong and determined to live.

Violet was heartbroken that William was not here to share our happiness. There is still no news of him and I fear she has now abandoned all hope, finding it easier to accept that he is dead than to wonder how he can be alive, but unable or unwilling to write. I understand her reasoning. Nevertheless, I find myself unable to contemplate the possibility. This has less to do with hope, rather more to do with stubbornness. I do so want little Ivy to have a family.

February 17th

An unsettling day. This morning Mother said something that astonished me. I wish to record her words here, lest I should later think I imagined them.

She must have heard Ivy crying. Mother's hearing is still acute, though her wits are scattered. She emerged from her room to enquire about the noise. She believed there must be a cat trapped in the house somewhere and Mother cannot abide cats. I told her one of the servants had brought a new baby up to Beechgrave. I felt uncomfortable telling a lie, but the truth is far too complicated for Mother to comprehend and I had no wish to distress her.

Much to my surprise, she asked to see the baby. Ivy's persistent crying indicated she was still at Beechgrave, so I could think of no good reason to refuse Mother's request. I left her waiting outside her room while I hurried off to fetch Ivy. I found Violet pacing the floor with the fretful baby in her arms. She apologised for the din, then I told her Mother wished to make Ivy's acquaintance. Violet looked anxious, so I tried to reassure her with a smiling confidence I did not feel. Taking Ivy from her arms, I asked her to accompany me.

Violet followed reluctantly as I carried Ivy along the corridor. Fortunately, the brisk movement seemed to pacify the child. When I presented her, Mother pulled back the shawl to peer at Ivy's face, then turned her attention to Violet. She looked her up and down, almost as if she were seeing her for the first time.

'Is this baby yours, Hatherwick?'

Violet looked from Mother to me, at a loss, so I answered quickly, 'Yes, Mother. She's called Ivy. Ivy Hester. After me.'

Mother looked surprised. 'Is there a father?' she asked sharply.

'He died in the war,' I explained, with a sidelong look at Violet.

'Ah!' Mother said, studying Ivy's face again. 'A dead war hero . . . Just like my own dear boys.'

I thought I should faint with shock, but knew I must answer straight away. 'Yes, Mother. Like poor Arthur and Eddie.'

'So much death,' Mother said, shaking her head. 'Take her away. She reminds me of my dead babies. I simply cannot bear it.' She rubbed her temple, saying, 'I think I shall go mad, Hester.' Then she gazed at me, her eyes quite lucid and said, 'I shall!' With that, Mother turned her back on us, shut herself in her room and locked the door.

I have knocked several times in the last few hours, but she has not responded.

February 25th

Mother has stopped playing the piano. I do not know which was worse: listening to her accompany music only she could hear, or this ominous silence. It is almost as if Arthur and Eddie have died again, as if a last musical link with my brothers has been broken. The silence is so final.

Mother has not played for several days now and I cannot bring myself to ask her why. I suppose I fear the answer. Or no answer.

I went to the music room today and took up my viola which has lain untouched for months. I tuned it, then played my part of a Brahms sonata, one Mother and I used to enjoy. I hoped the sound would lure her from her room, either to chastise me for my poor playing or to accompany me.

She did not appear.

I was unable to complete the piece – itself incomplete without Mother's contribution. I replaced the viola in its case, then sat down and wept. I had thought I was done crying, but grief appears to be a reservoir that never empties. Memory refills it constantly.

I believe I hoped Mother might yet appear to comfort me, as Nanny Dryden used to do when I woke crying after one of my bad dreams. I sat waiting, but Mother did not come. None of my ghosts appeared. Not Father, nor Arthur, nor Eddie. Walter Dowding did not come, nor did William Hatherwick. No one came. Not even Nanny Dryden.

I was roused eventually from my stupor of self-pity by the distant sound of little Ivy crying. As I dried my eyes, it struck me forcibly that ladies' handkerchiefs are quite inadequate nowadays. How can such small squares of lace absorb the outpourings of grief this war has occasioned? As I thrust the ridiculous scrap of cloth into my pocket, I recalled Violet standing in the kitchen of Garden Lodge after William had enlisted, mopping her face with her coarse linen apron.

I set off along the corridor in the direction of Ivy's nursery, where I found Violet trying to console her. I took the baby in my arms and held her red, tear-stained face up to mine – no doubt equally red and tear-stained. She stopped crying and in the silence that followed, we regarded each other solemnly. I smiled first. It is impossible to contemplate that fierce little soul for more than a few moments without feeling grateful.

I shall not play the viola again. I have no heart for music now. What should have been a consolation serves only to remind me – and, I fear, Mother – of all that we have lost. Thus we must add to our long list of war casualties the blessed consolation of music.

Sometimes I look at little Ivy and envy the emptiness of her infant mind. I wish I could erase mine and begin again, with a fresh start, new born, like her. Would a man without memory be a happy man, I wonder? If we did not always look back, could we move forward, unhindered by a crippling sense of loss?

I shall begin again. I must. Ivy and Violet are my future now. My new family.

THE BEECH WOOD

When all hope was extinguished, she came to us, to the wood, to finish something that had begun here. There was no body to inter. Instead she buried his love, concealed it in a place known only to the birds and small creatures who seek sanctuary among our boughs.

She had chosen a container to keep out wind and weather, a humble tin decorated with flowers. Now she stood, hesitating, at the foot of the largest tree, one on which so many had declared their love. She spread her arms and leaned against the trunk, embracing it, feeling with her fingers, like a blind woman, for the lovers' hearts and initials crudely incised on the smooth bark.

She released the tree and went to sit on the wooden swing that had hung from the beech's arm since before she was born. The branch creaked as it took her weight and the leaves rustled above her head. Looking up, she saw the perfect hiding place, but it was out of reach. Undaunted, she stood and bound the tin to her body with her woollen shawl, then, grasping both ropes, she lifted one foot and placed it on the wooden seat. As she leaned back to draw up her other foot, she began to swing. Kicking her skirts aside, she straightened up and swung back and forth, gripping the ropes, gazing up at the dark hole in the grey bark.

When the swing came to rest, she let go of one of the ropes and withdrew the tin from the folds of her shawl, which slithered undone and fell to the ground. Leaning against the taut rope, she reached out and pushed the tin *into the hole. She heard it tumble a little way and knew it would never be found.*

She descended from the swing, retrieved her shawl and flung the soft wool round her shoulders, then she stood for a moment, observing the silence. Lifting her head, she regarded her hiding place and murmured, 'May light perpetual shine upon you.' His love consigned to perpetual darkness, she left the wood, her footsteps slow and heavy.

We guarded her treasure for nearly a hundred years, but even we are not immortal.

WILLIAM

July 8th, 1916

He assumed he was dead. All he could see was sky, so blue and bright, it hurt his eyes; sky that stretched so far, it seemed infinite. He remembered sky. Sky was what you saw when you looked up from the graves. He couldn't remember much else, but he recalled that you saw a lozenge of sky, as narrow as a coffin. All else was mud and stench, things broken, dead or dying. Since he could not account for the vast expanse of blue above, he assumed he must be dead.

He tried to feel something in response to this surprising new knowledge, but found nothing in his heart save a great emptiness, a void as infinite as the blue above. When he thought of death, he remembered noise, indescribable noise, noise to drive a man mad, but here, now, there was silence. He wondered if perhaps he was deaf, not dead. For reasons he could not comprehend, dead seemed more likely.

He hadn't thought death would be so peaceful. Gratitude overwhelmed him and tears blurred his vision. As they trickled over his face towards his ears, he realised he must be lying on his back. As the salt water travelled, his face began to sting on one side and he noted – as if it were a matter of small consequence – that he was in a good deal of pain. He began to wonder if perhaps he was *not* dead.

He tried to lift a hand to his face, to ascertain if he still had a face. A memory of faceless men struck him with the force of a blow. As his hand drew an arc in the air, he examined his arm, as if it belonged to another man, then lowered his eyes to look at the rest of his body. It seemed to be caked in a dark substance, mostly brown, but red in places. He looked not like a man, but a creature made of earth, or one that lived in the earth. He thought of moles and knew – unaccountably – that he'd been responsible for the death of hundreds. Then he thought of men and knew he'd killed them too. His tears flowed again.

He regarded his filthy hand, poised in the air and spread his fingers. As the mud cracked, sprinkling his face with dust and small clods of earth, it revealed streaks of skin beneath, pale and branched, like the roots of a plant. He observed his hand, forgetting his pain for a few moments, absorbed in the action of moving his body and the sensations it provoked.

He felt sure now he must be alive, but he had no idea where he was nor how he came to be there. He lay still, overcome by a desire to sleep, but feared that if he slept, he might lose his tenuous hold on life, so he stared unblinking at the sky, willing himself to remain conscious. As he watched a cloud's stately progress across his field of vision, he knew there would be no rain. He didn't know why he felt so certain, how he could tell, just by looking at the sky.

His certainty brought him inexplicable comfort, a comfort soon dispelled when he realised he couldn't remember his name. Panic rose from his stomach to his throat as he acknowledged he didn't know who or what he was. His body jack-knifed and, as he sat up, he turned his head to one side and vomited.

He was able to walk. He'd taken an inventory of his body and found a deep gash in his neck and superficial wounds on an arm and leg. One side of his face was too painful to touch, but he had no idea what had caused the injury or if it had left him with a recognisable face. He staggered on, covering the marshy ground slowly, fearful that he might fall and be consumed by the bog. He thought he'd seen a man drown in mud, but that was surely impossible. It must have been a dream, a very bad dream.

He acknowledged that he was indeed deaf. The world he walked through was silent, blighted, hellish. For some time – he had no idea how long, but the sun was high enough in the sky for him to long for shade – he'd seen no feature on the landscape other than ruined buildings and blasted trees, black, leafless, with broken or amputated limbs. Sometimes, when he passed the trunk of a dead tree, he would lean against it, panting, and touch the scorched wood in a gesture of tenderness, then he moved on.

At the crest of a low hill he came upon a writhing, knotted bole where the earth had been eroded from its tangled roots. He stopped to pay his respects to the tenacity of the tree which stood sentinel at the roadside, bearing witness to the devastation of the village below. The nameless man laid his hand on the gnarled bark while his memory groped for a name. Finally, it came.

'*Crataegus laevigata.*'

The faint sound of his own voice, deep and hoarse, startled him, but his spirits rose a little to think his hearing was returning.

As he plodded onwards, the eerie silence was broken only by the raucous croak of an occasional crow. After some hours, he came upon a stand of living trees, their smooth, grey bark unscathed. He knelt at the foot of one of them, overwhelmed by a sense of familiarity, of joy, of love for these living things. Gasping, he named them, '*Fagus sylvatica*', before passing out.

He awoke, shivering and damp, his head throbbing. The ground beneath the trees was dry, so he assumed he was drenched in sweat. He struggled to his knees, then crawled, dragging himself over tree roots. Clinging to a trunk for support, he got to his feet and launched himself along a path through the trees.

When he emerged from the wood, stumbling and blinking in the sunlight, he saw a large building in the distance, a grand mansion that for a moment seemed familiar, even though he felt sure he'd never seen it before. As he approached, he saw that much of the roof had fallen in and one corner of the house appeared to have been blown away, exposing the interior like a doll's house. A conical turret still stood, but there was no glass in the many ornate windows.

He wondered if he might find food in the garden or at least water. Fixing his eyes on the ruined building and his hopes on a walled garden, he limped towards the abandoned house.

Climbing over rubble where the walls had been breached, he entered a formal garden. As he registered beds full of wilting flowers and vegetables, he knew at once what work needed to be done, knew the garden had been neglected for many weeks. He didn't know how he knew this. As he trod weedy gravel paths searching for something to eat, he recognised the foliage of potatoes, spinach, sorrel, the ferny leaves of asparagus and carrots, the flower heads of bolted lettuce gone to seed. He knew the lettuce had flowered because it hadn't been watered, but he didn't know how he knew such things.

He saw some plants covered with netting and dropped to his knees, knowing there would be good food beneath. He dragged the netting off, pulling up plants as he did so in his desperate efforts to get at the red fruit he'd spied. He crammed strawberries into his mouth and laughed with relief as the warm juice ran down his chin. When he could eat no more, he looked for a container to collect the remaining berries. As he cast an eye round the garden, he noticed the gravel paths led to the centre of the garden where a headless stone deity presided over a broken fountain. The water no longer flowed, but some lay in a pool beneath.

He lurched towards the fountain, removing his mud-encrusted khaki tunic and undershirt. He dropped them on the path, reached up to his swollen neck and tugged at the leather bootlace irritating his wound. Without stopping to consider their significance, he tossed two tags into a flowerbed, then sat down on the edge of the fountain to remove his boots. He shed his remaining clothes, opening up wounds as he pulled at scabs of dried blood. Pale, naked and bleeding, he stood and stared down at the surface of the water, curious to see what he looked like, anxious to know if he would recognise himself.

The gaunt face that gazed back at him seemed scarcely human. The eyes of a hunted animal looked out from sockets ringed with blood and dirt. Turning his head, he saw that one cheek looked flayed, like raw meat. He plunged his hands into the stagnant pool, dispersing his reflection, then washed off the dirt and strawberry juice. When he removed his hands from the water, he was surprised to note they were still brown, tanned to the wrists, as if they belonged to a body other than his.

He stepped into the fountain and lay down. The water was warm and slimy with algae. A gentle breeze riffled the surface and brought the scents of roses and lavender to his nostrils. He knew he should find a lavender bush to make some sort of dressing for his wounds because the oil in the leaves would help him heal. He didn't know how he knew this.

He climbed out of the pool and sat on the edge, staring at his discarded bloodstained clothes. Turning away, nauseated, he bent and picked up his boots, then dropped them into the pool where he rinsed off the dried mud. When they were clean, he set them in the sun to dry and hobbled along the path towards outbuildings tucked away at the edge of the garden, storerooms where he knew (but how?) that he might find tools, perhaps even some old clothes. As he passed a flowerbed hedged with lavender, he plucked handfuls of leaves and flowers, then crushed and rubbed them to release their scented oil. Wincing, he pressed the leaves against the wound in his neck.

When he got to the door of one of the outbuildings, habit made him hesitate as he reached for the handle. He knocked, smiling at the courtesy of a wet and naked man presenting himself at the door, then opened it and walked in. The storeroom was dark and musty, festooned with cobwebs. Looking round, he saw what he wanted. Some canvas, a ball of twine and a sharp knife to cut it with. He could use the knife to defend himself if the need arose. But why, he wondered, might he need to do that? How could he know he had enemies, yet not know who they were?

He opened a tin and found string, scissors and a pencil. Another contained envelopes of harvested seed and some empty printed packets. He recognised the illustrations, but not the names of the flowers: *penseé, oeillet, pois de senteur, verveine* . . . As he studied the packets, his hands started to tremble, then his whole body began to shake. It was as if he stood on the brink of an abyss, about to descend once more into darkness, a darkness where he would understand everything, but the knowledge would kill him. He thrust the seed packets back into the tin and shut the lid, his chest heaving.

Looking round for anything that might be of use, he pounced on a brandy bottle, thick with dust, but it was empty. An old overcoat with no buttons hung on a peg beneath a frayed straw hat. He put the bottle and his other finds into the deep pockets of the coat, then tore the canvas into strips. As he bound up his wounds, he placed sprigs of crushed lavender against his skin, then put on the coat. He cut a long piece of twine and tied it round his waist to keep the coat closed, then donned the hat and went out into the garden again in search of a well.

When he found it, he turned the winch handle, lowering the empty bucket until he heard it hit the water. When the bucket felt heavy, he wound it back up again and set it down. Cupping his hands, he drank the cold, fresh water until he could swallow no more, then immersed the brandy bottle in the bucket. He waited for it to fill, then carried it back to the fountain where he sat down again and struggled into his damp boots.

He explored the garden, filling the hat with onions, young carrots and peapods, which he then covered with a layer of gooseberries, plucked from a warm south-facing wall. When the hat was full, he turned his back on the kitchen garden and headed for the front of the house and the long drive he knew would lead to a road. The sun was sinking now and he thought he should head north, but he wasn't sure why.

At the end of the drive he found buckled wrought iron gates swinging on their hinges. He pushed one open and set off along a rutted lane. Arriving at a crossroads, he studied the names on the fingerpost, but they meant nothing to him. Keeping the sun on his left, he set off in a northerly direction.

He found an empty barn to sleep in. When he woke, he breakfasted on water that tasted of brandy and a few gooseberries, then he continued north. When his hat was almost empty, he put the remaining food in his coat pockets and placed the hat on his head to shade his face. The skin had become painfully taut as it had crusted over, so he strove to keep his face immobile.

The sky remained clear but he thought he could hear distant thunder, thunder that continued throughout the day, thunder that he knew could not be thunder, but his mind baulked at identifying the sound. He increased his pace and walked on, veering away from the sound. After a last meal of raw onion, he lay down under a hedge, his stomach protesting.

He woke to find an old woman standing over him, scowling and wielding a pitchfork. He sat up slowly, his hands raised in a gesture of submission. The peasant woman said something guttural and unintelligible. He spread his hands. 'I'm afraid I don't understand.' He pointed to an ear and said, 'Deaf,' then he tapped his chest and said, 'English.'

At the word, the old woman lowered her pitchfork. She rattled off more questions, to which he could only shrug and shake his head. As he got to his feet, his hands still raised, the buttonless overcoat fell open, revealing his nakedness. The woman's eyes widened, then she burst into gales of wheezy laughter, revealing a mouth almost entirely lacking in teeth.

He thought it politic to join in, though smiling hurt his face a good deal. It must have started bleeding again for the woman pointed and exclaimed. She indicated a building, possibly a farmhouse, a few hundred yards distant, then laid a hand on her generous bosom. 'Reynaud. Simone Reynaud!' she said in a loud, clear voice, as if addressing someone simple-minded. '*Et vous?*' She regarded him, not unkindly, as he tried to remember his name, any name.

Defeated, he extended a shaking hand and, with a small bow, said, '*Fagus. Fagus sylvatica.* At your service.'

HESTER

Sharpitor V.A. Hospital
Salcombe
Devon

March 2nd, 1917

My dear Hester,
Thank you for your last letter. I was sorry to hear Cicely has not rallied, but scarcely surprised. When I lost Walter I thought I should not be able to carry on without my only son and your poor mother has lost two. If it were not for my work here, I believe I too might succumb to melancholy.

I must apologise for this tardy reply, but I have very little leisure. I would not have it otherwise. To be both busy and useful is a great comfort. Though I can do nothing now for Walter, I can tend to other mothers' sons and that is both a privilege and a consolation.

I am writing to ask for your help in solving a mystery. Among the many Tommies convalescing here, there is a man with no name, no number and apparently no memory. He was patched up in France some months ago and we admitted him knowing only that he's English and suffers from amnesia and shell shock.

I wanted to put the matter before you because certain evidence suggests someone at Beechgrave might be able to identify this man. His accent suggests he comes from the Bristol area. He's a talented artist and has shown me sketchbooks filled with drawings of a house and gardens that look very much like Beechgrave. He has sketched the house from all angles, so I doubt he is copying something he has seen in a book. He is evidently drawing from memory. When questioned gently about his sketches, 'Tommy' (that's our name for him) claimed he had no knowledge of the name or location of the house. Its external appearance is apparently all he can remember. I enclose one of his sketches for you to examine.

We have supplied him with all the sketchbooks we can muster in the hope that some memory will surface that will enable us to identify him and return him to his family. I am anxious to find him a home because there is really nothing more we can do for him, although the peace and quiet here are always beneficial for the nervous cases. He has recovered well from his wounds, but there has been no improvement in his mental state. Time might heal these wounds, if only his memory would return, but at the moment he has no past and no future. He is lost in some sort of mental No Man's Land and there can be no question of sending him back to the Front, poor man.

I doubt a physical description will be very useful, but he is dark, with rather fine brown eyes. He is tall, with a ruddy complexion that suggests he enjoyed an outdoor life before he enlisted. He's intelligent and observant, but as he has no memory, one can only guess at his education. Not a university man, I think. He much prefers to be outside and spends a lot of time walking around the grounds, observing flowers, birds and insects. Oddly enough, he remembers the names of these and even knows some botanical Latin, but he can recall nothing about his life before he was wounded.

If you think our Tommy might have some connection with Beechgrave, I shall suggest we take a photograph to send to you. I could have asked him to draw a self-portrait, but his face was burned on one side and I hardly think studying his reflection would be good for his spirits. Looking-glasses are in any case scarce items here and for good reason. Some of these poor boys have no idea what frights they look – and that is much the kindest thing.

So, Hester, I hope you can shed some light on our mystery man. I've grown rather fond of him and should be delighted if we could send him home to his family, who must believe him dead by now.

I shall be going on duty in a few minutes, so I must close. Give my best regards to your mother. She has had so much to bear – as have you, my dear Hester.

Yours ever sincerely,
Ursula Dowding

Beechgrave House
Yatton
Somerset

March 4th, 1917

Dear Mrs Dowding,
I was delighted to receive your letter. It is very good of you to make time to write to me when I know you must be quite worn out with nursing.

I was very interested to hear Tommy's story. The sketch you enclosed certainly looks like Beechgrave. It must have been drawn by someone who knows the house well, though the ornamental gardens were dug up in 1915. We try to grow as much food as possible now.

It so happens that a member of our garden staff was reported missing in action on the Somme and I wonder if Tommy might be this man. His sister is Mother's lady's maid and I have taken a personal interest in the family, so with your permission, I should like to visit as soon as possible. I propose to travel on Wednesday and stay in a local hotel. Please say nothing to your man. I should hate to raise his hopes in vain. If Tommy is one of ours, I shall arrange to have him brought back to Beechgrave.

Forgive these hasty lines. I must make my travel arrangements and ensure Mother is cared for in my absence.

Till Wednesday then.
Sincerely yours,
Hester

WILLIAM

March 7th, 1917

He'd been told to expect a visitor. They had mentioned a name, but it meant nothing to him. He didn't get visitors. Other men did because they had families. He knew he might have a family and must have had a job before the war, but now anyone who ever knew him must think him dead. And that's how he felt sometimes, on bad days. Like a dead man. But a dead man would have had a name.

They called him Tommy Gardener because he spent so much time in the garden. He felt better outdoors and it got him away from the worst of the nerve cases. His nightmares were bad, but mostly he was all right during the day, which was more than could be said for some of the others. Door frames were lined with rubber, window sashes were cushioned with thick felt and heavy carpets covered the floors, but still the slightest noise would set off some poor devil.

It was peaceful in the garden at least. As he weeded and tidied, he named the plants to himself. Otherwise he didn't have many memories. Nothing at all before the old peasant woman took him in and tended his wounds. She lived alone, her menfolk gone or dead, he assumed. He helped her with her vegetable garden and the few goats and hens she had left. Then one day he was arrested as a deserter and they sent him back to England. It was shell shock, they said. He'd been fighting in a war.

They put his photograph in the papers, to see if someone would come forward to claim him, but his face was burned on one side and his hair had grown long in France. He doubted his own mother would have recognised him – if he had a mother.

Since it was clear from his accent that he hailed from the West Country, he was sent to a convalescent hospital in Devon. He recognised nothing, but when he came across pencil and paper, he started to draw his dreams. Not the bad ones, which were indescribable: men drowning in mud, severed limbs, rats gnawing at the entrails of dead men. Those he tried to forget, though he knew they would return when he slept. He had other dreams of a grand house with a large garden. He drew what he could remember of them on scrap paper until someone gave him a sketchbook. He filled it quickly with detailed drawings of a house that could not have been his home, yet somehow he knew it meant more to him than home.

Drawing stopped him from going mad. The sketches were all he had for memories, those and the plant names. They said he must have been a gardener to know so much Latin, so they allowed him to work outside. The other men sat on the lawn, reading and smoking, or they walked by the river, but he preferred to work. It comforted him and the birdsong always raised his spirits, but there were times he felt so lonely, so completely friendless, he wished a shell had blown his head off.

Today he had a visitor, the first in six months, apart from the padre. They said the visitor was a lady, so he shaved carefully and scrubbed his broken nails. He wondered what she wanted, then decided he didn't care. A visitor was a visitor. He'd be pleased to see a new face, though he doubted she'd be pleased when she saw his.

He wondered if she would be young. Or even pretty.

He stood up as Nurse Dowding showed his visitor into the library and then retreated to wait by the door.

The young woman wasn't pretty, but there was something about her, an air of intelligent composure that he liked. She didn't flinch when she looked at him, but she was upset, he could see that. Tears started into her eyes, so he looked away, uncomfortable with anyone's pity. There were others so much more deserving of it. After all, he was one of the lucky ones.

The visitor cleared her throat, extended her hand and said, 'My name is Hester Mordaunt. How do you do?'

He shook her hand, saying, 'I'm afraid I don't know who I am, but they call me Tommy Gardener.'

She managed a little smile, then swallowed and said, 'I am pleased to inform you that I know who you are.'

He tried to reply and failed, then reached for the back of a chair to support himself. Hester quickly sat down in another chair, thus granting him permission to sit.

When they faced each other, she said, 'You used to work for me. You were Head Gardener at Beechgrave House in Somerset and your name is William Hatherwick.'

'*William?* My name is William?' He laughed, delighted. 'You're certain? Certain that's who I am?' His hand touched his livid cheek. 'My face—'

'Quite certain. If your face had been obliterated, Mr Hatherwick, I should have known you from your voice.'

'William Hatherwick . . .' he said, as if trying out the name. He folded his arms and nodded, smiling. 'It's a good name.'

'And you were a very good worker. I gather from Nurse Dowding that for the time being there's no question of sending you back to the Front, so I should therefore like you to return to Beechgrave to resume your duties. You have a home there, a house known as Garden Lodge.'

He looked blank at the name, then his eyes lit up. 'Do I have a family, Miss Mordaunt?'

She appeared to struggle with her feelings, but when, finally, she spoke, her voice was steady. 'Your parents are dead, but you have a younger sister, Violet. You also have a niece, Ivy. She's a baby. Just a few weeks old.'

His broad smile stretched the shiny scar tissue taut across the bones of his face. He turned to Nurse Dowding, beaming. 'Did you hear that, Nurse? I'm William Heatherwick and I have a family!'

'It's Hatherwick,' Hester said, correcting him gently.

He nodded, still smiling. 'Takes a bit of getting used to after all this time. I'd given up hope, you see.'

She put her head on one side and regarded him earnestly. 'You remember *nothing*? Nothing at all?'

'No, Miss Mordaunt, I'm afraid not. But that won't prevent me from giving satisfaction as your Head Gardener. I haven't forgotten my trade. I've been working in the garden here and studying. I've made good use of the excellent library here, haven't I, Nurse Dowding?' he said, looking to her for corroboration.

'Indeed you have, Mr Hatherwick.'

He smiled at her gratefully. 'I remember all my plants, their names and how they grow, what conditions they like. For some reason I can still remember all that.'

'Do you remember the beech wood?' Hester asked, watching him closely.

He frowned. 'Beech wood?'

'There's a copse of old beeches. One of them is known as the Trysting Tree.' She paused, but saw no flicker of recognition. 'You don't remember it?'

'No, I can't say I do. But I remember the Latin name for beech. *Fagus sylvatica.*'

'Well, that's something,' she replied, trying to smile. 'Names and dates have been carved on the bark of this tree. By lovers. Someone carved this Latin phrase on the Trysting Tree,' she said, reaching into her pocket and handing him a scrap of paper. 'Perhaps you know what it means.'

He unfolded the paper and read aloud, '*Crescent illae crescetis amores.*' Looking up, he said, 'This is not the name of a plant.'

'No, I think not.'

He shook his head. 'Then I'm afraid I can't help you, Miss Mordaunt,' he said, handing the piece of paper back to her.

As she stood up, she crumpled the paper in her fist and dropped it into a waste basket, then turned away and began to issue instructions about travel arrangements. William Hatherwick expressed his profound gratitude and was dismissed.

Later, as Nurse Dowding poured tea in the kitchen, she said, 'Hester, that Latin quotation, the one carved on the tree. I believe it's from Ovid. It means, *As these letters grow, so will our love.*'

'Yes,' her young friend replied wearily. 'I know.'

HESTER

March 9th, 1917

Violet and her brother have been reunited. She greeted us with many tears on our return and I left them alone together. The journey quite exhausted me and I was glad to retreat to the sanctuary of my room, where I made up a parcel of William's gardening books, which I have since returned to him. I included the old seed packets I found inserted between the pages. I felt I should return everything to William that is his, as far as it lies within my power. He has lost so much.

Violet says he does not remember her at all, but seems delighted with baby Ivy. He will not remember George Flynn either, but I am sure Violet will deal with any awkwardness in a tactful fashion. She is as concerned as I about William's mental stability. After all he has endured, the return to Beechgrave might yet overturn his mind. We must be careful not to overtax it with unnecessary information. His physical wounds healed long ago and he appears to have come to terms with his facial disfigurement, but he is now in the habit of addressing people with his face averted, to spare them the sight of his scars. This is doubly sad. Never a man to shirk responsibility, nor indeed the truth, William Hatherwick's eyes used to meet mine.

I am reluctant to lose Violet's services, but her brother will need someone to look after him. She says he doesn't need her to live in, but he will need someone to keep house for him. I think if I take on more of Mother's care and perhaps even some of Ivy's, Violet would be able to cook and clean at Garden Lodge whilst continuing to live at Beechgrave. She says William will appreciate the solitude at Garden Lodge. He craves silence which acts as balm to his troubled spirit.

So silence shall be our watchword. It will restore William's peace of mind and perhaps one day his memory.

Silence, then.

It is all for the best.

THE BEECH WOOD

It has been our burden and sometimes privilege to bear witness. For centuries we have accepted gifts. Confidences. Confessions. Tears have watered our roots, their falling gentler than summer rain. We have seen acts of passion, of violence, self-slaughter even. We have observed and absorbed much grief.

On a dark winter's day, two women, one weeping, one silent, committed a tiny body to a grave beneath our canopy. Prayers were said. They gathered fallen leaves and moss to cover the newly turned earth so there should be no sign, no memorial, save initials graven on our bark. Then they left, one woman leaning heavily upon the other.

The child is forgotten now. Those who remembered are long dead. But we remember. While we stand, we shall not forget, nor shall we judge.

Were we human, we should pity.

Were we human, we should weep to see what we have seen.

PART FOUR

PART FOUR

ANN

After Connor kissed me, I stopped sleeping altogether. Well, that's what it felt like. I don't think it *was* anything to do with Connor, but that's when the serious insomnia started: after we'd stood under the beeches and I'd told him I knew I'd forgotten something.

Each morning, as the grey light appeared at my window, I was convinced I'd lain awake all night. I grew to dread the solitary robin's song, herald of the dawn chorus, knowing that was it for another night. The long day had begun.

I took to drinking red wine before bed, sometimes sherry. I even tried Phoebe's sleeping pills, but they all had the same effect, or rather, no effect. I would fall into bed exhausted, sometimes a little drunk. I'd sleep, then an hour later I'd be awake again, my mind teeming, my stomach churning.

Eventually I worked out what the problem was and it had nothing to do with my furtive feelings for Connor. I dreaded my dreams. I dreaded the return of the nightmares I used to have as a child, after my father left. And I dreaded sleep itself, because I didn't know where I might find myself when I woke.

🌿

'I've started sleepwalking again.'

'Good grief!' Phoebe looked up from her breakfast cereal and gaped at me, spoon poised in mid-air. 'You haven't done that since— well, since you were very small.'

I poured myself another cup of tea, watching my hands, willing them not to tremble. 'Last night I found myself in the kitchen at 3.00 a.m. I didn't remember getting up or coming downstairs.'

'Oh, Lord . . .'

'So I think I might start taking the key out of the back door at night. If I put it in a drawer, it will make it harder for me to find. More tea?'

Phoebe passed me her mug. 'But that won't work, will it? If your conscious mind knows where the key is, your unconscious mind will know where to look for it. Would you like me to hide the key?'

'There's not a lot of point, is there? If I decide to go walkabout, I can still get out through the front door.'

'I must have a key to your room somewhere. I could lock you in if you can bear it. That's what I used to do. You hated it!'

'I'd hate it now. And supposing you needed me in the night or there was some emergency? No, I just have to crack my insomnia. I'm sure that's the cause.'

'Do you know what's keeping you awake?'

'Well, *now* I think it's probably fear of sleepwalking, but originally . . .' I spread honey on some toast and ate without enthusiasm.

'What? Something happened?'

I swallowed a mouthful of toast and said, 'I had a very bad dream. About Sylvester. At least, I think it was him. There was a man and it wasn't Jack.'

Phoebe eyed me over the top of her mug, a knowing glint in her eye. 'Connor?'

'No, this man was dark. And very tall. A giant.'

'Sylvester wasn't tall.'

'He would have seemed tall to me when I was a child.'

'Ah. So you were a child in this dream?'

'Yes.'

'What happened?'

'I was out in the garden, looking for something.'

'Here? Looking for Sylvester?'

'No, for something I'd lost.'

'And did you find it? In the dream, I mean.'

'I don't remember. But I did find something . . . Something awful.'

'What?' Phoebe asked, looking apprehensive.

'I don't remember, but I think that might be why I can't sleep. My mind won't let me, in case I have that dream again and I *do* remember.' I pushed my plate aside. 'I'm not making much sense, am I?'

Phoebe said nothing, but fidgeted in her chair as if she'd rather be somewhere else. In her studio painting, perhaps. Irritated, I found myself wishing I was talking to Connor instead, seeing concern in his eyes, rather than the squirming embarrassment I saw in my mother's, but I plodded on, trying to make sense of the random thoughts generated by my weary brain.

'That must have been what happened to Ivy, mustn't it?'

Phoebe stared at me. 'I don't follow.'

'She must have discovered something, or remembered something that changed things. Changed *everything*.'

'I suppose so,' Phoebe conceded. 'But to react like that, she must have been quite fragile, mustn't she? Of a nervous disposition.'

'The thing is, she wasn't. Connor said she was one of the first women to train in horticulture. She'd been a young woman in a man's world. That must have been tough. Then, when she lost her adult daughter, she stepped in as a surrogate mother for Connor *and* stood up to his father when Connor wanted to follow in her footsteps. She always sounds tough as old boots, not the sensitive type at all.'

'And yet something knocked her sideways, poor old thing.'

I stood up and started to clear away the breakfast things while Phoebe sat in ruminative silence. I considered returning to bed for a few hours to catch up on sleep but rejected the idea, fearing a daytime nap would make insomnia even more likely.

As I loaded the dishwasher, Phoebe suddenly said, 'What on earth do you think about when you're lying awake at night?'

'Work . . . The garden . . . I think about how nice it will look in the summer. But mostly I think about Sylvester. Whether he's dead or alive. And if he *is* alive, whether it matters to him if I am.'

Phoebe didn't reply immediately. She appeared to weigh her words, then said, 'I'm absolutely convinced that *wherever* he is now, your welfare still matters to him.'

'You really think so?'

'I *know* so. He loved you, Ann.'

'But he left.'

'As I have frequently observed,' Phoebe said loftily, 'life stinks.' She hauled herself to her feet, reached for her stick, then shuffled out of the room, breathing heavily.

Clumsy with tiredness, I broke a glass while loading the dishwasher, then, as I gathered up the pieces, I managed to cut myself. Applying Elastoplast one-handed to a bleeding thumb, I wept a little, for no particular reason.

I could feel myself unravelling, like a piece of old knitting.

Connor and I behaved as if nothing had happened. He did not presume, he exerted no pressure, nor did he sulk. He was as cheerful and friendly as ever, but also watchful, waiting for a sign. Clearly it was up to me to indicate if there was to be a shift in our relationship. Probably all I needed to do was speak, touch him, perhaps just smile invitingly and we would pick up where we'd left off in the wood.

I did none of those things. Insomnia made me too tired to think straight. I knew what I wanted, or thought I did, yet I did nothing, telling myself it was impossible to conduct a romantic relationship under Phoebe's nose. If I was going to make a fool of myself with a younger man, I didn't want an audience, let alone one as critical as my mother.

So I let things drift – long enough for Connor to conclude our kiss had been a whim on my part, an unprofessional gaffe on his. I watched myself throw away an opportunity, as if someone else was directing my life, someone too confused and frightened to know what she was doing.

My confusion was perhaps understandable. Years of living alone and many months of celibacy had undermined my sexual self-confidence, yet desire persisted. And that was what Phoebe would say, angry and maudlin after her third gin. 'Don't believe what they say about old age, Ann. You never stop *wanting*. You learn to go without, but you never stop noticing what other women have and you don't. Youth. Beauty. Health. Husbands. Lovers.' I might have added 'Children'.

But what did I *fear*? My own emptiness and need? Other people's? Did I see Connor as a threat to my shaky equilibrium, my fragile sense of self-sufficiency? I suppose going without must be habit-forming. I allowed myself to want, but not to have. I watched, though. And Connor waited.

As spring wore on and the weather improved, we were able to spend more time outdoors and made good progress in the garden. I knew the end of the project was in sight, but Connor always seemed to find more jobs that needed to be done.

One day he decided to build a compost bin, recycling bits of the old shed that had been crushed by the fallen beech.

'The wood's perfectly sound,' he explained, 'and the bin will blend in better if we use old wood. And cost nothing.'

'I shudder to think what we owe you in man hours,' I said as I sorted through the heap of broken wood, removing nails with pliers.

'And I shudder to think what I owe you in gin and Rioja, not to mention all the food I've put away.'

'It's kind of you to see it like that, but we owe you big time.'

He took a long piece of wood, examined it, then laid it across the arms of a garden bench, saying, 'It's been a pleasure, Ann. I'll be sorry when it's all over, but pretty soon it will be. The garden's ready now. And waiting.'

I looked round at the pale new leaves, the breaking buds and the white flowers on the fan-trained pear trees, the first fruit to blossom. 'It *is* waiting, isn't it? And it's been such a long wait. But finally the time has come. It's waking up.'

Connor didn't reply, but gazed at me for a moment as if he wanted to speak, then evidently thought better of it. Bending over his piece of wood, he began to saw.

We continued to work together in silence.

Connor was always a pleasure to watch, at ease with his tools and materials. I admired the unhurried and meticulous way in which he worked, his easy grace as he swung a hammer or stooped to pick up a wheelbarrow. I derived a sensual pleasure from the sight of a man trusting his body, using it skilfully. It soothed me in a way, aroused me in another. When we worked together I would sometimes stand, my trowel or secateurs idle, and watch Connor surreptitiously, hypnotised by the rhythm of his digging or raking.

Once he must have sensed my gaze, because he looked up from his digging and his eyes met mine. I meant to look away at once, but didn't. It seemed pointless to pretend.

He straightened up and said, 'You look tired. Still not sleeping?'

'No, not much.'

'Maybe you should rest. It's good to have company, but I can manage.'

'Yes, I know, but I like to be outdoors, listening to the birds. There's so much activity now. It's . . . reassuring.'

'Spring's here again,' Connor said, leaning on his spade.

'Yes, it's the continuity, isn't it? Yet every year spring is just as exciting.' He nodded, smiling. 'It reminds me—' I stopped, unsure whether to continue.

'Of what?'

'Of my father. Being out here and helping in the garden. I think he must have found me little jobs to do. I remember being very happy out here, before—' Again I faltered.

'Before he left?'

'I was happy enough, but I suppose he and Phoebe must have been miserable.'

'You were only five. You might have noticed, but you couldn't have understood.'

'No.'

'And it wasn't your fault he left.'

'I know that now, but years later I used to wonder why I hadn't been enough. Why he hadn't wanted to stay for my sake. I'm sure if I'd ever had kids I'd have wanted to hold it together for them.'

'He probably tried.'

'Yes, I'm sure he did.'

I knelt down again and bent over a tray of plants and began to tease them out of their plastic compartments. One by one, I dropped them into the holes I'd dug for them, then I filled in around them with loose soil, patting it down carefully.

Connor was silent for a while, then said, 'Perhaps Sylvester thought you'd be better off without him, you and Phoebe. Or – if you don't mind my saying so – maybe he was just a selfish sod.'

I sat back on my heels and dusted soil from my hands. 'Well, that would be the obvious explanation. But somehow I don't think he was.'

'Phoebe might have a different view.'

'Well, she didn't ever *say* he was. Selfish, I mean. She never mentioned him, let alone criticised him. Everything I know about Sylvester, I had to wheedle out of her. She didn't seem to hold a grudge as so many abandoned women do. She just wanted to move on. And she did.'

'Did you?'

I looked up at him, surprised. 'You think I haven't?'

He shrugged. 'I'm just asking the question – and maybe I shouldn't. But whenever you mention your father, I find myself thinking you and Phoebe ought to talk. *Really* talk.'

I bent over again and started to dig more holes with my trowel. 'Oh, there are loads of things Phoebe and I need to talk about. Her future mainly, but she won't hear of it. We don't *talk*, my mother issues *decrees*. The latest is, she's not celebrating her seventieth birthday.'

'You're kidding? When is it?'

'Next week.'

'Could we throw a surprise party?'

'The surprise would be, she'd walk out.'

'You're not going to let her get away with this?'

'No, I'm scheming.'

Connor smiled appreciatively. 'If you need a co-conspirator, you know you can count on me.'

'Yes, I do. Thank you for being so understanding. About everything.'

He waved a muddy hand, dismissing my thanks and resumed his digging in silence. I watched him for a moment, then went indoors to make tea and scheme some more.

Phoebe was adamant she didn't want a party. She said variously that she couldn't afford it, we didn't have room, she didn't want people to know how old she was. She even tried, 'I've got nothing to wear.' She didn't volunteer what I suspect was the real reason: her fear that people might not come. Phoebe had been out of circulation for so long, she must have wondered if her old friends and colleagues would make the effort to trek down to darkest Somerset for what she referred to as 'a pensioner's knees-up'.

'Half the old crowd are dead,' she claimed. 'And if the art critic from the *Guardian* is to be believed, so am I!'

Phoebe forbade me to organise any kind of celebration, but when I remonstrated with her, she said she might enjoy a nice little dinner with Connor.

'That's a lovely idea. Am I invited?'

'Of course. You'll be doing the cooking.'

'Dinner at *home*? Oh, *Mum*!'

'I'm not dressing up! And I can't afford to pay restaurant prices for the quantity of booze I intend to drink. You're a jolly good cook, Ann. Make us something special. Get in a few bottles and invite Connor. I like that boy and he likes us. It'll be fun! But tell him, no presents. He can't afford it. I forbid him to waste any money on an old trout like me. But a special evening, just the three of us, raising a glass to seven decades . . . Well, that might be very pleasant. Can I leave it with you?'

Phoebe left it with me.

'I can't buy *anything*?'

'Shhh! Keep your voice down. She'll hear you.'

Connor and I were drinking tea in the kitchen, waiting for the rain to stop.

'Can I give her something if I don't spend any money?'

'I suppose so. But she really doesn't want anything, just your company.'

'Well, that's very sweet of her, but it's also very boring.'

'I know, but she doesn't want any fuss. She hates being another year older, with so little to show for it. Well, that's the way *she* sees it. The rest of us think she's a hero to try to keep working.'

'That sketch she did of me – it was good, wasn't it?'

'Yes, it was, by any standards.'

'She says she wants to paint my portrait.'

'Let her. If you're prepared to sit for her, that is. It's hard work, harder than you might think. And she can be a real bully if she's not happy.'

'Can't wait,' Connor said amiably. 'But is there really no way I can cheat with a present? What can I give her that doesn't cost money?'

'I don't know. She's made it very hard . . . Do you own a suit?'

'A *suit*?'

'Yes. Could you dress up a bit for dinner? I think she'd enjoy that. She once said she thought you'd scrub up well. Her phrase, not mine. If you wore a suit it would make the occasion seem a bit more special.'

'You'd dress up too?'

'Of course.'

'Okay, you're on. But I have to give her *something*,' Connor said, frowning. 'She'll be seventy!' After a moment, his face brightened. 'Do you think you could get her out of the house for a couple of hours on the day? Take her shopping or something?'

'She hates shopping, but I could drag her off to the hairdresser. She'd probably like to have her hair done for her birthday.'

'Could that take a couple of hours?'

'Easily, if I take her into Bristol.'

'Great! Make the appointment, but don't tell her what I'm up to.'

'What *are* you up to?'

'It's going to be a surprise. For both of you.'

'Will you need a key?'

'No, I'll be working outside.'

'On what?'

'I'd rather not say.' He tapped his head, looking mysterious. 'The concept is still evolving. But I'll need a photo of Phoebe. Full-face, nice and clear. And if you can find a profile shot as well, that would be handy.'

'I'm intrigued. Will you need anything else?'

'A chainsaw. But don't worry about that, I'll bring my own. Any more tea in the pot?'

On her seventieth birthday I presented Phoebe with champagne, an outrageous Vivienne Westwood hat I picked up on eBay and *Classic English Gardens*, a book Connor had wanted to buy for her himself. The text was by the Victorian gardener Gertrude Jekyll and was illustrated with watercolours. The book demonstrated the art of 'painting with plants', something we hoped would appeal to Phoebe.

She was thrilled with my gifts, especially the hat, but Connor's upstaged all of mine. And it cost him nothing but sweat.

When the doorbell rang I insisted Phoebe answer it to greet her solitary guest. She was wearing a purple trouser suit at least twenty years old, but it still fitted her, which flattered her vanity. It looked good with her freshly cut and blow-dried hair and a new red lipstick. I'd encouraged her to buy some glamorous sandals (heels had been out of the question for years) and I'd lent her some big statement jewellery. I told my mother she looked a million dollars and I wasn't lying.

I was in the kitchen setting out champagne glasses on a tray when she called out, 'My God, it's a Strippergram!' Horrified, wondering if Connor had bribed a mate to do the honours, or worse, he was doing them himself, I rushed to the front door where a tall man in a tuxedo stood, his top half almost obscured by a bouquet of flowers.

'Sorry to disappoint you, Phoebe,' Connor said, lowering the flowers. 'It's only me. Happy birthday!'

'You've been spending money on me, haven't you? That's too bad. I gave the *strictest* instructions.'

'Not a penny. These,' he said indicating the flowers, 'are for the cook. If they happen to brighten up your sitting room a little, Phoebe, that's just a happy side effect. These flowers are most definitely for *Ann*.'

As he presented them to me, Phoebe and I stood open-mouthed, surprised less by Connor's generosity than by his transformation. He too had had his hair cut and it now formed a thick mat of curls on the top of his head, revealing neat ears and a strong, thick neck. The new style made his shoulders look broader – or maybe that was the tux. I hoped he hadn't gone to the expense of hiring it, at the same time acknowledging, if he had, it was worth every penny in entertainment value.

Phoebe took the words right out of my mouth. 'Connor, you look *gorgeous!*'

He bent his burnished head and said, 'Thank you, Phoebe. So do you. And so does Ann. I don't believe it's ever been my privilege to dine with two such beautiful and talented ladies.'

'Oh, bollocks to that,' Phoebe said. 'Come on in and give me a kiss. I'm seventy. We must make the most of what little time I have left.'

I laughed out loud, but Connor spread his arms wide and enfolded Phoebe in a hug. Looking at his face over her shoulder, I could see his pleasure was genuine. I felt both grateful and jealous.

'Champagne!' Phoebe called as she released him. 'Such lovely flowers! I think I might paint them. Ages since I did a still life. I love iris. Those blues and yellows just light up the room! So glad they were for Ann, though. I really didn't want any presents.' Phoebe didn't see Connor's eyebrows shoot up, nor the conspiratorial look he gave me.

I jerked my head in the direction of the kitchen, indicating he should follow. He nodded, then turned and escorted Phoebe to her fireside chair. Once she was settled, we went into the kitchen where I started to undo the flowers. 'Connor, you shouldn't have spent so much! You know what she said.'

'They're for *you*.' I rolled my eyes, but he protested. 'They are! I've no idea when your birthday is, so this is an early present. Or belated. Whichever . . . Happy birthday, Ann. You know, I've never seen you in a dress before. You look stunning,' he said, bending to kiss me on the cheek.

He smelled as good as he looked. 'I need some champagne,' I said faintly. 'In the fridge. Glasses over there.' As he tackled the bottle, I searched for a large vase. 'Did you already own the tux? It looks terrific.'

'It was my brother's. It fits me now I've bulked up a bit. I used to be a skinny lad, but Ivy said one day I'd probably be built like Kieran, so I should keep it. We got rid of the rest of his clothes. Very evocative things, clothes,' he added, as he filled three glasses. 'You don't realise it when people are alive, but after they've gone, you notice their clothes smell of them. I had to get this cleaned a couple of times.' Connor didn't explain why and he didn't need to.

I carried the flowers through and he followed with the champagne. Phoebe clapped her hands as we entered and beamed while we toasted her good health. Then Connor cleared his throat rather self-consciously and said, 'Ladies, would you care for an evening stroll? There's something I'd like to show you.'

'What – *now*?' Phoebe asked. She looked at me. 'Will dinner keep?'

'Oh, yes. It's mackerel pâté for starters and I haven't put the Beef Wellington in yet.'

'Isn't it getting a bit dark, though?' Phoebe asked, looking puzzled.

'We can take a torch,' Connor answered. 'And I shall lend you my arm. We shan't be going far.'

I stared at Connor, dying to know what was afoot. His smile was teasingly enigmatic.

'Should we take our glasses?' Phoebe asked.

'*Definitely*. Right, follow me, ladies. There's someone I'd like you to meet . . .'

Connor led the way through the garden with Phoebe on his arm. We all carried a glass of champagne and I brought up the rear with a torch which we didn't need while we were close to the house, but as soon as we moved away from the lighted windows, the darkness closed in.

We moved through the shrubbery in the direction of the fallen beech. I smelled sawdust and my heart began to beat faster as I tried to guess what Connor had been up to.

He stopped, turned to me and swapped his glass for the torch, which he kept directed at the ground. He took Phoebe's arm again and asked her to close her eyes, then he led her to a spot which he appeared to choose precisely. Lifting the torch, he shone it straight ahead and revealed a massive wooden face.

'You can open your eyes now, Phoebe. Happy birthday!'

The flat, cut surface of the upended tree stump had been carved and a face – a smiling, almost laughing face – peered out through sculpted foliage that formed a rampant mane framing the face, so that the creature appeared to be half-human, half-vegetation.

'My God,' Phoebe said. 'It's a Green Man!'

'Green *Woman*,' Connor corrected her. 'Look at it carefully . . . Remind you of anyone?'

Primed with the knowledge of the photographs, I'd seen the resemblance straight away, but Phoebe wasn't far behind.

'It's *me*!' she squealed. 'Ann, do you see? It's me as a Green Woman! Look at that nose. Couldn't be anyone else, could it?' She looked up at Connor and, sounding almost accusatory, said, '*You* did this?'

'Yes.'

'How?'

'Chainsaw. Chisel. Ann lent me some photos.'

Phoebe approached the face, as big as a table, and laid her hand reverently on a sharp cheekbone. 'I don't know what to say . . . And I can tell you,' she said, turning and wagging a finger at Connor, 'that's a first!'

'You don't have to say anything, Phoebe. I just hope you don't mind me vandalising your tree stump.'

'Mind? I *adore* it. To be commemorated in this way . . . as an ancient spirit of rebirth and regeneration . . . This is just *wonderful*!' She turned to us and said, 'I wish to make a libation.' She raised her glass. 'To the spirit of this venerable tree, which isn't really alive and isn't quite dead. Rather like me,' she added with a wink. 'I now bless this sculpture, this beech wood, my daughter and my friend,' she said, tipping her glass towards Connor. 'Long may they all flourish!' With that she poured champagne over the forehead of her wooden alter ego. Connor stepped forward and did likewise, saying, 'Happy birthday, Phoebe', and then I emptied mine.

'Happy birthday, Mum. May you have many more.'

We watched as the liquid trickled down over the Green Woman's brow, into her eyes and out again, as if she wept, but wept for joy.

Phoebe sniffed noisily and said, 'Well, I think we all need another drink. Several, in fact. Let's go back now and eat Ann's lovely dinner.' She reached for Connor's arm again and leaned on him, more heavily this time. He raised the torch to light the way.

I hung back to take a last look at the Green Woman. It was difficult to see much detail now. She was just a pale face looming out of the darkness, but this was no unfriendly spirit to be feared. This was just my mother, laughing in the moonlight, delighted with her new incarnation.

A good deal of food and wine was consumed, after which we subsided happily on to the sofa and armchairs. I put Phoebe's favourite Cole Porter CD on and we sat in companionable silence. I thought she was too exhausted to talk, but Phoebe surfaced to say, 'I've had *such* a lovely time . . . Lovely food, lovely wine, lovely company – and as for my presents! So very thoughtful, both of you. Thank you so much. And when I think I said I didn't want to celebrate . . . You know what? I'd like to do it all over again! I wouldn't even mind braving that idiot hairdresser again. And I could certainly drink all the champagne again. One birthday is not enough,' she announced. 'Not when they're this much fun. Wouldn't it be nice to have *two* birthdays, like the Queen!'

'Ivy had two birthdays,' Connor said. 'But she only celebrated one.'

'Your Ivy?'

'Yes. Her official birthday – the one she celebrated – was the ninth of February. But if you look in the Hatherwick family Bible, you'll see it's recorded as October sixth the previous year.'

'How very odd.'

'Do you know how the confusion arose?' I asked.

'Not really. Ivy said the Bible was wrong, but no one liked to correct it. Hester told her it was Violet's mistake. She was the one who recorded the Hatherwick "hatched, matched and despatched", but for some reason she was way out with Ivy's birth.'

'That's very odd,' I said, considering. 'How do we know it was Violet who was wrong?'

'Hester showed Ivy the entry in her own journal recording the birth.'

Phoebe frowned and shook her head. 'How could Violet have made a mistake like that?'

'Maybe she was ill. Puerperal fever or something. Women had a rough time of it in those days, didn't they?'

I leaned back in my chair and closed my eyes, struggling to make sense of the latest piece of the puzzle. 'Was October the sixth someone else's birthday? William's? Or Hester's?'

'No, not as far as I recall.'

'So why on earth did Violet get it wrong?'

'Search me.'

'Well, much as I like Hester,' Phoebe said, 'I think that was out of order, insisting she was right and Violet was wrong. I should think a mother would know when her own child was born!'

I opened my eyes and sat bolt upright. It was as if Phoebe's last words had flipped a switch in my brain, turning on a light. 'She *would*, wouldn't she . . . ? I think Ivy's mother *was* right.'

'So why did Hester get it wrong?'

'She didn't.'

Connor and Phoebe looked at each other, then stared at me, their faces blank.

'You've lost me,' Connor said. 'Why did *Violet* get it wrong then?'

'She didn't.'

'Oh, don't be maddening, Ann!' Phoebe said, losing patience. 'Whatever do you mean?'

'There were two babies.'

'*What?*' Connor and Phoebe spoke in unison.

'There must have been *two*. Violet and Hester both gave birth, one in October and one the following February.'

After a stunned silence, Connor was the first to catch on. 'And one of the babies must have *died*,' he whispered, his eyes shining. 'Hester's, I suppose. Then for some reason she adopted Violet's baby . . . then gave her the birthday of her own child.'

I shook my head. 'No, that wouldn't have worked. There's a discrepancy of four months in the dates. I think *Violet's* baby died in October and I presume she didn't tell anyone. Perhaps it was a late miscarriage or more probably a stillbirth. It must have been for her to record it in the Bible.'

'So you're saying Violet lost her baby and recorded the day of its birth – and death – in the family Bible?' Phoebe said. 'Meanwhile *Hester* was still pregnant – pregnant with a child she would later adopt!'

'Perhaps that was the real reason Hester shut up Beechgrave,' Connor said. 'She was pregnant and needed to go into seclusion.'

'Of course! And her mad mother wouldn't have noticed what was going on!' Phoebe announced. 'The two young women must have hatched a plot to pass off Ivy as Violet's child. Extraordinary!'

'So Violet would have had to fake pregnancy until Ivy was born. That would be easy enough, I suppose,' Connor said. 'But why did she agree to it?'

'Money? Or gratitude perhaps. Hester didn't turn her out when she discovered she was pregnant. Violet was working up at the big house by then, looking after Mrs Mordaunt. And who else could she have turned to but Hester? Her father was dead; William was away fighting. Maybe the father of her baby was also away at the Front. Is a father named on Ivy's birth certificate?' I asked, looking at Connor.

'No.'

'Very likely killed, then.'

'So, let me get this straight,' Phoebe said carefully. 'You think Violet was so grateful for Hester's support, she was prepared to pose as Ivy's mother in order to save Hester from disgrace.'

'Well, that's my theory, but I think there could have been another, more personal reason.' Phoebe and Connor looked at me expectantly. 'Hester's baby was Violet's niece.'

'William's child!' Phoebe exclaimed.

'Who else? No man features in Hester's diary after Walter's death. But it's full of William. She promoted him in his absence. She fetched him home from hospital. And don't forget the love letters we found in the biscuit tin. Written on *seed packets*. Addressed to *My dear H* and signed *W*.'

'You know, there's probably a way to prove all this,' Connor said, getting up from the sofa and going to the corner of the sitting room where we kept the box of archive material. 'If you're right, Ann, William must have been home on leave about nine months before Ivy's birth date, the one Hester gave her.' He took out a volume of Hester's journal and started leafing through the pages. 'Got a calendar?'

I jumped up from my chair and almost ran to the kitchen where I grabbed the calendar. As I returned, Phoebe beckoned me to come and sit beside her on the sofa. 'Quick, quick, quick! I can't stand the suspense! Count back forty weeks from – what was it, Connor? February the ninth?'

'No, Mum, it's thirty-eight weeks from conception. Trust me, I know about these things.'

Phoebe threw an arm round my shoulders and squeezed. Flipping over calendar pages, we counted back the weeks, then had to refer to the small printed box of last year's calendar.

I looked up at Connor, whose tall, waiting form loomed over us, his face eager. 'If Hester's baby went to term and William was the father, he must have been home on leave around the end of May or the first week of June, 1916.'

'He arrived home on the twenty-fourth of May,' Connor said, his eyes shining. 'And on May the twenty-seventh Hester wrote, *Something has happened that never should have happened. Something terrible. I am lost, quite lost.*'

Phoebe let out a jubilant cry and hugged me. 'Oh, you clever, clever girl! Isn't she marvellous, Connor?'

'Yes . . . Yes, she is.' He shut the journal and lifted a large hand to watery eyes. Wiping them, he said, 'I don't suppose you have another bottle, do you, Ann? I think I'd like to raise a glass to my great-grandmother. My *real* great-grandmother. To Hester Mordaunt . . . God bless her.'

HESTER

July 13th, 1917

I have been much occupied with plans for the new Beechgrave Convalescent Hospital and the task of engaging suitable staff has left me little leisure to write my journal. However, I have made some important decisions which affect the lives of several souls at Beechgrave and I wish to record the circumstances that led to them.

Violet has for some time pleaded with me to be allowed to return to live at Garden Lodge so she can care for her brother. William is in good physical health, apart from being a little hard of hearing. However, he is very troubled mentally. His attacks of melancholia, though intermittent, are severe. According to Violet, the worst problem is his nightmares in which he appears to relive his terrible experiences on the Somme battlefield.

Matters came to a head when William handed her their father's shotgun and asked her to keep it here at Beechgrave. He gave no reason for this request and Violet says none was needed. She believes he is in danger of taking his own life.

William's sense of isolation must be acute. He lives alone and still remembers nothing at all about his life before he was wounded in France. He is not mentally fit to return to the Front, yet feels he should be 'doing his bit', even though he is in charge of food production here at Beechgrave – vital employment now.

Violet is very concerned. She suspects William is not eating properly and thinks she should be present in the house at night, when his attacks are most likely to occur. I suspect she wishes to make sure he is locked in overnight. We know he walks around the grounds when he cannot sleep – I have seen him from my bedroom window when I too am similarly afflicted – and Violet thinks he shows an unhealthy interest in the lake for a man who cannot swim.

I can spare Violet, but I should miss little Ivy a great deal. I also question the wisdom of removing an infant from her home to take her to live with someone prone to nocturnal fits of screaming and sobbing. I cannot think Ivy will thrive under such conditions and Violet does not disagree. It would surely be better for Ivy to continue to live at Beechgrave with daily visits from Violet. I have no reservations about this arrangement since Violet and I have shared Ivy's care since she was a baby.

I wish to do all I can to support the Hatherwicks and keep the family together. It has been a source of consolation to Violet – and to me – that Ivy has a loving uncle determined to be as good as a father to her. To see William, himself so weak and vulnerable, cradle that little child has been one of my chief joys. I will never deprive them of each other's company, but I believe the best thing for Ivy would be for me to become her legal guardian. I shall never marry now and have no relative likely to outlive me. I should therefore like to make Ivy my heir by formally adopting her and giving her my name. In the event of my dying before Ivy reaches her majority, the Hatherwicks would become joint guardians. I shall make financial provision for all of them.

I intend to stipulate these conditions in my will and I do not expect Violet to raise any objection. She knows how much I love Ivy and I am sure she will be relieved to know that the child will be provided for, for life. I have therefore made an appointment to discuss these matters with the family solicitor. I anticipate surprise, disapproval and idle assurances that I might yet marry, even though the few able-bodied men who survive the war will have their pick of young, healthy, even wealthy women. I am twenty-five and under no such illusions, nor do I care to marry. The Hatherwicks are the only family I have now apart from Mother, who on her worst days has no idea who I am and addresses me as if I were one of the servants we dismissed in 1916.

Mother is living in the past and so, for much of the time, is William, but Violet and I must look to the future. Ivy's future.

CONNOR

'Should we wake her?' Connor said, looking down at the dark curly head resting on his shoulder.

'No, she looks perfectly comfortable. Let her sleep,' Phoebe said. 'The poor girl's shattered. She's been cooking and cleaning all day and she hardly sleeps at night.'

Connor looked up. 'Chronic insomnia, she says. And sometimes she sleepwalks.'

'Really?' He lowered his voice. 'Is there something on her mind?'

'I suppose so.'

'Do you know what's bothering her?'

'No idea. Is that bottle really empty?' she asked abruptly.

Connor smiled. 'It was the last time you asked me. I'll say this for you, Phoebe, you can certainly hold your liquor.'

'Oh, pain keeps me sober,' she grumbled. 'The amount I've put away tonight would fell the average woman, but the first bottle just takes the edge off for me. After a few more drinks, I'm ready to party!'

Ann stirred and Connor looked down at her again. 'She should be in bed.'

'No, don't disturb her. Let her sleep on the sofa. Come and sit over here,' Phoebe said, tossing him a rug. 'And cover her with that. The fire's dying down now. She might wake if she gets chilly.'

Connor struggled out from under the dead weight of Ann's sleeping body and lowered her gently on to the sofa. He removed her shoes, lifted her feet up, then covered her with the rug, tucking it in around her.

Settling into an armchair, Connor said, 'Do you know the present I would really have liked to give you, Phoebe?'

'No, what? What could possibly top that brilliant carving? I can't wait to get out there in daylight to have another look at it.'

'What I really wanted you to have was one pain-free day. One day when you could throw your stick away and stand and paint all day.'

'Well, that's jolly decent of you, but do you know, given the choice of one pain-free day and the Green Woman, I'd take the Green Woman – no question! That will last and give me pleasure for years. As for painting . . . Well, I *can* still do it. I'm an old hand and I know how to cut corners. Cheat honourably. But there's little joy in it now.' She sighed. 'Painting was never easy for me – it's damned hard work! – but the struggle used to be worth it. I had faith in the enterprise, it wasn't just about *endurance* . . . But today,' she said, brightening, 'has been about lots of other things. And all so exciting! That news about Hester . . . ' Phoebe whistled. 'It knocked you sideways, didn't it?'

'It did. When I began this research, I didn't think there'd be any big revelations for *me*. I'm still struggling to take it all in. We've got no proof, of course, but it all adds up.'

'Do you think finding out Hester was her mother was what tipped Ivy over the edge?'

'I don't think so. How could she have found out after all that time? There's no clue in the archive. Hester even lied in her diary, so I think she would have covered her tracks pretty thoroughly.'

'Maybe there *was* something, but it got destroyed in the fire.'

'Well, even if there was, why would Ivy start a bonfire? She *loved* Hester. She owed her comfortable upbringing and her career to Hester, who paid for her training.'

Phoebe narrowed her eyes. 'Clutching at straws here . . . Maybe she was angry that the blood relationship was never acknowledged?'

'That's possible, but Ivy must have realised she hadn't missed out in any real way. After all, Hester made Ivy her heir. If she did discover the truth at the eleventh hour, I don't see why she'd have wanted to destroy the evidence, not to mention the rest of the archive.'

'So the mystery remains unsolved.'

'Afraid so. In fact, it just got more complicated.' Ann stirred again on the sofa and a little moan escaped her lips. 'I think we're disturbing her,' Connor whispered. 'Perhaps I'd better get back to the servants' quarters.'

'Oh, no, must you? This is such fun! Stay and have some cocoa.'

Connor raised an eyebrow. 'Late night cocoa, eh? I've heard about women like you.'

Phoebe snorted with laughter, then clamped her hand over her mouth. 'Come on,' she whispered. 'Let's adjourn to the kitchen and leave Ann to sleep in peace. Cocoa calls.'

Seated at the kitchen table, nursing her mug, Phoebe said, 'Why are you so obsessed with the past, Connor?'

'I'm not really, I'm obsessed with family. *My* family. But my family are all dead, so I don't actually have a family any more. And I'm unlikely ever to have another.'

'Why do you say that? You're young. You might be *head* of the family now—'

'More like last man standing,' he said with a wry smile.

'Indeed. But there's no reason why you shouldn't found a new dynasty of Grenvilles.'

Connor shifted in his chair. 'Actually, there *is*.'

'Oh dear . . .' Phoebe set down her mug. 'Have I put my great big foot in it?'

'No, I don't mind talking about it. Especially with someone who might understand what I'm talking about.'

'Are you sure? It won't have escaped your notice that I'm not the most tactful of people.'

He laughed. 'Yes, I had noticed! It's one of the things I like about you, Phoebe. You take no prisoners.'

'That's because bloody cancer took me prisoner years ago,' she growled. 'What people don't realise is that even if you're cured, it's still a life sentence. A life sentence of fear and in some cases, a life sentence of after effects.'

'Yes, I know.' There was something about the way he said the words that made Phoebe look up and search his face. Connor met her eyes and said, 'I *do* know, Phoebe. You remember when you talked about the children who kept you going? Kids having chemo? Well, that was me. They saved my life when I was seven, but I'll never have children of my own and I've always known that. It's never really bothered me, but when my brother was killed, Dad was doubly heartbroken. We lost Kieran – who was engaged to a lovely girl, very keen to start a family – and Dad lost his future grandchildren. He was left with me – the runt of the litter and a waste of space as far as he was concerned. I didn't even want to be a soldier.'

'Oh, Connor, I'm so sorry . . . I'm kicking myself now for going on and on about my problems. Me and my big mouth!'

'Don't apologise. You have every right to talk about what happened to you. You're still suffering the after effects.'

'So are you. No children . . . That can be a very big thing in a man's life, as I know to my cost.'

'Sylvester?'

'He wanted a big family. He was Madeiran. Family was sacred to him. I lived with the pain of a man who desperately wanted children and eventually I gave in.' Phoebe reached across the table and laid a hand on Connor's arm. 'Don't underestimate what you've been through. Children unborn, unthought of . . . they can still have a powerful effect on the mind.'

'I'm not going to argue with you, Phoebe.'

'But, you never know, you might marry a woman with children. You might *acquire* a family.'

'I might, but it's not something I want. Not consciously anyway. I've known the score since I was a teenager, so I've never even thought about being a father. I found it tough enough just being a son.' He stared gloomily into his mug, then set it down. 'A family is something I know I can't have and probably couldn't afford. But as I got older, I thought a lot about my own family. My roots.'

'Perhaps it was because you went into horticulture,' Phoebe said, smiling at her own pun.

'Yes. The *other* family business, apart from war. Did I tell you, Ivy trained at one of the first horticultural schools to admit women? She was very proud of that. We had a lot in common: a love of gardens and a consuming curiosity about the past, who we were, where we'd come from. When she died, there was unfinished business and I want to get to the bottom of it if I can – not just for Ivy, for me. I want to get to grips with the past.'

'Can one ever really do that?' Phoebe asked softly. 'Can't say I've had much success in that department.'

'Well, the past is *past*. It's known. I mean, it can't *change*, can it? But the present and future . . . Well, who knows? I'm not anxious about my future. I'll take what comes. When you've been that sick as a child, you grow up quickly and learn to count your blessings. But I suppose it's my tidy nature. I like to clear things up. Gardens. Family trees. Disorder bugs me. Meaninglessness bothers me. I know why my brother died, but what did he die *for*? Did his death make a difference to anyone apart from his family and his mates in the army? I don't know. Don't suppose I'll ever know. So I look for meaning, for cause and effect. And I continue in my valiant and probably doomed efforts to subjugate Nature,' he said with a cheerful grin, 'because I need order. I need to feel as if I have some control, even though I learned when I was very young that we don't, we really don't. Control is just an illusion. Your own body can turn on you and your big brother can be blown to bits, just doing his job. So I like to create something out of nothing. A garden from a wilderness. I also like answers. Solutions to mysteries. Stories that have a beginning, a middle and an end.' He leaned back, clasped his hands behind his head and sighed. 'Did that make any sense at *all*?'

'Perfect sense,' Phoebe said, nodding vigorously. 'Have you talked to Ann about all this?'

'No.'

'You should.'

'Why?'

'Because it's her issue too. She's not childless by choice, you know. She and Jack tried for years. Tried everything. She was prepared to adopt, but he wouldn't hear of it. Wanted his own flesh and blood. And now that's what he's got – which must make Ann feel even worse, I should imagine.'

'She doesn't talk about it?'

'Not to me. But then I've never been the kind of mother a daughter could confide in. Too wound up in my own selfish concerns. Ann's a *much* nicer person than me. Takes after her father. She accepted the limitations life imposed on her. I didn't. I was greedy. I wanted it *all*.'

'And did you have it all, Phoebe?'

'Most of it! But other people sometimes paid the price for my fun and games. And for my career. I was no good as a wife or mother, no good at all. But I think I was quite a good artist. For a single parent, anyway.'

'Was? You still are, surely? Don't talk about yourself as a has-been. Who knows, maybe the best is yet to come.'

'Which reminds me . . . Are you still drunk enough to agree to sit for a portrait? I want to paint you. Be warned though – it's hard physical work being a model and I'm a tyrant. I go on and on until I get what I want.'

'How can I refuse? Sounds like it will be a laugh a minute.'

'Thank you! But don't think I'll have forgotten by the morning. Your fate is sealed, I'm afraid.'

'I won't have to take my clothes off, will I?'

'You can if you wish, but I shall only be painting your face.'

'You're on.'

'Excellent! Now, I'm off to bed. I need my beauty sleep. You can let yourself out, can't you?'

'Of course. Will Ann be all right on the sofa?'

'Oh, yes, I should think so. Best not to disturb her.' As Phoebe struggled to her feet, Connor stood up to assist her. She laid a hand on his arm and said, 'Do me a favour, will you, Connor? Keep an eye on Ann. She's . . . unsettled. Unhappy, I think. Not sure why . . . It could be something to do with this divorce business, I suppose. But I'd like to think there's someone else looking out for her.'

'Of course. You can count on me.'

She patted his hand. 'I know I can. Thank you for a wonderful birthday.'

'It's been my pleasure, Phoebe.' He bent and kissed her on the cheek. 'Sleep well.'

'Oh, I shall, don't worry. I shall take one of my magic pills. I just hope Ann sleeps too. She really needs it.'

'I'll leave a lamp on in the sitting room, so she knows where she is if she wakes, then I'll let myself out. 'Night, Phoebe.'

'Good night, Connor.' She turned away and began the slow and painful climb up the stairs.

When, some time later, Connor woke, he had the distinct impression there was someone in the studio with him. His heart juddered, then common sense reasserted itself. Sitting up, he called out, 'Phoebe? Is that you? Is something wrong?' When no one answered, he tried – more in hope than expectation – 'Ann?'

As his eyes grew accustomed to the darkness, he noticed a pale face at the window, looking in. Startled, he clutched at the duvet before he realised it was Ann, solemn-faced, hollow-eyed, regarding him. Wrapping the duvet round him for warmth and decency, Connor got out of bed and approached the window. Ann didn't react, didn't appear even to see him. Turning away, she set off across the courtyard in the direction of the beech wood.

Connor shuffled over to the studio door. Pulling it open, he called out, 'Ann, are you okay?' She didn't look back. Even before he registered the pale soles of her stockinged feet in the moonlight, he realised she was sleepwalking, with no coat or cardigan over her sleeveless dress.

Connor cast the duvet aside and hurried back to the chair where he'd left his work clothes. He pulled on a pair of jeans and a sweatshirt, then slid his bare feet into wellingtons. Grabbing the torch Ann kept under the sink, he raced out of the studio, slamming the door behind him. He ran through the garden, looking to left and right, but a gut feeling told him Ann would be heading for the clearing in the wood that had so disturbed her, the spot where the Trysting Tree once stood and where all that was left of it now lay.

That was where he found her, apparently staring into space. Ignoring the carved tree stump, Ann gazed higher, where the tree had once stood. She stood still for several moments, trembling. Connor wondered if she was just shivering with cold or if she was in the grip of fear again. He was about to approach when she wheeled round suddenly and began to walk away, very quickly, towards Connor who was watching from a distance. Oblivious to his presence, Ann broke into a run and would have collided with him, had he not side-stepped out of her path.

Connor was so surprised, it was a few seconds before he started to run after her, calling her name. He couldn't remember if it was dangerous to wake a sleepwalker or if that was just one of Ivy's old wives' tales, but he knew Ann wasn't safe running blind, so he ran and overtook her, turned and then blocked her way. She ran straight into him.

He dropped the torch and enfolded her flailing body in his arms. Holding her firmly, he spoke in a calm, even voice, as if trying to soothe a child. He could see her feet were muddy and bleeding where stones and tree roots had ripped her tights, then her skin. When she stopped struggling, he said evenly, 'You've hurt your feet. They need attention. I'm going to carry you back to the house, okay?'

Ann gave no sign of understanding his words, but allowed him to lift her chilled body without protest. Settling her securely in his arms, he strode back towards Garden Lodge where he found the back door standing open. Light from the sitting room spilled into the dark kitchen.

As he entered the house, he kicked off his wellingtons, then carried her in and set her down on the sofa. He grabbed a newspaper and put it under her bleeding feet, then arranged the discarded rug round her shaking shoulders. The stove was still alight, so he opened the door and threw on another log. He turned to look at Ann and said, 'I'll be back in a minute.' She stared into space, white-faced and unresponsive.

Connor hurried back to the kitchen where he filled the washing-up bowl with warm, soapy water. While the tap was running, he opened cupboards looking for a first aid kit. He thought of calling out to

Phoebe, then remembered she'd taken a sleeping pill. He locked the back door, pocketed the key, then took the stairs two at a time.

In the bathroom he found plasters and a fleece dressing gown hanging on the door. He picked them up and thundered downstairs again.

When Connor entered the sitting room carrying the washing-up bowl, with a towel over his arm, a pink dressing gown slung over his shoulder and a box of Elastoplast in his mouth, Ann looked up, alarmed. 'Connor! What on earth is going on?'

Relieved to see some colour back in her face, he set the bowl on the floor and removed the plasters from his mouth. 'This is for your feet. You need to wash them.'

She looked down at her shredded tights. 'Oh my God, what happened?' she said, lifting her muddy feet off the newspaper. 'They're *bleeding!*'

'You went walkabout outdoors. I found you sleepwalking in the beech wood. Phoebe and I left you in here, fast asleep on the sofa. We didn't want to disturb you. You'd dozed off leaning on me hours ago. I don't suppose you remember.' He offered her the dressing gown. 'Put this on. You're frozen.'

'We drank champagne . . . It's Phoebe's birthday, isn't it? But I saw someone in the wood,' she added, shivering violently.

'The Green Woman. It was my present for Phoebe.'

'Oh yes . . . But there was someone else. Wasn't there?' She looked confused and Connor could see she was close to tears.

'I didn't see anyone, but I think *you* did. Or thought you did. Come on, get your feet into this water while it's still hot,' he said pushing the bowl towards her.

Ann ripped what was left of her tights away from her feet and placed one foot gingerly in the water, then the other. 'You say I *saw* something?'

'No, there was nothing to see. You just stood there, staring into space. You seemed calm enough to begin with, then you took fright and ran away. I followed and grabbed hold of you. I was worried you'd put an eye out running through the wood in the dark.'

'*Dark?* But in my mind it was *light*. Almost light anyway. It was morning.'

'Can you remember what made you run?'

She was silent for a moment, then her face crumpled. 'No, I can't!'

'Do you think it's something you've dreamed up? Or was it something that actually happened?'

'I don't know! How *can* I know, Connor? Stop asking me all these stupid questions!' she said, burying her face in her hands.

'Sorry. I was just trying to help.'

She reached out and grasped his hand. 'I know you are. I'm sorry. I'm just . . . frightened. And I don't even know what I'm frightened of.'

'Nothing can harm you, Ann. You've got me and Phoebe looking out for you. What's the worst that can happen?'

'My memory could come back.'

For a while he didn't reply, then he said gently, 'You think that's what this is about? Something bad actually happened – but so bad, you wiped it?'

'I think so.'

'And you think your memory's coming back?'

'Yes. Something is getting closer. Creeping up on me. It's as if I'm being stalked by my own memory.' She covered her face. 'Is this what it feels like when you're losing your mind? Please help me, Connor. I can't bear it!'

He dropped on to his knees in front of her and she launched herself at him, throwing her arms round his neck, her feet still immersed in the bowl of water. She clung to him, sobbing, so he held her until she was calm again, then he reached for a box of tissues and placed it beside her.

She grabbed a handful and began to mop up. 'I'm sorry to blub all over you like this.'

'Don't worry about it.'

'I haven't slept in days. Well, not properly for a couple of weeks now.'

'Yes, Phoebe said.'

'So I suppose I must be overwrought.'

'I imagine so.'

'Now I've started sleepwalking, everything seems so much worse. I'm afraid to go to sleep. Phoebe offered to lock me in my room, but I can't bear the thought of being trapped . . . And with these thoughts!'

'I have a suggestion to make. Just for tonight.' Ann looked up, her eyes so full of apprehension, Connor wanted to hold her again. Instead he lifted her feet out of the water and started to pat them dry with the towel. 'Now, don't go getting the wrong idea here, but what I suggest is, you allow me to stay in your room, with the door locked and the key in my pocket. If you've got a spare duvet, I'll kip on the floor, but don't worry if you haven't. I can sleep anywhere.' He opened the box of plasters, extracted a few and began to apply them to the cuts on her feet. 'You won't be able to get out, but hopefully you won't feel too bad about that because you won't be alone. Chances are, you'll go out like a light as soon as you get into bed after all your nocturnal wanderings. You might actually get a good night's sleep – well, what's left of the night. What do you think?'

'I think you're kindness itself, Connor. And your kindness makes me feel very guilty. And rather foolish.'

'Oh. That wasn't the idea. I was hoping you'd feel reassured. Protected.'

'I do.'

'Good! So it's settled then?'

'Yes. It's settled.' As he applied a final plaster, she said, 'There's just one thing, though.'

'What's that?'

'I'm not letting you sleep on the floor.'

'It's not a problem. I really don't mind.'

'But I do. I want you in the bed. Please.'

'Oh. I see . . .' Connor blinked several times, then a slow smile spread across his face. 'Right, that's absolutely fine, because I also want you in the bed. No – don't get up. You're not walking on those feet, not after all the trouble I've taken with those plasters. I'm carrying you upstairs, no arguments.' He bent down and slipped one arm round her waist and the other under her knees. 'Put your arms round my neck and hold tight.'

He swung her up into the air and as he did so, she giggled. Exhausted now, Ann rested her head on his chest. By the time they reached the top of the stairs, she was almost asleep. Connor laid her down gently on the bed and, as she stirred, he whispered, 'You're sure now?'

'Oh yes. I'm sure.' She propped herself up on one elbow and watched him undress. 'My goodness, that didn't take long. Only two garments?'

'I got dressed in a hurry when I saw you heading for the wood.'

She got off the bed and turned her back to him so he could unzip her dress. As she wriggled out of it, he said, 'I forgot – I need to lock us in.' He strode over to the door, turned the key and removed it from the lock.

Slipping under the duvet, Ann laughed as she regarded him. 'Well, there's nowhere you can hide it on your person.'

'Close your eyes. I'm going to hide it somewhere secret so you won't be able to get out.'

'Don't worry, I won't be going anywhere. My feet hurt too much to walk. In any case, here is where I want to be. And *here*,' she said, throwing back the duvet and patting the mattress, 'is where I want *you* to be. Hurry up, Connor, before I fall asleep.'

Tossing the key into a corner of the room, he covered the floor in two strides. 'There'll be no sleeping on my watch. Not for a while anyway.'

She giggled again and took him in her open arms.

It was not the last of the laughter.

ANN

When I woke Connor was gone. It was very light and I knew I must have slept late into the morning. As the events of the previous night came back to me, I felt disappointed that I'd woken alone, until common sense reasserted itself and I realised Connor had wanted to spare me embarrassment. *He* might have withstood a ribbing from Phoebe, but he knew I wouldn't have taken it so well. He'd no doubt risen early and returned discreetly to the studio.

As I sat up in bed, I registered aches and tenderness in various parts of my body. Accounting for them wasn't difficult, apart from the soreness of my feet. Swinging my legs out of bed, I examined them and remembered Connor administering first aid, then I remembered why he'd had to do it. I lay down again and hauled the duvet back over me, wishing Connor hadn't left me to start the day alone.

The sound of lively voices drifted up the stairs, along with the aroma of frying bacon. Suddenly hungry, for bacon and the sight of Connor, I got up, showered and dressed quickly, then went downstairs to the kitchen.

'Ah, you've decided to join us at last! Connor, slice some more bread and I'll shove a few more rashers in the pan. Did you sleep well, Ann? I assume you must have done, lying in till this hour.'

Phoebe's cheerful prattle eased my embarrassment at seeing Connor again. He gave me no special look, nor did he avoid my eye. It was clearly business as usual, but I still felt at a loss, not knowing what he might have told Phoebe about my sleepwalking.

As I limped over to the table, Connor quickly pulled out a chair for me and I was able to sit before Phoebe noticed I was having trouble walking. He poured me coffee, set the mug in front of me and said, 'You slept, then.'

It wasn't a question because he knew I had. Eventually.

'Yes, I did, thank you.' I looked him in the eye. 'I had a wonderful night. The best in a very long time.'

His expression remained serene. 'Must have been all that champagne.'

'I always say champagne cures whatever ails you,' Phoebe said, chipping in. 'And if it *doesn't*, well, you're probably past saving.' She dished up the bacon on to a plate, then handed it to Connor, who deposited it in the middle of the table. 'Tuck in! This is brain fodder, Ann. Connor and I were in the middle of an investigation,' Phoebe said, pouring coffee and splashing some on to the table in her clumsy excitement, 'and frankly, we need your help. You're the one with the brains.'

'Thanks,' Connor mumbled, his mouth full of bacon sandwich.

'We need to put *all* our heads together because we're actually no nearer to solving the Mordaunt mystery, despite the shocking events of last night.'

I looked up at Connor, alarmed, wondering what my mother knew. He held my eyes, shook his head almost imperceptibly, then said, 'I take it, Phoebe, you're referring to the identity of my great-grandfather.'

'Yes, of course! There's so much more to think about now we know about William. The plot thickens!' Phoebe said with relish.

'Okay, fill me in then,' I said, relieved to be able to focus on the details of a hundred-year-old love affair. It meant I could postpone thinking about Connor and the incident that had finally brought us together. 'What do we know about Hester and William in later life?'

'The information's patchy,' Connor said. 'Mostly hearsay. If Hester kept any diaries, they're missing.'

'Missing, presumed burned?'

'Yes. There was just one fire-damaged journal covering a period in the 1920s. It was half-burned and not a single complete page was legible, so I got rid of it. It stank the place out.'

'Do we know how William died?'

'TB. Ivy said he died in a sanatorium, but he'd been ill for many years. It wasn't just his mind that was affected by his experiences in the trenches. His lungs and hearing were damaged too. Hester's health also declined after William's death, but if he was the love of her life, that adds up.'

'Poor old Hester,' Phoebe said, shaking her head. 'She saw an awful lot of death, didn't she? Far too much.'

'It must have taken its toll,' Connor admitted. 'She lost most of her family during the war, then her mother and Violet died in the Spanish flu epidemic.'

'No!' Phoebe was aghast. '*Both* of them?'

'Afraid so. After the war Spanish flu killed more people than the Black Death. So by 1919 Hester's only connections with her past were William and little Ivy. She sold the Beechgrave estate in various parcels during the 1920s, but retained some of the houses on the estate. She and Ivy lived in one and William stayed on as a tenant at Garden Lodge with a housekeeper to care for him after Violet died. Eventually, Hester paid for his care in a sanatorium.'

'Maybe she sold Beechgrave to pay for his care,' Phoebe suggested.

'That's possible. Ivy assumed Hester's generosity stemmed from her affection for the Hatherwick family. She had no idea her adoptive mother – as she thought – was caring for a dying lover.'

'So we're pretty much dependent on what Ivy told you about her family,' I said, clarifying. 'There's little documentary evidence left.'

'That's right, apart from the odd letter or photo that survived the fire.'

'Did William ever get his memory back?'

'Yes, a few days before he died. Well, that's when he told Hester he finally remembered everything. I think memories might have been coming back to him for some time,' Connor said, with a glance at me. 'But Ivy always said he got his memory back after she sent him a letter.'

'After *Ivy* sent a letter?'

'Yes. Hester apparently gave her all the credit for restoring William's memory.'

'What was the letter about?'

'Gardening.'

'*Gardening?* Phoebe exclaimed.

Connor shrugged. 'That's what she said. She was away at college, just a kid, only seventeen or so. She wouldn't have been discussing his war experiences, not in 1934.'

I shook my head, puzzled. 'I find it hard to believe Ivy would have destroyed the letter – *her* letter – that brought William's memory back.'

'At the time of her death, Ivy was apparently trying to destroy *everything*,' Connor said grimly.

We all fell silent. The bacon sandwiches were finished and the coffee pot was empty. Connor and Phoebe looked at me expectantly and I suddenly felt overwhelmed with tiredness. Then my mother did an odd thing. She reached across the table and took my hand. Squeezing it, she smiled and said, 'Come on, Ann! We're counting on you. Aren't we, Connor?' she added, nudging him with her elbow.

He looked at me then, the veil of circumspection cast aside. 'I really appreciate what you've done for me, Ann, but you can quit any time.'

'No, she can't! What are you saying? I want this mystery solved before I pop my clogs,' Phoebe said, rapping the table.

'Shhh, Mum! Let me think. God, the *pressure*,' I said with a smile at Connor. 'So, to summarise . . . We're certain it was a letter from *Ivy* that restored William's memory? *All* of it?'

'That's what she said.'

'Then he must have remembered what Hester meant to him before the war . . . He must have realised they'd lost *years*.'

'Seventeen,' Connor said. 'And all because Hester never spoke of their love.'

'Yet somehow a letter from *Ivy* brought everything back . . .'

We sat in silence again, contemplating the wasted, loveless years William and Hester had endured, then another thought struck me.

'Connor, do you remember that jolly letter with the inkblots? Ivy's first letter home from college, wasn't it? We wondered why she'd sent a tear-stained letter home, especially as she didn't seem particularly homesick. I wonder . . . Perhaps those weren't *her* tears.'

Connor frowned. 'Whose could they be?'

'I'm wondering if they were William's.'

WILLIAM

October 2nd, 1934

When the latest fit of coughing had subsided, William sat up in his hospital bed, his head thrown back, gasping for breath. His heart pounded as if it would burst out of the frail vessel that contained it and he laid a hand on his bony chest to calm it, as he might have quietened a fretful child. Never one to dwell on regrets or opportunities missed, William pushed away the fleeting but familiar thought that, if he'd had his own child, he might have loved it even more than he loved his niece – though he could scarce imagine how, since he was sure he loved Ivy as if she were indeed his own child.

He rallied at the thought of Ivy and reached for her recent letter which he kept to hand on the bedside table with the books and newspapers brought by Hester, with which he whiled away the tedious hours of an invalid's day.

Fumbling with the envelope, William extracted the two sheets covered in Ivy's untidy handwriting and began to smile, anticipating the pleasure of rereading her cheerful words. He sat back and perused the letter again.

Waterbury Horticultural School
Wheatley
Oxon.

September 30th, 1934

Dear Uncle Will,
Hurrah! I have now completed my first two weeks'
training and thought you might like to hear what I've
been up to.

If you saw me in my uniform, you'd hoot with
laughter. It's certainly going to take some getting used
to. Students and teachers, all female, work side by side
wearing identical uniform: green breeches with green
knee stockings (very itchy), shirts buttoned right up to
the neck, with a tie and a green smock over the top. We
look a sight, but the clothes are very practical.

This week we picked bushels of apples and pears and
stored them. We learned about the care and use of tools
and collected leaf mould from the woods. (Oh, how I miss
our beech wood!) We also potted early strawberries, mostly
King George and The Duke.

One of the jolliest jobs was bunching asters for the
Saturday market in Swindon. We took sandwiches and
tea in a Thermos and set out our stall selling cut flowers,
fruit, rooted cuttings and flower seedlings in boxes –
forget-me-nots, pansies and primulas. We sold all our
stock and could have sold the fruit twice over!

I struggle to rise early, but you'll be pleased to hear
I haven't yet been late for breakfast, which is delicious.
Porridge with cream, followed by fish or sausages, eggs
and all the bread and marmalade you can eat. I also

drink a gallon of tea. I find I'm always hungry and thirsty here. It must be all the fresh air and hard work.

Now I must ask your advice, Uncle Will, because I have an essay to write. It concerns the construction of a rockery for a town garden. I must choose twelve suitable plants. I've already made my selection but I wondered which you would have chosen? I want well-behaved plants that will not overrun a modest plot within a few years. Do let me know your thoughts so I can compare your no doubt superior selection with mine.

It's been a tiring day, so I will close now, sending love to you and Hester. I miss you both dreadfully and must confess I've shed a few tears late at night when all the others are fast asleep. But don't worry about me, I shall soon get used to my new life. I'm too busy to be miserable for long. Thinking about how many sausages I shall consume at breakfast cheers me up no end!

I do hope your health is no worse. I look forward to a little letter from you soon, if you can manage it. In the meantime, I shall continue to work hard. I'm determined to make you and Hester very proud of me.

All love,

Ivy

When he'd finished reading, William glanced at the date of the letter and decided he should reply. Ivy was waiting for a response to her query and in any case, it would be a pleasure – albeit a tiring one – to write. When a nurse brought him some tea, he asked her to set notepaper and an envelope on the table by the window, left wide open to admit the copious fresh air deemed beneficial in the treatment of tuberculosis. She helped him into his dressing gown, then supported him as he made his way to the table. Remembering what he wanted to write, William sent the nurse back to his bedside cupboard to fetch one of his old gardening books, a volume on the cultivation of alpine plants.

He sat and turned the pages until he found the list he was looking for, then laid the book open on the table. He unscrewed the top of his fountain pen and began his reply to Ivy. A breeze lifted the pages of the book and began to turn them. William turned them back, found his place again and resumed his letter, but another gust of wind, stronger this time, lifted the pages again. As he looked up, irritated, William saw a brightly coloured piece of paper fly up in the air, twist, then drift down to the floor where it lay at his feet. He put down his pen and, as he bent to retrieve the paper, saw it was a seed packet. As his fingers grasped the paper, he cried out, then let it go, as if the packet had burned his hand.

William got to his feet, his chest heaving and stared at the packet on the floor. He staggered as memory engulfed him like a tidal wave, obliterating the merciful amnesia that had protected his shattered mind for seventeen years. Remembering, he lifted his hands to his head and clutched at it, as if he feared the sudden flood of knowledge might cause his skull to explode. He let out an agonised cry and sank back on to his chair, turning his head from side to side, incredulous.

Sobbing, William leaned forward and pillowed his head on his arms, resting his wracked body on the table. Ivy's letter and his reply lay unregarded beneath him, absorbing his tears, until the nurse looked in on him again. Seeing her patient's pitiful condition, she summoned a doctor immediately.

THE BEECH WOOD

They sought consolation among us, separately, not expecting they should meet. Grief drove them towards us and towards each other. Both had lost so much, yet there was still something that could not be taken; something both still had to give.

Afterwards, they regretted what had happened, but in the midst of decay and death, life goes on. The cycle is eternal, inexorable, like the rising of the sun, the phases of the moon.

They were young. Alive. They did not understand, but obeyed the imperative. Death had no dominion over them and so they found the consolation they sought – not with us, but with each other.

WILLIAM

May 27th, 1916

Even before she came into sight, his sharp ears detected sounds: the sweep of her skirt over the mossy floor of the wood, the cracking of fallen twigs beneath her feet. He turned, quickly concealing the packet behind his back, though as it was wrapped in oilcloth, no one could have discerned the contents. When he saw it was Hester Mordaunt, he removed his cap and dropped the packet into it, then greeted his employer.

She was walking with her head bowed and at the sound of her name, she looked up, startled. Her serious expression vanished and was replaced briefly by a joyous smile. She then composed herself and said, 'Mr Hatherwick. William . . . Please accept my condolences. I was so very sorry to hear of your father's death. I have not liked to call. I thought you and Violet were best left alone to grieve. She has seemed quite distraught.'

He nodded. 'She has indeed taken it badly, but she says you were a great comfort in his final days, Miss Mordaunt.'

'Oh, *Hester*, please! Have you forgotten?' she asked with a smile. 'We might not have seen each other for a while, but you have often been in my thoughts. Family and friends still living are even more precious now so many have departed and I count you and Violet among my friends.'

'Thank you,' he replied with a slight bow. 'Violet has spoken warmly of your generosity.'

'Oh, it was nothing. I grew fond of your father. He was an excellent worker and a kind man. He seemed very concerned about Violet's future, so I did my best to settle his mind. I told him her position at Beechgrave is assured.'

'I fear I can do nothing to repay your kindness other than promise that when I'm able to take up my father's duties, I shall fulfil them gladly and gratefully, to the very best of my ability.'

'I know you will, William. And I hope that day will come very soon.'

He didn't reply and in the silence they shared, both acknowledged privately how remote the end of the war still seemed, how difficult it was to recall peacetime.

'Thank you for your last communication,' Hester said with a shy smile.

He looked uncertain. 'I'm afraid I don't remember—'

'Your sketch. You sent me a little sketch of your trench garden. I was delighted to receive it. I do miss getting letters from the Front. There used to be so many and so many I had to write. But there's no one now. My brothers . . . Friends . . . It seems as if everyone's gone. Your sketch meant you were *alive*, so I was very glad to receive it. And it was such a charming sketch. I showed it to Violet and we discussed your excellent draughtsmanship.'

He looked uncomfortable and stared down into his cap. Hester feared she'd embarrassed him with the compliment, but eventually he said, 'I'm sorry there was no letter to accompany the sketch. It's difficult to find the time, not to mention the paper. I had to tear a page out of my sketchbook.'

'Yes, of course. I understand. I really didn't expect a letter. It was very good of you to think of me at all when your father was ill and Violet so troubled. I should not have mentioned it. That was selfish. Please forgive me.'

William looked up, his expression pained. 'Miss Mordaunt . . . Hester . . . I *did* write to you.'

Her eyes widened. 'You did? But . . . but I never received any letters.'

'That's because I never sent them.'

'Why not?'

'They weren't the sort of letters that could readily be sent.'

Hester frowned. 'I don't understand.'

'If you'd read them you would understand.'

'Where are these letters? I do hope,' she said, her voice unsteady, 'you didn't destroy them?'

'No. I kept them.'

'Where are they now? May I read them? I should very much like to read any letter you wrote me, however old.'

William said nothing, but slowly extracted the packet from his cap. He stared at it, as if trying to decide what to do.

'Are those my letters?' Hester asked faintly.

'Yes. But they aren't proper letters. It was hard to find paper. And in any case . . .' His voice tailed off, but then he drew himself up and said firmly, 'They could not be sent. I mean they could not be *read*.' He made a derisory sound and looked down at the packet in his hand. 'They should never have been written!'

After a long pause in which Hester struggled to order her thoughts, she asked, 'Why do you have them with you? Were you intending to destroy them?'

'No. I was going to hide them. Here, in the wood. I couldn't bring myself to destroy them.'

'And you couldn't bring yourself to give them to me?'

'No.'

'But *why?*'

'Because it would have been wrong.'

'I don't understand. If you've kept them for so many weeks—'

'Months.'

'Why won't you keep them any longer?'

'Because I know I shall not return. I feel it in my bones. I cannot explain it, but I know this is the last time I shall speak to you, Hester, the last time I shall see Beechgrave and my home.'

Tears started into her eyes. 'You cannot know that! It's mere superstition. Please don't say such dreadful things, William. We must never abandon hope!'

Ignoring her, he continued solemnly. 'I wished to dispose of anything that might prove an embarrassment to my family after my death, or an embarrassment to you. So I was going to hide these letters in the Trysting Tree. There's a hole in the trunk, high up. No one would ever have found them there and no one would ever have known. Apart from me.'

'Would you show me the letters? Please.'

He looked up and fixed her with dark, expressionless eyes. 'Know that you ask this of a dead man.' He swallowed and went on. 'And it is a dead man who complies with your request. Do you understand?'

'I think so.'

He regarded her a moment longer, then put down his cap and slipped the string off the packet. As he unwrapped the contents he let the oilcloth fall to the ground, then stepped forward and handed Hester some seed packets.

She was so astonished, she laughed. 'But these are just seed packets!'

'The ones you sent me,' he said simply. 'Open them up. Read the sweet peas first. Violet told me you liked our sweet peas, so that was the first one I wrote.' As she shuffled eagerly through the empty packets, he laid a hand on her arm and said, his voice low and urgent,

'Remember, Hester: it is a letter from a dead man. Remember that and forgive.'

She looked into his face but his eyes were cast down – in shame, she thought. As he turned away, she continued her search. When she found the sweet pea packet, she set the others down. The packet had been opened carefully along its sides so that she was able to open it out like a book. Inside, the paper was covered with small, neat handwriting executed in pencil. The letter began 'My dear H'. As she peered at the tiny words, all colour left her face. As Hester read on, a whimper escaped her lips and, blinking away tears, she put a hand up to her mouth. When she'd finished reading the packet, she bent and picked up another and read that, then another. In the end she abandoned her reading because she could no longer see through her tears. She let the packets fall and as they fluttered to the ground, she covered her face with her hands.

William stepped forward, clutching his cap. 'Forgive me, I would not have made you weep, not for the world! You must understand it was my intention you should never know. And you never *would* have known if we hadn't met today.'

She looked up, her cheeks wet, her expression earnest. 'Then I thank God we *did* meet! I thank the God I can scarcely believe in that I met you today, William. That you had the courage to show me these blessed, blessed letters! I thank God I shall not die believing no man ever loved me. But most of all, I thank Him that *you* will not die before I have told you that your love is requited. That I think of you every day – every *hour*! That I pray fervently you will be spared, that you will come home to Violet and to *me*, William, because if the day comes when I cannot look upon your dear face, I shall be a dead woman mourning a dead man.'

She stooped and quickly gathered up the seed packets and clutched them to her breast, dislodging a little silver brooch in the shape of a daffodil. William saw it fall and bent to retrieve it. As he straightened up, they stood very close, close enough for him to hear how her breath came unevenly, close enough for her to feel the warmth of his upon her face.

He dropped the brooch and took her face in both his hands, staring at her in mute appeal. He felt rather than saw her nod. As he kissed her, she let the packets fall so she could take him in her arms. She clung to him, sobbing between kisses, forbidding him to leave Beechgrave, assuring him she was his, would always be his, in life and in death, but that he must not – *must* not – die, not now they had found each other, now that they both *knew*.

William buried his fingers in her hair and silenced her with another kiss. Combs and hairpins worked loose, allowing her long hair to tumble down her back. He groaned in ecstasy and took her firmly round the waist, crushing her to him, so he could feel her breasts against his chest. She said his name over and over, pressing her face against his neck, her mouth searching for his skin.

He took hold of her arms and held her away from him, his eyes wide. 'Hester, you must go. Now. Leave me here. Go now before we— before it's too late. *Go!*' He released her and stepped back.

She stood, dishevelled and confused, expecting to feel ashamed, but there was no shame, only a terrible hunger, something as primitive, as all-consuming as the grief and anger she had known when her brothers died. 'William . . . There is more, isn't there? Is that what you're afraid of . . . ? Tell me. Is there more?'

He hesitated, then nodded. 'Much more. But it would be wrong, Hester. Wrong in every way you can imagine.'

She tossed her loose hair away from her face and said, 'This war is wrong. What happened to my brothers was wrong. And so is what's happening to my poor mother. Going back to the Front is wrong, William, I know it! I cannot believe anything we do in the name of love can be more wrong than this wicked, wicked war. Can it?'

'No, my dearest love,' he said with a sad smile. 'It could not be more wrong than this godforsaken war.'

'Then I am satisfied. And you, I think, are not. If there is more, William, I want it. If we can be more to each other, then that is what I desire, above *everything*. And I do not care if the world thinks us wicked. It will be a wicked world that judges us!'

Still he hesitated, a look of agony contorting his features. She grasped his hand and pressed it to her breast. 'Kiss me, William. Take me in your arms and love me. Love me as if we both might die!'

He looked into her eyes for a long moment, a moment in which his resolution faltered. He withdrew his hand and stared down at the ground, then he spun on his heel and walked away to the centre of the clearing where he stood and surveyed the circle of beech trees that surrounded them. Hester watched, not breathing, as he gazed up at the tree canopy, then solemnly addressed the beeches, calling on them to witness his vow. He swore to honour and protect the woman he loved for as long as he should live, then he turned, took Hester's hand and led her, unresisting, to another part of the wood: a sunken dell, thick with moss and bluebells, where light hardly penetrated and the only sound was the gentle rustling of leaves in the treetops.

THE BEECH WOOD

Afterwards, he gathered up the forgotten seed packets and pressed them, wordlessly, into her hands. They searched in vain for her brooch and he told her he would give her another, a brooch instead of a ring, something she could wear openly, something to remember him by, if he should— But there she raised a finger to his lips and silenced him.

We watched as they parted: he agitated, already conscience-stricken; she dazed, unseeing, like one who walks in her sleep. We watched as, hearts and bodies now conjoined, they went their separate ways.

PART FIVE

PART FIVE

WILLIAM

October 4th, 1934

William wept for two days. Even then it was some time before he was able to speak coherently, but the nursing staff had seen this sort of reversal before. They knew what had happened. After seventeen years the poor man's memory had returned and one of the things he was remembering was the Battle of the Somme in which he'd been wounded. In view of William's already frail physical condition, it was considered doubtful whether he would survive the shock, so they sent for Hester Mordaunt.

When she arrived, he lay in bed, skeletal and still, as if the consumption had already wreaked its final havoc, but the doctor said his patient was only sleeping. Hester asked if she could sit by the bed and wait. Permission was granted and she sat in her coat, trying to ignore the cold draught from the open window.

She removed her gloves and regarded the father of her child, wondering yet again just how much William had remembered. His fits of terror and weeping suggested he remembered the battlefield, but would he remember what had happened at Beechgrave? As she waited anxiously, Hester wrung her gloves in her lap, trying to decide if total recall would be even worse than total amnesia. If, when William woke, she discovered he was still suffering from partial amnesia, how much – if anything – should she tell him?

William's dark lashes flickered and he moved his head. His thick curling hair was greying now and his gaunt, scarred face looked much older than his fifty years. As he opened his eyes, Hester leaned forward, smiling with relief. Curbing an impulse to take his hand, she said, 'How are you feeling? I've been so worried about you. They let me sit with you so you'd see a familiar face when you woke.' He looked confused and gazed around the room in which they'd isolated him out of consideration for other patients. 'You've been moved,' Hester explained. 'They thought you needed peace and quiet.'

'I'm not in France, am I . . . ? I was wounded . . .' His hand travelled to his neck where his trembling fingers found an old scar.

'No, you're in England. In a sanatorium near Bath. You've been here for some weeks now.'

'Ah . . . I remember.' He began to cough violently and it was some moments before he could speak again. 'It's very good of you to come, Hester. Thank you. You come often, don't you?'

'As often as I can.'

'Why?'

'*Why?*'

'Yes, why? Why do you visit so often?'

'Because you're family, William! You and Ivy are the only family I have left now.'

He considered this for a moment and said, 'In what way am I part of your family?'

Hester wondered if he'd set a trap for her, but she thought it unlikely. She could see the direction the conversation was heading and it would be difficult to avoid telling a lie, but she had no idea if William was ready for the truth or if he had already remembered it.

'I think of you as family because I'm Ivy's legal guardian.'

'And I'm her uncle.'

'That's right,' Hester agreed eagerly, grateful to be spared, if only temporarily, the ordeal of confession.

A young nurse entered bearing a tray of tea and slices of bread and butter. She put down the tray and helped William sit up in bed. Hester got to her feet and rearranged the pillows behind him with a professional competence. The nurse nodded her thanks.

'You've done this before, I think.'

'Oh, yes. I used to work at Beechgrave Convalescent Hospital. I think I still know how to make a bed,' she added with a smile.

The nurse settled William back on his pillows and placed the tray in front of him. 'Now drink your tea while it's hot, Mr Hatherwick. And eat your bread and butter. I've cut it nice and thin for you, so do your best, won't you?' Without waiting for a response, she turned away and said in an undertone to Hester, 'Try to get him to eat something.'

Hester sat down again. William stared at the cup and saucer as if he wanted to drink, but hadn't the strength to lift it.

'Would you like me to help you?' she asked. 'Can I hold the cup for you?'

'No, please don't trouble yourself. I'm not thirsty.'

'You should try to eat, though. That nurse will nag you if you don't.'

'She certainly will.' His smile was half-hearted, but Hester was overjoyed to see it.

'Try to eat just a little, William.'

'In a moment,' he replied, shutting his eyes. They remained shut for some time and Hester thought he might have fallen asleep, but he opened them again and, looking directly at her, said, 'Why did you never marry, Hester?'

Astonished, Hester found herself answering before she'd considered the possible import of the question. 'I nearly married. I was engaged at one time, to a sweet young man. Walter Dowding. He was killed in 1916. He was the son of Ursula Dowding, the woman who nursed you at Sharpitor. That's how we found you. Mrs Dowding recognised your sketches of Beechgrave and wrote to me.'

'And you've never loved another?'

Hester looked away and laughed nervously. 'Oh, I didn't love Walter! I *thought* I did. For a while anyway. But now I don't believe there was any love on either side. It was just a suitable match. Our parents were old friends, you see. Poor Walter's death saved me from a loveless marriage.'

'You haven't answered my question.'

'Did I love anyone after Walter?' Hester looked down at her hands resting in her lap and noticed they shook. Clasping them tightly she said, 'Yes, I suppose I did. But he . . . he was also lost in the war.'

'Missing in action?'

'That's what the telegram said.'

'And you loved him?'

'Good gracious, this is quite an interrogation!' Hester said, still avoiding his eyes. She stood up and removed the untouched tray. 'Why the sudden curiosity?'

'You loved this man? The one who went missing?'

Hester took her seat again and studied William's face, but he was gazing into space now, his expression unreadable. 'He was the only man I've ever loved.'

'If he'd lived, would you have married?'

'We had no plans to marry. I had no idea my feelings were requited. He didn't declare his love until the day before he left for the Front and by then it was . . . too late.'

'A sad story.'

'Yes, but common enough,' Hester said briskly. 'Violet's sweetheart didn't come home either and they *did* have plans to marry.'

William's chest rose and fell as he appeared to gather himself. 'You should have told me.'

'About Walter Dowding?'

'About who I was.'

'I did, William. The day I found you, I told you who you were.'

'But not *what* I was.'

She looked puzzled. 'I don't understand. I explained that you were my Head Gardener and I promised to reinstate you at Beechgrave. Don't you remember?'

'Yes, I remember . . . And I remember you lost a brooch.' As Hester's hand flew up to her mouth, her intake of breath was audible. 'It was silver. A daffodil, I believe. The catch was broken. We looked but we couldn't find it. I found it the following day and took it away to France with me, intending to mend it for you. I don't know where it is now. I lost it. I'm sorry, Hester. I wouldn't have lost it for the world.'

'You *remember*?'

'Everything, I believe. Too much.'

'Did something happen? They told me you were writing a letter to Ivy and were suddenly overcome. They assumed it was memories of being in battle. No one said—'

'I haven't told anyone. They don't know that everything has come back.'

'Everything?'

'I gave you my love letters in the wood. They were written in pencil inside the seed packets you sent me for my trench garden. I believe I sent you a sketch?'

'I still have it.'

'I wanted to write to you, but I knew it would be very wrong, so I allowed myself the pleasure of writing letters, but I spared you the shame of receiving them. What happened to them? The seed packets?'

'When I'd finally given up hope of your ever coming home, I put them in the Trysting Tree.'

'*Crescent illae crescetis amores.*'

'So it *was* you!'

'I carved that on the bark before I left for France. I didn't expect to return, but I knew the tree would flourish, if not our love. How did you hide the packets in the tree?'

'I put them in a tin and dropped it into a hole, high up.'

He nodded, almost imperceptibly. 'I know the one. But how did you get up there? Did you take a ladder?'

'I stood on the swing.'

'Ah, I'd forgotten that . . . And they're still there, my letters?'

'Yes.' She looked down at her hands and the ruined gloves they held. 'We'd had no news of you, William. And there was no body to bury. It was my way of commemorating your death and . . . our love. The Trysting Tree seemed to me the right place. The *only* place. I could come and pretend it was your final resting place. I thought, if you could have chosen, that's where you would have liked to be buried.'

'You know me well, Hester. I often thought of that wood when I was in France. After I came home, I stood beneath the Trysting Tree many times, but I didn't remember its significance. Not until the other day.' As he reached across the eiderdown, Hester leaned forward and took his hand in both of hers. 'Why didn't you tell me what I meant to you?'

'I wanted to but I didn't know how. And then I didn't know if I should. When you first came back to Beechgrave, I waited for your memory to return naturally. I thought being at home again, working in the garden, would have a restorative effect. It seemed safest just to wait. If your mind had chosen to forget the past, I assumed reminding you of it, of what you'd suffered, would be very painful for you, dangerous even. Months later, when it seemed clear you wouldn't regain your memory, I could see no point in telling you what you'd once felt for me. If you no longer felt the same way, talking about the past would only lead to embarrassment and . . . and a sense of *obligation*. You weren't the same man.'

'But you felt the same way? About me?'

'Of course. I was the same woman.'

With some difficulty, he swivelled his head round and looked into her eyes. 'Do you still, Hester?'

'My feelings haven't changed since the day you left Beechgrave. Even before that. I didn't realise it at the time, but I think I probably fell in love with you at the Victoria Rooms in Bristol, in 1914.' She paused to see if he would remember.

'Women's suffrage.'

'Yes!'

'We attended a talk. With Violet. You were there with a friend, but as I recall, you'd lied to your mother about the nature of the talk. I think I gave you a leaflet . . . I don't remember why.'

'I'd told her I was going to a talk given by the National Geographical Society. You gave me a leaflet about a talk you'd recently attended, so I'd be able to mention a few convincing details. I was so grateful – and the collusion was such fun!'

William smiled. 'I was delighted to be of assistance. I didn't love you then, but I wanted to help you. To protect you. You seemed in need of protection.'

'Oh, I just needed *work*! And a better education. I was thrilled to be allowed to share your books. I realised if I'd been a man I might have wanted to become a scientist or a doctor. I really enjoyed running a convalescent home. I've never been so tired in my life, nor so happy. I knew you were alive and safe – from the war, at least – and I had a real sense of purpose for the first time in my life.'

'You should have married, Hester, and had a family.'

'I didn't marry, but I had a family. You, Violet and Ivy were my family.'

'That's hardly the same.'

'Perhaps not, but after the war women had to learn to live without marriage, live without men. I think we made a pretty good job of it under the circumstances. In the end, we *shamed* them into giving us the vote.'

William's wheezy chuckle gave way to a violent cough. Unable to suppress the fit, he waved Hester away and turned to face the wall. The nurse appeared and announced that Mr Hatherwick was tired and Hester should leave.

Standing at the end of the bed, gazing helplessly at William's prostrated form, Hester said goodbye, but he gave no indication he'd heard.

As she walked along a chilly corridor that smelled of death and disinfectant, Hester decided she wouldn't tell William about Ivy. His mind was already overwrought and the doctor had said complete rest was essential if, in his debilitated state, he was to survive the onslaught of his memories and an overwhelming sense of loss.

There was no way of knowing how William would respond to the news that his beloved niece was in fact his daughter. Such a revelation might overturn a healthy man's mind and William was very ill, probably dying. The question was, what was best for him? And what was best for Ivy?

Hester decided she would wait, wait until she felt certain that disclosure would be in both Ivy's and William's best interests, or until she had no choice but to tell him the truth.

She did not have to wait long, but before Hester could speak to William, she had to write to their daughter.

Wisteria Cottage
October 6th
My dearest Ivy,

I'm afraid I have some bad news for you, but not the worst. Uncle William's condition is no better. He has deteriorated to such an extent that I think you'd better come home as soon as you can. I haven't discussed this with him because I know he wouldn't want you to interrupt your studies. In any case, I don't think he realises how ill he is and I don't propose to tell him.

His doctor at the sanatorium has said we should prepare for the worst, but of course William could yet rally. There is always hope! He's in good spirits on the whole, but in very poor health, so I feel I have no alternative but to summon you. I cannot bear the thought that you and he might not see each other again.

I've written to your Principal to explain the situation. I told her William has been as good as a father to you, so at this time your place is at his bedside. It will do him so much good to see you, Ivy. You are always such a tonic!

Hurry home, my dear, so we can all be together again.

All love,
Hester

When Hester arrived, Matron advised against a visit as William's condition was now critical. Hester said that was why it was essential she speak to him. She declined to discuss the matter in any detail, but when

Matron enquired whether the conversation would lead to any agitation in the patient, Hester lied and said it would not. She was permitted to see him on condition that she keep her visit as brief as possible.

The sight of William lying wasted in the hospital bed, looking so much worse, came as a shock. The urge to keep her secret, to let him die in peaceful ignorance of her deception was overwhelming, but then his eyes flickered open and he attempted a smile. In the dying light from those hollow eyes Hester thought she saw the ghost of their daughter. She knew then that even if the knowledge hastened his death, William must be told he had a child.

She pulled up a chair and sat close to the bed. He was too weak even to lift a hand to take hers, so she took one of his, lifted it to her lips and kissed it.

'How are you today, my love?'

'Oh, I live the life of a log, but I'm holding on.'

'Good. I'm so glad, because I have some news for you.'

'Good news?'

'Very surprising news. You'll be shocked to hear it, but I think you'll consider it good news when you've had time to take it all in. At least, I hope you will,' she added nervously.

'Does this news concern you?'

'In a way, but really I want to talk to you about Ivy.'

He looked concerned. 'Is something wrong?'

'No, she's very well. In fact, she's coming home very soon.'

William closed his eyes. 'So they've told you I'm dying.'

'No, they've said you're very ill – but we both know you have the constitution of an ox!'

He opened his eyes again and frowned. 'Then why is Ivy coming home?'

'That's what I want to talk to you about, but they've told me I mustn't stay long, so please forgive me if I come straight to the point.' She sat back, arranged her hands in her lap, then looked up into William's enquiring eyes. 'You told me you remember our last meeting in the wood, before you went away to France.'

'Indeed I do.'

'And you remember what happened? *Exactly* what happened?' He nodded. Hester took a deep breath and said, 'I have to tell you now, William, that what we did that day had far-reaching consequences.'

His long, thin fingers clutched at the bedclothes. 'There was a *child*?'

'Yes.'

'And it died?'

'No. *Violet's* child died. She had a daughter who lived for only a few hours.'

'But I don't understand . . . Ivy—'

'She's your daughter. *Our* daughter. And that's why I've asked her to come home. You must spend some time with her knowing . . . who she is.'

When he was finally able to speak, William whispered, 'Does she *know*?'

'No. She was told what you were told. The story Violet and I concocted between us.'

'And she's coming to see me? Soon?'

'Tomorrow, I hope, if you're well enough. The college has granted her leave of absence.'

'Ivy is my *daughter* . . .' A slow smile began to spread across his emaciated face and then he began to laugh, tentatively, in happy disbelief, until the wracking cough took over.

Hester waited, dreading the appearance of a nurse who would order her to leave. When the fit had passed, she leaned forward, saying, 'I have a request to make, William. You will find it very hard to grant, but please, hear me out before you decide what to do. When you *do* decide,

I beg you to put our daughter's welfare first.' She took his hand again and pressed it to her cheek. 'I'm asking you to greet Ivy and talk to her as her *uncle*. Don't tell her about her parentage.'

'I don't understand. If you didn't want her to know, why did you tell me?'

'Because you had a right to know.'

'And Ivy doesn't?'

'She doesn't need to know *now*.'

He swallowed and, struggling visibly with his emotions, said, 'Hester, do you know what you're asking of me?'

'Yes, I do. She's my child too and I haven't acknowledged her as mine for seventeen years.'

'Was it the shame of being unmarried?'

She sighed. 'It was a lot of things. We'd had to assume you were dead. My mother was still alive and I couldn't foist public shame on her. After losing a husband and two sons, her sanity hung by a thread. I had no one else to turn to for advice or support, there was only Violet. She'd confided in me when she found she was expecting. In fact, it wasn't until she described her symptoms that I realised I was too. I thought I was just ill. So I told Violet we were in the same boat and that you were my baby's father. She was very surprised, but also very pleased and she agreed to help me.'

'Dear old Vi . . . No man ever had a more loyal and loving sister.'

'And no woman a more loyal and loving friend,' Hester replied. 'She helped me shut up most of the house and then I dismissed all the servants. Violet came up to live at Beechgrave and looked after my mother, but after she lost her baby, we decided it would be better for everyone if she pretended to be the mother of mine. I would later adopt her and raise her myself. That seemed less scandalous. I didn't want my sins to be visited upon our child.'

'Was Vi with you when Ivy was born?'

'Yes. I was naturally very frightened, but Violet knew what to do. She was a great comfort. I knew nothing at all about babies, but she did.'

'Our mother had five. Only Violet and I survived childhood.'

'Once you'd been found, I hoped we'd be able to marry one day and acknowledge Ivy as our child. Who was there to care if I was making an unsuitable marriage? People already believed I was as mad as my mother, adopting a servant's child as a substitute for marriage and motherhood. After the war, I didn't care what people thought! But you didn't remember me, let alone Ivy's conception, so there seemed little point in telling you the truth. Or telling Ivy. So I said nothing. I don't know if that was the right decision, but in seventeen years no one has suffered from my deception.'

'Apart from you.'

Hester sat in silence, her head bowed. Eventually she looked up and said, 'We don't have much time. A nurse might come in at any moment and send me away . . . I chose not to acknowledge my child and now I'm asking you to do the same. Ivy loves you. I don't believe she could love you more. But you could turn her world upside down – and mine, because Ivy's world is mine.'

'So I'm *never* to be acknowledged as her father?'

'She'll need time, William. *I* need time.'

'And mine is running out.'

'If your memory hadn't returned, you would never have known. You would have died in ignorance – and perhaps that would have been better, better for you. But your memory *did* return. And now you might die . . .' Her eyes began to fill with tears. 'How could I keep silent? After all these *years* of silence!' she added fiercely.

'No, you had to tell me, I see that. And I'm very glad to know our love resulted in that wonderful child. She's so like you, Hester. I never saw it before, but I can see it now. She reminds me of you when you were young, when you used to ask so many questions and complain you weren't allowed to arrange your own flowers. Ivy has that same quality of . . . *indignation*. She wants a fairer world and she's prepared to fight for it, isn't she?'

Hester smiled. 'We have every reason to be proud of our daughter.'

'And I'm so proud of her mother – how you managed on your own and took care of Vi.'

'No, she looked after Ivy and me. *And* my mother. She was wonderful.'

'I wish I'd been there to support you.'

'Never mind,' she said, squeezing his hand. 'You came home to us, that's the main thing.'

'So you'll tell Ivy about me . . . one day?'

'Of course I will. But I don't know when. It will be hard enough losing you so soon after I found you again – the *real* you, William. Allow me to deal with that before I have to confront Ivy with seventeen years of deceit and dissimulation.'

'She might not see it like that.'

'I don't want to take the risk. Not yet.'

William was thoughtful for a moment, then said, 'I think I'd like to write her a letter.'

'But, William—'

'One for you to give her *after* I've gone. Whenever you see fit. If I can't speak to her as her father, I'd like to write to her.'

'Yes, of course. I'll bring you some notepaper. Or would you like to dictate it to me? You shouldn't tire yourself.'

'No, I'll try to write to her myself. I'd like her to have something from me, something more than those old gardening books.'

'She'll treasure them, as I treasured them when you went off to war – and for the same reason, William. Ivy and I love you.'

He patted her hand and looked away. 'You'll give her my letter then . . . ? When the time seems right?'

'I will.'

'Thank you.' He closed his eyes and sighed. 'Oh, Hester, I'm so tired . . . You've given me a great deal to think about and I must sleep on it.' He opened his eyes and looked at her anxiously. 'You'll come again tomorrow?'

'Of course. Tomorrow and every day.'

'I don't think I shall be troubling you much longer. The nurses have stopped nagging me to eat and drink. In fact, they're being especially kind to me now. That doesn't bode well, does it?' he said with a crooked smile.

Hester swallowed a sob. 'Don't let's part speaking of death! We've had the gift of another day, another conversation together. I'm sure we shall have another tomorrow,' she added, unable to keep the note of doubt out of her voice.

'Let's hope so,' he replied, reaching for her hand. 'Goodbye, Hester. I'm so glad you found me. If I still believed in God, I'd thank him for letting me find *you*, even if it was seventeen years too late.'

'They weren't wasted years, William. In all that time you've been my dearest friend – and more, though you didn't know it. Your friendship was more than I dreamed of when you went off to the Somme, more than I dreamed of when Violet got the telegram telling her you were missing in action. We have so much to be grateful for! We have each other now and we have Ivy. We couldn't really ask for more, could we?'

William didn't respond at once, but appeared to consider her words, before saying, 'When he felt particularly pressed, when there was just too much to do in the garden, my father used to complain about "the smallness of time". That's what I'd ask for, Hester. More time. Time to enjoy our blessings.' Unable to reply, she gripped his thin, frail hand and he closed his eyes again. 'You'll look after her, won't you – my splendid daughter. Does she take after me, do you think?'

'Oh, yes. She has your eyes,' Hester said fondly. 'Those remarkable Hatherwick eyes. Dark and intelligent. Violet had them too. She had no difficulty passing Ivy off as her own child.'

He was already asleep, so she released his hand and studied it as it lay inert on the bedcover. She listened to his laboured breathing for a few moments, then got to her feet. Smoothing his hair away from his clammy forehead, she bent down to kiss him, so gently, he could not have felt it.

Hester walked over to the door, opened it cautiously, then turned back to look at William's sleeping figure. 'It wasn't wrong,' she murmured. 'We weren't wrong. It was the war that was wrong. Goodbye, my love.'

She waited for a response she knew would not come, then closed the door quietly behind her. Still clutching the handle, she leaned her forehead against the cool, painted wood, gathering her strength before setting off briskly along the corridor, her shoulders straight, her head high.

HESTER

October 7th, 1934

I fear William will not be with us for much longer. I suppose it's selfish of me to want him to live, prolonging his suffering when he cannot be cured and lives a miserable, bedridden existence. He no longer has the strength to walk in the grounds of the sanatorium and when I took him round in a wheelchair, it only exhausted him.

I've summoned Ivy by letter and we expect her some time tomorrow. I hope she won't be too late.

Today William couldn't stop coughing, so I held his hand and chatted to him about Ivy, trying to soothe him. As I left – under compulsion from that dragon of a ward sister – he handed me a letter. He was unable to do more than give me a speaking look before the uncontrollable coughing started again.

October 8th

Ivy was too late. William died yesterday, not long after I left him.

Ivy is broken-hearted, especially as she wasn't able to say a last goodbye. She's staying now until after the funeral and I shall be very glad of her company. We plan to walk together in the beech wood and share our memories of William.

When I saw him last, William was semi-delirious but he said he trusted me to do the right thing. I only wish I knew what that was.

My first duty will always be to Ivy. She is happy and settled at college and doing well. She will need time to adjust, not only to the loss of her uncle, but to the final severing of ties with the Hatherwicks and Garden Lodge, which I've decided to sell. It will be a very difficult time. We both need time to think and grieve.

ANN

'You think the tears were *William's*?' Connor looked at me in disbelief, then stood up. 'We need more coffee. Or maybe you need less, Ann,' he added, taking the empty coffee pot over to the sink.

As he refilled the kettle and switched it on, Phoebe leaned across the breakfast table. 'Are you on to something?'

'I don't know. Maybe . . . Connor, when did William receive that letter from Ivy?'

'A week before he died. She wrote to him from college, but he didn't reply and they never saw each other again.'

'How do we know William didn't reply?' I asked, watching Connor spoon coffee into the pot.

'That's what Ivy told me.'

'But there's an envelope, isn't there? An empty envelope with Ivy's real name, which you said no one would have used. If William wrote to her *after* his memory returned, he might have addressed her as his daughter. As Ivy *Hatherwick*.'

'That's a good point! I don't suppose there's any way of dating the envelope?' Phoebe asked.

'No, there's nothing on it but her name. It was obviously delivered by hand.' Connor brought the full coffee pot over to the kitchen table. 'Shall we adjourn to the sitting room, girls?'

'Good idea!' Phoebe said struggling to her feet. 'I could do with the exercise. My arse was taking root.'

'Go and see if you can find that envelope, Connor. I'll bring the coffee through.'

As he headed for the sitting room, Phoebe followed, calling out after him, 'Tip everything on to the floor. Let's have a good old rummage!'

I loaded our mugs and the coffee pot on to a tray, deep in thought. By the time I'd warmed some milk in the microwave and carried everything through, Connor had found the envelope and Phoebe was examining it closely.

'Good-quality paper. And lined. A bit feminine, don't you think? And far too posh for William. He wouldn't have been able to afford stationery like this.'

'But Hester would,' I said, setting down the tray on the coffee table.

'It's not her handwriting,' said Connor, seated on the carpet, surrounded by mounds of yellowing correspondence.

'Do we know whose it is?' I asked handing him a mug.

'No. And we don't have any actual letters from William for comparison.'

'Yes, we do, we have lots.'

'We do?' He blinked up at me, surprised. Despite the caffeine intake, Connor's lack of sleep and his exertions of the night before appeared to be taking their toll.

'The seed packets.'

'Of course!' He reached across the floor, grabbed a large envelope and tipped out the contents. Opening a packet carefully, he examined the tiny writing. Phoebe peered over his shoulder, while I knelt beside him on the carpet.

There was a tense silence before Phoebe announced, 'It's not the same. *Damn.*'

'But it's *similar*,' Connor countered. 'And if you consider this was about twenty years earlier and written in a trench, in pencil, possibly under fire . . . He was also writing something he never intended anyone to read.'

'Whereas that envelope,' I said, pointing, 'might have contained his final communication with Ivy.'

'What makes you say that?' Phoebe asked, sipping her coffee.

'Well, it's probably Hester's notepaper.'

'I don't follow.'

'Why would William be writing on someone else's expensive notepaper? He must have had his own paper and envelopes at home.'

Connor sat bolt upright. 'But he wasn't *at* home!'

'No, he was in hospital.'

'And Hester brought him in the wherewithal so he could write a last letter to Ivy before he died! It all adds up!' Phoebe said, delighted.

'Well, possibly . . . Do you think it *is* William's handwriting on that envelope, Connor?'

He examined the two words again. 'Could be. He was dying. Writing in bed, presumably. It *could* be the same hand. But if William was writing to Ivy on his deathbed, what would he want to say?'

'Fond farewells. The usual stuff,' Phoebe said dismissively. 'How much he loved her, I suppose.'

'He must also have told her she was his daughter.'

'Hang on, Ann – we don't *know* that.'

'Yes, we do. The envelope is addressed to Ivy Hatherwick. Her legal name was Mordaunt. He surely must have been writing to *tell* her she was his daughter.'

'Well, in that case,' Connor said, 'she never got the letter.'

'She must have,' Phoebe insisted. 'We've got the empty envelope here.'

Connor shook his head. 'Unless you think Ivy was hiding something from me, we know she didn't have any idea who her real parents were.'

'That's right. Not until she read William's letter.'

'But she didn't read it, Ann! Hester can't have given it to her. My grandmother wouldn't have lived a lie. She *couldn't*. She was a deeply moral woman, a churchgoer all her life. She thoroughly disapproved of Hester's atheism! And why would she have asked me to research her family tree if she knew there were some dodgy skeletons in the cupboard? Sorry, but you're wrong. Ivy had no idea whose child she was.'

'Not until the day she died.'

'*What?*' Phoebe and Connor spoke in unison, staring at me.

'I believe Ivy must have found this letter on the day she died. I've no idea where, but I think it must have turned up somehow after a lifetime of being hidden – by Hester probably. It might have been her notepaper. If so, she must have given it to William. He probably told her why he wanted it. For some reason Hester didn't hand the letter over, but decades later, Ivy found it, read it and discovered who she was.'

'And then set fire to the family archive? *Why?* She adored Hester. And if the "uncle" she'd loved all her life turned out to be her dad – well, why would she be angry about that? It doesn't make any sense! Having Hester and William for parents was no more shameful than being the lovechild of Violet and some unknown dead Tommy.'

'Oh, *no* . . . That's what it was. *Shame*.' The shock of realisation was so great, I thought for a moment I was going to be sick.

'Ann, are you okay?' Connor put an arm round me. 'What's wrong?'

'Don't you see?' I swallowed and said, 'If William told Ivy he was her father . . . I mean, if he *only* told her he was her father . . . Don't you see? As far as Ivy knew, *Violet* was her mother!'

'Oh, Jesus . . .' Connor let me go and his arms fell to his sides.

'Ann, please explain!' Phoebe said testily. 'I can't keep up.'

'Hester never acknowledged Ivy as her own child. We know Ivy believed she was Violet's child, of father unknown. William was dying when he wrote. Confused, possibly delirious. What if he didn't explain who Ivy's *mother* was? If he didn't actually name her? What would Ivy have thought? How could she have made sense of it all? After all, she was in her nineties.'

'Oh, Lord . . . I see what you mean,' Phoebe said.

I was watching Connor, concerned about his pallor. I laid a hand on his arm. 'You knew her very well. How would she have taken the news that she was apparently the product of brother and sister incest?'

'She would have been appalled. Completely appalled.'

'You said she wasn't one to live with secrets. Suppose she thought she'd discovered that her whole life was one big shameful secret, one her conscience-stricken father felt he must reveal on his deathbed—'

'She would have destroyed the letter . . . She might have destroyed everything.'

There was a long and terrible silence in which no one moved, then Connor's shoulders seemed to sag and his head fell forward. I knelt up and put my arms round him, holding him tight while his body shook with silent sobs. Phoebe struggled to her feet and, leaning on her stick, she laid her free hand on his head and stroked his hair, murmuring.

My mother and I shed tears for Connor while he wept for Ivy Hatherwick, who lived and died in ignorance of who she was, who never knew how much her mother had loved her, nor how much she'd wanted to protect her.

IVY

24th November, 2013

Ivy Watson threw another log on to the dying fire and replaced the fireguard. She picked her way carefully through the photo albums, letters and postcards strewn on the floor of her small sitting room and settled down again in her armchair. She lifted one of the old albums on to her lap and turned its heavy, ornamented pages. She decided Connor must have a picture of the old Trysting Tree, so she removed the photo of the ancient beech, making sure she didn't bend it with her clumsy fingers.

As she extracted the corners from the small card triangles holding the photo in place, Ivy saw an envelope had been tucked behind. As she turned it over, she was astonished to see the envelope was addressed to *Ivy Hatherwick*. Curious now, she opened it and removed a single sheet of notepaper. At once she recognised her Uncle William's handwriting and noted that the letter had been written the day before he died. Ivy settled back in her armchair, but she'd read no more than a few lines when she suddenly shot forward, her hand covering her mouth. As she continued to read, her eyes widened and she emitted a small whimpering noise.

October 7th, 1934

My dearest Ivy,

*I understand from Hester that you have been given
leave to come home from college. I so look forward to
seeing you again, my dear, but I fear I might not, so I've
decided to write to you. If you are reading this letter, it's
because I am dead and Hester has had to give you my
final communication.*

*I am very ill and preparing to quit this world.
Before I go, I must act according to my conscience, which
troubles me greatly. I have something to tell you that will
cause you great consternation. I wish to acknowledge the
truth about your parentage. Your mother didn't want you
ever to know, but now, as time runs out for me, I believe
I must tell you the truth, however unpalatable.*

*The facts are simple. Our situation was not. I
loved your mother and she loved me, but our love was
forbidden. Marriage was quite impossible. On a single
occasion, just before I left for France, we succumbed to
our mutual passion. You were the consequence.*

*I recalled nothing of this until a few days ago when
my memory returned in its entirety. Since then I have
been trying to come to terms with a past that was until
that moment unknown to me. When I came home, I was
told you were another man's child and so all these years
I've loved you as my niece, but I don't think I could have
loved you more, had I known you were my own child.*

*My strength is failing and I must close now.
Remember your loving 'uncle' and try to forgive your
father's sin. It was committed in the name of love, in
the face of probable death. It is in the face of imminent*

death that I write to you now, to claim you — finally and proudly — as my child. I deeply regret what happened and how it blighted your poor mother's life, but I do not and could not regret the great gift of your birth.

My dearest Ivy, please try to find it in your heart to forgive me.

Ever your loving father,
William Hatherwick

Ivy crushed the letter into a ball, held it tightly in her fist for a moment, then threw it on the floor. She leaned back, clutching the arms of her chair and wept for a long time.

After she'd composed herself, she bent down, her breathing still unsteady, and retrieved the letter. She spread it out on her lap and read the words again, hoping they might have changed, that she had been dreaming, that her aged brain had simply misunderstood. But the words remained the same and there was no other construction she could put upon them.

She was the child of incest. Violet Hatherwick had been in love with her own brother and it was for this reason no father had been named on her child's birth certificate. Ivy's happy, fatherless childhood had been a lie, her parentage an abomination. Hester had evidently tried to shield Ivy from this terrible knowledge by hiding the letter, but truth will out. Oh, why had she not simply destroyed it, so Ivy could die in ignorance of her tainted blood?

Wiping her eyes, Ivy looked down again at the letter. How dare William ask for forgiveness? She would not, *could* not forgive such wickedness. His confession had destroyed the pride she took in her family, wiped out all her happy memories. It was all lies!

But no one else need ever know. Connor must never know. Ivy would make sure of that. When she died, the dreadful secret would die with her. She would protect her beloved grandson just as dear Hester had protected her. But Hester had only *hidden* the truth. Ivy would destroy it. *All* of it.

She got to her feet and staggered towards the fireplace. Setting the fireguard aside, she threw William's letter on to the fire and watched it burn. When there was nothing left and the flames had died down, she turned and surveyed the family archive spread out on the floor and dining table. She bent down and grabbed some letters and photographs and hurled them on to the fire. As she gathered up the piles of photos and consigned them to the blaze, she began to weep again, but she stood and watched with something like relief as the photos buckled, then burst into flames . . .

ANN

Connor was subdued for the rest of the morning. Upset and, I suspect, embarrassed by his emotional response to what was ultimately just a theory about Ivy's discovery, he set about packing up the archive into its cardboard boxes. I offered to help and we worked in leaden silence while Phoebe took a leisurely bath. Afterwards he went out into the garden to do a few maintenance jobs and I cleared away the breakfast things.

Some time later, he put his head round the back door and said, 'I think I'll call it a day, Ann.'

'But you'll stay for lunch?'

Avoiding my eyes, he said, 'I won't, thanks. There's still loads of stuff I need to do for the website launch and I really need to get on top of paperwork. It's a busy time of year and I've got more jobs than I can handle at the moment.'

'Well, that's a nice problem to have. Are you launching the website soon?'

'In a few days probably.'

'So shall we celebrate? Next weekend? I dare say Phoebe will insist on more champagne.'

'Okay. That sounds great,' he said, attempting a smile.

'I think the garden's just about ready for me to take over now, so we should celebrate the end of the project. Take some photos. Raise a toast.'

His smile was a bit more convincing this time. 'Yes, let's do that. Next weekend it is.' There was an awkward pause in which Connor looked uncomfortable. Staring down at his muddy wellingtons, he said, 'Ann, you do know it's nothing to do with . . . what happened last night?'

'Of course. I just wish now I'd kept my big mouth shut about Ivy. I wasn't thinking how it would affect you. I'm so sorry.'

'No, I'm just overreacting. She meant such a lot to me.'

'I know, and to think of her in such a state of turmoil, alone and so very angry . . . It's horrible! But, you know, I could be wrong. There might have been another reason. Maybe you should try to believe there was.'

'But you can't really do that, can you? Un-know something. Forget what you don't want to remember. Isn't that why Ivy burned the archive?'

'*Would a man without memory be a happy man?*'

'What do you mean?'

'That's what Hester wrote in her diary. I wonder if William was happier before his memory returned?'

'I don't know, but I'll never be able to look at a photo of Ivy without thinking how she might have felt during those last few days in hospital . . . She was so *proud* of her family. She loved them so much. She didn't remember much about Violet, but William and Hester were her world.'

'She might have died with her love for Hester intact.'

'You think so?'

'Well, she still thought of her as a protective adoptive mother.'

'Who'd colluded with covering up incest.'

'Maybe she *didn't* think that. But even if she did, knowing why she destroyed the archive allows *you* to move on, Connor. It's an ending to the story. We don't know if it's the real ending, but it *is* an ending. Without it you'd spend the rest of your life wondering, trying to make sense of what happened. And I really can't recommend spending another forty years trying to come up with motives for apparently inexplicable actions.'

'You mean Sylvester?'

I nodded. 'I wish I could have got inside his head somehow, even if it turned out he was a lying, cheating scumbag with a second family in Madeira. Maybe if we'd ever known the truth, Phoebe and I would have been closer. Fonder. We could have shared the hurt.'

'You really think she doesn't know?'

I looked up, astonished.

'Forgive me for pointing this out, Ann, but you only know what your mother's told you.'

'Just like Ivy . . .' I murmured.

'Just like Ivy.'

An uncomfortable silence was broken by Phoebe calling out from upstairs.

'I'd better go and see what she wants. Come back at the weekend, Connor. We've got lots to celebrate.'

'I'd like that. I don't have to wear the tux again, do I?'

'Not unless you want me to struggle to keep my hands off you.' Phoebe called out again, more impatiently. I took a step towards him, stood on tiptoe and kissed his mouth, then turned and ran upstairs.

Long before he turned up for the champagne celebration, I knew Connor was up to something. I was searching for a book in the studio, a compendium of William Morris designs, and it wasn't on the bookcase where I kept all the volumes currently in use for work. There was no gap where the book should have been – *would* have been if I'd just taken it off the shelf – which struck me as odd. It looked as if someone had closed up the books to disguise the fact that one was missing.

I went back into the house and found Phoebe extracting pages from her most recent sketchbook.

'Ah, there you are! Come and tell me which of these poses you think would be best for Connor's portrait. I've made up my mind, but I want to see if you agree.'

She showed me three sketches, allowing me time to consider each one.

'Is it going to be a portrait in oils?'

'Oil pastel. Quicker and easier for me.'

I nodded and studied the sketches again. 'Well, they're all good.'

Phoebe allowed herself a satisfied smile.

'I'd reject the full-length pose though. His height distracts from his face.' After more consideration I said, 'The profile, I think. That's all you really want. Head and shoulders. You need the set of his shoulders – it's so Connor. But profile is good because you see all the determination in the nose and jaw. You can see he's a fighter. The full-face sketch just looks . . .'

'Handsome.'

'Yes. And Connor's so much more, isn't he?'

Phoebe beamed.

'I take it I picked the right one?'

'I don't know, Ann, but you picked the same one as me. You have a good eye, I'll say that for you. Years spent drawing all those finicky plants, I suppose.'

Ignoring the slur, I said, 'Actually, that was why I came in. Have you borrowed one of my Morris books?'

'No. That would be Connor.'

'*Connor?*'

'He asked me if he could borrow a book, just for this week.'

'Why did he ask you and not me?'

'It's a surprise.'

'What is?'

'Whatever he's making.'

'Mum, what are you talking about?'

'Well, you aren't supposed to know, but he's working on a present for you. He wanted to borrow a particular book on Morris, so I said he could. You've got so many, I didn't think you'd miss one.'

'What's he making?'

'He wouldn't tell me. Said I'd blab,' she added indignantly. 'But the Green Woman will be a hard act to follow. I suppose we'll find out on Friday night.' She turned her attention back to the sketches. 'The profile is definitely the one. Heroic, but still vulnerable . . . Can't wait to see what he comes up with for you. Bound to be something interesting.'

Even before I learned Connor was making me a present, I knew what I wanted to give him: a photo album filled with pictures of Garden Lodge and the restoration of the walled garden. In addition to the usual before and after shots, I included a photo of Phoebe on a garden bench, sketching, wrapped in a blanket and sporting her tweed cap. There was one of Connor with a muddy face, grinning at the camera, brandishing his spade. Others showed the Green Woman, the beech wood and distant Beechgrave up on the hill, taken from my bedroom window. I'd recorded winter turning into spring, from bare branches against a pale sky, to trees smothered in snowy blossom. In the final photo, taken by Phoebe, I stood beside the massive stump of the fallen Trysting Tree, holding the rusty tin that contained William's love letters.

I printed out the photos, arranged them in the album, then inscribed it. I could have just given him a USB stick, but I thought Connor of all people would appreciate an album recording the last few months. I hoped it would compensate a little for the sad conclusion to Ivy's story.

When he arrived on a fine April evening, we were ready with champagne, a special gift and – for what we trusted would not be a last supper – his favourite fish pie. Connor turned up with two large holdalls and a carrier bag full of narcissi.

'I couldn't resist. The supermarket was practically giving them away, so I bought the lot. Hope you've got enough jugs and vases,' he said, handing over the flowers. 'Now, ladies, you must excuse me for a while. I have some business to attend to.'

'Business?' Phoebe asked.

'*Secret* business. I'll be back shortly to collect you.'

'What's going on?' I asked with a laugh.

'It's a surprise. This time it's for you, Ann.'

'For *me*?' I said, feigning surprise. 'Well, as it happens, *we* have something for you too. Shall we save it for later?'

'Yes, I need to get to work before the light goes.'

'We'll see you later then. For bubbly and surprises.'

He set off up the garden path, carrying his bulging holdalls. I was just about to shut the front door when he wheeled round suddenly. 'Can I borrow a ladder?'

'It's in the garage. I'll come and unlock it.'

Connor wouldn't allow me to accompany him to his mystery destination, so I left the ladder propped up against the garage door and returned to the house, where I found Phoebe arranging her flowers.

'Aren't they *gorgeous*? Wonderful to have them in such profusion. The house will be full of their scent soon.' She buried her face in some blooms and inhaled. When she emerged, she said, 'Shall we take a picture?'

'Yes, let's.' I looked round for my camera, but it wasn't on the shelf where I normally left it, so I went to look in the kitchen. It wasn't there either. I ran upstairs to see if I'd put it in my room. Drawing a blank, I came down again, calling out. 'You haven't seen my camera, have you?'

Phoebe appeared in the doorway. 'Did you leave it on the hall table?'

'No. I can't find it anywhere.'

'You took it out yesterday, didn't you?'

'Yes, but I'm sure I wouldn't have forgotten it.'

I spent the next few minutes checking every room again while Phoebe searched the sitting room thoroughly, but to no avail.

Putting my head round the sitting room door, I said, 'I'm going out to look for it before it gets dark.'

'Perhaps Connor will have spotted it.'

'Hope so,' I said, pulling on my coat. 'Could you put the oven on for the pie? I'll be as quick as I can.'

I closed the back door and headed over to the walled garden where I'd taken some shots the day before. One circuit of the path established that my camera wasn't there, so I went over to the studio and had a scout round, even though I was beginning to suspect I'd left the camera in the wood. I remembered putting it down to take a phone call, then, when it had started to rain, I'd headed back to the house, still on the phone. I reassured myself the camera was safe inside its waterproof case and should have come to no harm.

The light was fading fast and when I got there the wood seemed gloomy, almost forbidding. As I retraced my steps to the spot where I thought I'd taken the call, I heard a sound that stopped me in my tracks, a sound that was familiar, yet I knew I hadn't heard it in a very long time. Decades, possibly. It was the slow, rhythmic creaking of a branch of a tree. When the sound stopped suddenly, I set off in that direction, intrigued. I spotted the silver glint of the ladder, propped up against one of the beeches and hurried over to the clearing to ask Connor if he'd seen my camera. As I skirted round the Green Woman, something else caught my eye.

A swing was hanging from a horizontal branch of a tree and a man was standing on it, his back towards me, his head bowed.

I began to shake uncontrollably, then my knees gave way beneath me. As I sank to the ground, a sob rising in my throat, I saw what I had seen. I knew – finally – what I had always known.

I saw my father and I knew that he was dead.

THE BEECH WOOD

It was early when the child wandered into the wood. Dew still lay on the ground, but by then it was all over.

She had come to retrieve the doll she'd left by the swing, propped up among our tangled roots, so it could observe her as she swung back and forth, serenading us with nursery rhymes.

When she arrived in the clearing, the child's eyes were cast down, but watchful. She wished to avoid the gleaming, black slugs, as big as her father's thumb. But she wasn't afraid. This was her wood. The only other person who came here was her father. He'd hung a new swing for her when the ropes of the old one finally frayed.

The doll was where the child had left it, but it had fallen over, dislodged by some nocturnal creature. She didn't see the doll. Long before she reached the foot of the tree, she sensed she was not alone and looked up to see her father standing on the swing. She ran towards him, delighted to have company.

She stopped when she realised something was wrong. He was wearing his dressing gown and he was floating, like an angel. His slippered feet didn't touch the seat of the swing and his arms weren't holding the ropes, they hung loose at his sides. She couldn't see his face because his back was towards her, but his head hung forward, as if he were very sad.

The child stood still and waited for her father to move. When he didn't, she called his name in a small, high voice, then again, louder. The silence was broken only by startled crows, flapping their wings in protest.

She began to back away from the swing. Stumbling over a tree root, she regained her balance, then turned and started to run, with no thought for her abandoned doll, nor care for the slugs she crushed underfoot.

Not until she was out of sight did we hear the first of many screams.

PHOEBE

Someone was banging at the back door. Phoebe had just closed her eyes for a few moments while she waited for Ann to return and the loud noise had startled her. Annoyed her too. Why was Ann knocking on the door when it wasn't even locked?

Groaning, she hauled herself out of her armchair and reached for her stick. 'All, right, all right! I'm coming,' she grumbled as she shuffled into the kitchen. Yanking the door open, she protested, 'Why on earth didn't you—' but the question died on her lips as Connor almost fell into the kitchen carrying Ann, who was whimpering, her eyes wild. 'For God's sake, Connor, what happened? Is she all right?'

His face almost as pale as Ann's, Connor gasped, 'She knows! Her memory's come back. She *knows*, Phoebe! And you know too, don't you?'

She blinked at him, unsure whether he was angry or just afraid. 'Yes. I know,' she admitted. 'I hoped Ann never would.'

Connor staggered into the kitchen and shut the door behind him with a vicious kick. 'She's in shock. I'm putting her to bed and I'm going to sit with her. Make a hot water bottle. And some tea. But ring a doctor first.' He didn't wait for a reply, but pushed past Phoebe and mounted the stairs, carrying Ann.

Phoebe fetched the phone from the hall and sat at the kitchen table to make the call. Someone took her details and said a doctor would ring back shortly. She laid the phone down, went over to the sink and filled the kettle. As she leaned against the worktop, waiting for the water to boil, her eyes fell on the fish pie Ann had made.

Phoebe turned the oven off and buried her face in her hands.

By the time the doctor rang back, Ann was calmer, but still unable to speak, so Phoebe explained that she thought her daughter had probably experienced a flashback to the time she found her father's body hanging in the wood.

The doctor said Ann would need rest and, when she was ready, she might benefit from counselling. He assured them that she had suffered no physical harm, but her mind would need time to recover. Registering Phoebe's age, he asked if she would be able to cope on her own. She scoffed at his concern and hung up.

Phoebe looked up at Connor, sitting on the other side of the bed. 'Did you hear all that?' He nodded. 'Poor thing,' Phoebe whispered. She lifted a hand towards Ann's head, but appeared to change her mind. 'Better not disturb her. The doc said she needs to rest.'

'I'm going to sit up with her all night, so if you want to get some sleep, that's fine by me. I can call you if she wakes.'

'I'm not tired. I want to be here if she wakes up. That's the least I can do,' Phoebe added ruefully. 'There's a fish pie downstairs. Are you hungry?'

'No. Are you?'

'No. I feel like I'll never be hungry again.' She shook her head. 'But Ann went to such a lot of trouble to make it. All for you. She's very fond of you, you know.'

'Yes. And I'm very fond of her.'

Phoebe studied the sleeping face. 'She was a beautiful little girl. Exquisite. And so intense. That's the Madeiran blood. She was her father's daughter.'

'Why did he do it, Phoebe? I'd like to understand. I think I might be more use to Ann if I knew what actually happened.'

She sat in silence for some moments, staring into space, her face blank. Eventually she said, 'I suppose I might as well tell you. I haven't spoken of it in . . . almost forty years.' She sat back and folded her arms. Fixing her eyes on a point in the middle of the floor, Phoebe said, 'The marriage was already over by then. There had been a stupid row . . . I might have been a bit drunk. I went to bed and took a sleeping pill, so I knew nothing till Ann woke me up the following morning, pulling at the bedclothes, hysterical.'

'Did she see him *die?*'

'No, thank God. The post-mortem established the time of death. He'd been dead for hours when she found him.'

'Did Sylvester suffer from depression?'

'Oh, yes. He'd always had a tendency to mood swings. He was mercurial. Unbearable in the winter. You'd think we were living in Siberia, the fuss he used to make about the weather! So I encouraged him to spend time abroad, for the good of his health and the business. He imported wine and he was away a lot. Well, I'm not faithful by nature and I'm easily bored. Opportunities presented themselves . . . I'm not proud of what I did, but they were just flings, not relationships. They meant very little to me. Sylvester was the only man I ever loved, but he found that hard to believe. He couldn't understand *hurting* people you loved . . . But just look at what *he* did! What he did to Ann and me! Yet I know he really loved us. He was ill, you see. Very ill. And I had no idea . . . It took me a long time to forgive him, but in the end I did. I'm still working on forgiving myself.'

'He found out you'd been unfaithful?'

'No, he didn't suspect a thing! He was a trusting soul. No, it was more complicated than that and I didn't handle it well . . . I had an abortion, you see. Sylvester was furious. Heartbroken. He'd wanted another child for years and I'd refused. This one was an accident, but he'd guessed I was pregnant. I was throwing up and couldn't work. So I got rid of it. In Sylvester's eyes that was murder. I'd murdered a child, *his* child. I should have left it at that, said no more, but I thought the truth might make things easier for him.'

'I'm guessing it didn't.'

Phoebe looked at Ann and murmured, 'When does the truth ever make anything easier?'

'What did you say?'

'I told him the truth, which was that the baby wasn't even his.'

Connor winced.

'What else could I say? I didn't want him thinking *he'd* lost a child. He hadn't.'

'But he took it badly?'

'The marriage didn't recover. Nor did Sylvester. He moved into the spare room and started putting things in order. Filing. Accounts. I assumed he was preparing to leave me, which was what I deserved, so I didn't say anything. Nor did he. We both suffered in silence.'

'You didn't realise he was cracking up?'

'No, I was used to his black moods. They'd always passed. Eventually.'

'And Ann knew nothing of all this?'

'She was only five. If she'd overheard anything, she wouldn't have understood. But I should have seen it coming. It was all too much for him. The abortion. The infidelity. I think he even began to doubt whether Ann was his child. But he said nothing, just went quietly mad. Towards the end he was very tender with Ann. Spent a lot of time with her. I thought he was trying to compensate for landing her with a monster for a mother, but he was saying goodbye. He wanted her to have good memories of him. And he succeeded. She didn't remember any of what came afterwards. Until today.'

'Why didn't you ever tell her what had happened to him?'

'I couldn't explain because she'd forgotten! How do you tell a five-year-old her dad has hanged himself, if her brain is telling her it didn't happen? Everyone said her memory would come back eventually, so I just played along. What else could I do? I was beside myself. Don't you see, I loved Sylvester and I'd *killed* him!'

'No, Phoebe.'

'As good as! I drove him to suicide.'

'That tendency must have been there already. Plenty of men have survived unfaithful wives. You might have contributed to his depression, but you weren't responsible for his death.'

'It's very kind of you to say so, Connor, but I haven't changed my mind in forty years. I'm guilty as hell.'

He regarded Phoebe's ravaged face and said gently, 'How did you cope with Ann – after she found him?'

'She had hysterics, then she went to sleep. Out like a light. She slept for a very long time, then when she woke up, she seemed all right. Normal, almost. I remember she was very hungry, but she said nothing about Sylvester. So I rang Dagmar – she's my agent – and asked her to come and take Ann back to London for a few days. She'd been to Dagmar's flat before and knew her well, so I made out this was a special treat and told Dagmar to spoil her rotten. The minute Ann was gone, I took the damn swing down.' Phoebe looked up, her eyes filling with tears. 'He must have stood on it . . . before he jumped.'

'That's why Ann had the flashback. She saw me standing on a swing.' Phoebe looked perplexed. 'I made one for her. As a present.'

'Oh God, you didn't!' Phoebe exclaimed.

Ann stirred and they watched her sleeping figure anxiously until she settled again.

Connor sighed. 'I had no idea what a swing would mean to Ann.'

'No, of course you didn't. I'm sorry, that was stupid of me.'

'I'd hung it in the wood and I was testing it for weight. I wanted to make sure it was safe.' He bowed his head and looked at his hands. 'If I hadn't made that swing—'

'No, don't blame yourself! It's probably better she knows what happened. It was a brain bomb waiting to go off at any time.'

'When she came back from London, did she ask about the swing?'

'No, that's what was so very odd. She didn't mention the disappearance of the swing, but if she'd wiped the incident *completely*, she would have asked what happened to it, wouldn't she?'

'Did she ever mention it?'

'No, never. Then after she'd been home for a few days, she asked me when Daddy was coming home. That's when I realised. She didn't remember anything. I didn't know what to say, so I just played for time. I concocted some story about Sylvester going away for a long time. Abroad, for work. She asked me again and I stuck to my story, then after a few weeks, I told her Daddy wouldn't be coming home any more. She asked if we were getting divorced. God knows where she'd heard the word. School, I suppose. I didn't even know if she knew what it meant, but I said, yes, we were. I told her Daddy had decided he didn't want to live with us any more – which was true. I said he'd gone away and I didn't know even where he was – which was also true, in a way. It seemed the kindest thing to say. She was so very young and her brain seemed to be protecting her from the horror, so I thought I should too. I knew I'd have to come clean one day, but I thought it could wait until she was older, until she had a chance of understanding why Sylvester did what he did. Somehow the opportunity never arose. Then once she was an adult, I didn't want to tell her because . . .' Phoebe hesitated.

'Because of the abortion.'

'Yes. She and Jack went through so much trying to conceive a child. How could I tell Ann I got rid of a baby with scarcely a second thought? It just became impossible to talk about it, *any* of it. There were so many lies! Eventually the lies were so old, they seemed like the truth.'

Ann stirred again, tossing her head back and forth on the pillow.

'I think she's surfacing,' Phoebe hissed.

'Maybe she's thirsty.'

'Hungry, more likely. It's been hours since she ate anything and she only grabbed a bite at lunchtime.'

They continued to watch as she rolled over in bed, mumbling. Connor thought he caught his name, then decided he'd imagined it. As Ann's eyelids began to flicker, he said in an urgent undertone, 'You have to tell her, Phoebe. All of it. She has to understand what happened. She *will* understand, if you tell her.'

She stared at him, dull-eyed and exhausted. 'You really think so?'

'You treated Sylvester badly, but not Ann. You never did anything other than try to protect her from the trauma of what she'd witnessed, but couldn't possibly understand.'

'She might not see it like that.'

'Maybe she won't, but you still have to tell her.'

'Yes, I know. I've always known . . . I think perhaps you'd better leave us now, Connor. Would you mind? I'd like to be alone with my daughter.'

'Of course.'

'You might bring me a whisky. In a while. Not yet. And pour one for yourself. It's been a long day.'

He got to his feet, still watching Ann. 'I'll put that pie in the oven. She'd want us to eat it, wouldn't she?'

'Oh, yes! She made it with such loving care. She had to make an extra trip to the supermarket because she'd run out of nutmegs. I said you wouldn't have noticed.'

'Damn right I wouldn't.'

'Ann said that wasn't the point. She wanted to do it *properly*.' Phoebe shook her head. 'I love that in her. Her *thoroughness*. The attention to detail. It's beautiful.'

'You should tell her.'

'I will when she wakes up. I'll tell her everything . . . You won't forget to bring me that whisky, will you? I'm going to need it. Gin for the good times, whisky for the bad times, eh?'

Connor was almost out of the room when he heard a sharp intake of breath and the rustle of bedclothes. He spun round to see Ann sitting up in bed, staring at Phoebe.

'*Mum . . . ?* Is something wrong?' she asked, frowning. 'Where's Connor?'

'He's still here,' Phoebe said, pointing towards the door.

'I was about to put your fish pie in the oven,' he said, approaching the bed again, glad to see recognition and relief in Ann's eyes.

'We can all have a lovely midnight feast!' Phoebe announced with a fixed smile.

Ann looked from Phoebe to Connor and said, 'What happened in the wood?'

'Tonight?' he asked.

'No. When I was five.'

'Phoebe will explain. I'll be downstairs if you need me.'

He closed the door behind him and began to descend the stairs. Glancing at his watch, he saw it was almost 2.00 a.m. Still a long time till dawn, but at first light he would go up to the beech wood and take down the swing before Ann had a chance to set eyes on it again.

ANN

By the time Ann arrived at the clearing in the beech wood Connor had already taken down the swing. She stood at a distance, watching him, trying to remember what life was like before yesterday; before Connor rang the doorbell on a rainy January morning and asked to view the house; before he'd come to seem so very necessary in her life. She couldn't remember that time. There was only now.

She walked on towards him, stepping carefully on the mossy ground, heavy with dew. She made no noise, but he looked up, suddenly alert. Winding long pieces of rope round the swing seat, he said, 'You're up. How are you feeling?'

'Very strange. Fish pie for breakfast was a new experience. It tasted surprisingly good.'

'You can't beat home-made.'

As he bundled the seat into a holdall, Ann said, 'No, don't. Show me. I'd like to see it.'

'You're sure?'

'Yes, I'm sure. Phoebe said you borrowed one of my books on William Morris.'

'For the decoration. I know you love what he does with plants.'

'How do you know that?'

'Phoebe said. She explained about the Morris room. How he was your hero.'

She smiled. 'You like Phoebe, don't you?'

'I think I love Phoebe.' He held Ann's eyes. 'But not as much as I love you.'

She said nothing and looked down. When she felt able to speak, she said, 'Show me what you made.'

He unravelled the ropes again and displayed the wooden seat. A pattern of carved beech leaves curled around the edge and in the centre it said *Ann de Freitas 2015.*

'I wanted to make something to remind you of the time we spent here. And I'm not really up to making garden benches.'

She traced the shape of a leaf with her finger. 'It's beautiful, Connor. Such a thoughtful present. Thank you.'

'I didn't know—'

'No, of course you didn't.'

'And I wanted to give you something that would last.'

She looked up into his face. 'Oh, believe me, you have . . . If it's not too much trouble, I'd like you to hang the swing back up for me. It belongs here.'

'No trouble at all.'

He bent to put to the seat down. As he straightened up, Ann put her arms round his waist and laid her head down on his chest. He folded her in his arms and they stood in silence until she said, 'Phoebe always said he loved us. She insisted on that. I suppose that love just wasn't enough.'

'If you're very ill, sometimes it's not. My dad didn't love me enough to stop drinking.'

'She talked about him recently. Sylvester. I'd brought the subject up. I said I wondered if he ever thought of me, the way I often think about him. She said something rather odd. It seems even odder now that I know.'

'What did she say?'

'She said, "I'm absolutely convinced, wherever he is now, your welfare still matters to him."'

'I think she believes that.'

'Do you? I wish I could.'

'You could try. Can't do any harm, can it?'

'No, I suppose not.'

She laid her head down again and they listened to the silence of the beech wood until Connor whispered, 'Could you use some coffee? Let me make you some.'

'That would be nice.'

He took her hand and they walked through the wood, past the laughing Green Woman, into the spring sunlight.

Connor looked up at the cloudless sky and said, 'It's going to be fine.'

'Yes,' Ann replied. 'I think it is.'

THE BEECH WOOD

She has remembered what she saw long ago, what she found. There was a dark place in the wood and in her heart, a place that held secrets. Now nothing is hidden. Now she can grieve. Forgive. Love. Her life is full.

We, who have lived long, have borne witness to these things.

Were we human, we should rejoice.

Were we human, we should weep to see what we have seen, see what we see.

ACKNOWLEDGMENTS

I'd like to thank the following people for their help and support in the writing of this book: Tina Betts, Clare Cooper, Amanda Fairclough, Lorna Fergusson, Margaret Gillard, Amy Glover, Philip Glover, David J. Hogg, Bill Marshall, Erica Munro, Joanne Phillips, Sally Salmon and Katherine Wren.

I would also like to thank the staff of the National Trust at Tyntesfield, Somerset.

ABOUT THE AUTHOR

Linda Gillard lives in North Lanarkshire, Scotland, and has been an actress, journalist and teacher. She's the author of eight novels, including *Star Gazing*, shortlisted in 2009 for Romantic Novel of the Year and the Robin Jenkins Literary Award. *Star Gazing* was also voted Favourite Romantic Novel 1960–2010 by *Woman's Weekly* readers.

Linda's fourth novel, *House of Silence*, became a Kindle bestseller and was selected by Amazon as one of its Top Ten 'Best of 2011' in the Indie Author category.

Find out more about Linda at www.lindagillard.co.uk.